HELL IS BEYOND
THE DEAD END SIGN . . .

where the unfinished demolition begins; on the wasteland where children no longer go to play, the desolation on the outskirts of a city.

* * *

Shanifa!

No, it was impossible, and yet even her clothing, the
way her jacket swung in time with her movements,
implanted a terrifying certainty in his still-doubting
brain.

He tried to call her back, but only a whispered croak
escaped his lips. Her footfalls were fainter now; soon
she would be lost to him. He found the place where
she had passed through. Hurrying, oblivious of the
deep puddles of muddy water that filled his shoes, he
stumbled blindly in Shanifa's wake. He would not turn
back, wherever she went, even if she led him into the
bowels of this awful place which had been the hell of
his early childhood!

NOWHERE TO RUN . . . NOWHERE TO HIDE . . .
ZEBRA'S SUSPENSE WILL *GET* YOU—
AND WILL MAKE YOU BEG FOR MORE!

NOWHERE TO HIDE (4035, $4.50)
by Joan Hall Hovey

After Ellen Morgan's younger sister has been brutally murdered, the highly respected psychologist appears on the evening news and dares the killer to come after her. After a flood of leads that go nowhere, it happens. A note slipped under her windshield states, "YOU'RE IT." Ellen has woken the hunter from its lair . . . and she is his prey!

SHADOW VENGEANCE (4097, $4.50)
by Wendy Haley

Recently widowed Maris learns that she was adopted. Desperate to find her birth parents, she places "personals" in all the Texas newspapers. She receives a horrible response: "You weren't wanted then, and you aren't wanted now." Not to be daunted, her search for her birth mother—and her only chance to save her dangerously ill child—brings her closer and closer to the truth . . . and to death!

RUN FOR YOUR LIFE (4193, $4.50)
by Ann Brahms

Annik Miller is being stalked by Gibson Spencer, a man she once loved. When Annik inherits a wilderness cabin in Maine, she finally feels free from his constant threats. But then, a note under her windshield wiper, and shadowy form, and a horrific nighttime attack tell Annik that she is still the object of this lovesick madman's obsession . . .

EDGE OF TERROR (4224, $4.50)
by Michael Hammonds

Jessie thought that moving to the peaceful Blue Ridge Mountains would help her recover from her bitter divorce. But instead of providing the tranquility she desires, they cast a shadow of terror. There is a madman out there—and he knows where Jessie lives—and what he has seen . . .

NOWHERE TO RUN (4132, $4.50)
by Pat Warren

Socialite Carly Weston leads a charmed life. Then her father, a celebrated prosecutor, is murdered at the hands of a vengeance-seeking killer. Now he is after Carly . . . watching and waiting and planning. And Carly is running for her life from a crazed murderer who's become judge, jury—and executioner!

Available wherever paperbacks are sold, or order direct from the Publisher. Send cover price plus 50¢ per copy for mailing and handling to Penguin USA, P.O. Box 999, c/o Dept. 17109, Bergenfield, NJ 07621. Residents of New York and Tennessee must include sales tax. DO NOT SEND CASH.

GUY N. SMITH

DEAD END

ZEBRA BOOKS
KENSINGTON PUBLISHING CORP.

ZEBRA BOOKS are published by

Kensington Publishing Corp.
850 Third Avenue
New York, NY 10022

First Printing: March, 1996
10 9 8 7 6 5 4 3 2 1

Printed in the United States of America

But only a host of phantom listeners
That dwelt in the lone house then
Stood listening in the quiet of the moonlight
To that voice from the world of men.
                                        — *Walter de la Mare*

One

Disasters came in threes. Max Frame had been attempting to convince himself for most of the day that they didn't. It was a load of bull; they happened every day, everywhere, throughout the population of the world, unevenly distributed. Five hundred heart attacks daily, he had read somewhere; industrial and road accidents, fires, you name it. Hurricanes and floods killed thousands annually in tropical climates. There was no way you could group them, bracket them into triples. Except when they happened to you.

He glanced sideways, almost surreptitiously, at the slim, blond-haired girl wearing a floppy green tracksuit who stared fixedly ahead of her as though mesmerized by the repetitive swathes and monotonous whine of the windshield wipers as they fought valiantly against the driving sleet. But Shanifa neither heard nor saw them, he was only too well aware of that. She was entwining her fingers, a habit of hers that he found extremely annoying on most other occasions. On this one he could excuse her, sympathize with her.

Her thoughts were with her elder sister, who had been fighting for her life in the intensive care unit at the hospital since Sunday night. Mown down by a drunken driver as she crossed the road, Wanda should have been killed outright, pronounced dead at the scene of the accident. Fate had cruelly, temporarily, granted Wanda a senseless respite. Both legs broken, four cracked ribs, a smashed pelvis, innumerable lacerations, terminating in a clot on the lung by Tuesday. Today was Wednesday, the doctors had warned that she was unlikely to make it past Thursday. Tragedy number one.

"What's the matter with this bloody traffic?" Shanifa voiced her frustration. Her fears found a scapegoat in the double line of vehicles ahead of them which had slowly crawled to a standstill.

"It's the evening rush hour," Max answered. Whether we get to the hospital at six, or seven or even eight o'clock, it won't make a scrap of difference. Because Wanda won't know whether we've been or not; she's unconscious and never likely to be anything else. Except dead. "It's heavier than usual because it's Christmas week and late-night shopping to boot."

Silence except for the wipers and the idling engines in front and behind, clouds of exhaust vapors reducing visibility still further, stop lights winking angrily as drivers fidgeted with their brake pedals. The Fiat Uno directly ahead of them edged right up to a van, leaving a gap. Max did not ease forward; there was no point. Nobody was going anywhere at the moment.

"God!" Shanifa thumped her fists on her knees. She was close to tears.

Max sighed, thought about a cigarette but decided against it because Shanifa objected to smoking, was quite obsessional about it at times, and this could well be one of those times.

Disaster number two. Well, not *exactly* a disaster, more of a mishap, a routine minor accident in the life of most professional driving instructors. That idiot Taylor had scraped the side of the Fiesta yesterday, oversteered on a three-point turn and caught one of those low ornamental walls up on the Cedar Estate. Max was tempted to wind the window down, lean out and check one last time that it wasn't as serious as he had thought at first. He didn't because the exhaust fumes would have eddied in and the lashing sleet would have stung his face. And doubtless Shanifa would have complained, let her emotions rip in a bitter tirade. Then he would have become the scapegoat instead of the traffic jam.

The damage was nothing to worry about, just a deep scratch. An insurance job, some additional paperwork. Damn it, it wasn't as if Les Taylor had gone and run somebody over.

Like Wanda.

The second of three. Don't be so bloody stupid.

"She's not going to make it," Shanifa spoke suddenly, her tone surprisingly rational. She had stopped twisting her fingers together. "I know she isn't. I've known all along, before the doctors warned us."

"Nobody knows for sure." He turned to face her, saw how white her pert features were in the reflected glow of the headlights behind. He just checked himself in time from adding "Whilst there's life, there's hope." Instead he continued, "They said this morning that she was stable, didn't they?"

"That just means she isn't dead yet. God, she's on a life-support machine, Max. *Technically* alive. A heartbeat, nothing more. If they wanted to they could keep her that way for months. Years!"

The Uno's brake lights went out; it began to roll. The traffic was starting to move. Slowly.

Stopping again.

Okay, Max thought, Wanda's in a bad way, there's

no getting away from that. She might or might not make it; the odds are she won't. The car's been scratched. But the two are not in any way related. He almost spoke aloud in his attempt to get the message over to his doubting mind. The only remotely relevant factor was that both incidents had occurred within a few days of each other. Nothing else. If there *was* to be a third, then it might be something trivial: a flat tire, or the rented TV or the video packing up on Christmas morning when there wasn't a call-out service available. But neither he nor Shanifa would be watching it this holiday, anyway, so what the hell.

Max was overweight. Not a lot, fifteen pounds at the most; nobody else noticed it, not even Shanifa, or if she did, then she had not commented upon it. Like crunches, a midriff spread went with a driving instructor's job. You sat in a car all day, stopped off at a cafe for a sandwich at lunchtime, and you didn't exercise because you were too damned knackered at the end of the day. You smoked because of the stress factor; fools like Les Taylor had you reaching for a cigarette. Your average lifespan? Max did not know, had deliberately avoided finding out.

He tinted his hair and his close-cut beard; only Shanifa shared that secret. He had started to go gray fifteen years ago, had first noticed it just after his twenty-third birthday. Janice, his wife, had claimed that it made him look "distinguished." Christ, Janice approved of just about everything, and that made her the most boring woman he had ever been with. The only time he had ever known her to disapprove of anything was the day she found out about his affair with Shanifa.

If Janice had ranted and raved, slapped him, thrown something at him, then she might just have clicked up a notch in Max's waning admiration for her. Instead, she had gone to bed, sobbed for a whole day and a night, and then asked him if he wanted *her* to leave. Max had almost said "no" out of sympathy, but saying "yes" had made it an easy ride from there on. She went back to live with her mother; she had spent half the week at her mother's ever since they had been married, so now that had become a full-time instead of a part-time occupation.

The only thing Janice had refused him was a divorce, always hoping that he might have a change of mind. They had been separated long enough now, he could have forced the issue, but he hadn't. He did not really know why; certainly he did not want her back. But she would be awarded half the house and business which would have left him with barely enough to live on. Driving schools were in the depths of a recession, the run-of-the-mill ones, anyway. Boyfriends taught girlfriends to drive; friends instructed friends, freebie lessons that got the pupils through their tests simply because the bureaucrats wanted to reduce the growing waiting lists. Which was one of the reasons why some pissed-off kid had run down Wanda.

"The traffic's moving again, Max!" A reprimand for daydreaming, admonishing him because she knew that he wasn't grieving for Wanda.

"Sorry." Hell, I don't have to apologize. I'm a driving instructor and Shanifa can't even drive, isn't interested in learning, either.

Shanifa was the complete opposite of Janice. A council house background, Shanifa had left school at sixteen to work in the High Street cafe and was still there sixteen years later. No ambition. Max had had to work on her to get her to go out with him the first time. It was a month after that before they made love, and she wasn't all that good at it, either. Yet, for some totally inexplicable reason, he was wildly in love with her.

"They're bloody well stopping again!" Shanifa's near-hysterical shriek had Max banging the brake pedal so hard that he again left a gap between the Fiesta and the Uno in front. He almost apologized to her a second time. She was going through hell right now. The traffic was much heavier than usual, even for Christmas week. Maybe there had been an accident up ahead . . .

. . . Somebody run over . . .

"It's probably a lorry broken down, blocking the road." His off-the-cuff explanation was as much for his own benefit as Shanifa's. *Not* an accident. Because that would have been number three, justifying his phobia that disasters came in triples. But even if it was a pileup, it had nothing to do with either him or Shanifa; no way could you relate it to Wanda and the damaged car. He tried to shake off the spectre of his premonition but found himself peering into the murkiness up ahead, almost willing his eyes to see flashing blue lights.

Whatever the obstruction, it was not hindering the oncoming traffic, an unceasing flow of fast-moving vehicles that showered the stationary double queue with muddy surface water. Max restarted the wipers, tried not to listen to them.

The Fiat had edged up again, but he wasn't going to follow. In a minute or two everybody might start to roll.

"Surely we have to move soon; they won't let the traffic snarl up for much longer." Shanifa was biting the nail of her little finger. "It must stretch right back to the big island by now. Can't you edge out a bit, get into the opposite carriageway? We could go back to the island, find a way round."

"You have to be joking!" he snapped irritably. "Try a U-turn here and we'd be flattened underneath a dozen artics."

"Sorry I spoke."

Shanifa would sulk now, he predicted, probably wouldn't speak again until they got to the hospital. Whenever that might be. There was just the depressing hum of the wipers and the swish of passing cars and trucks, their headlights seeming to wink, mocking their less fortunate colleagues.

A thought crossed Max's mind. He tried to push it away just as he had attempted to dispel the nagging premonition of a third catastrophe. *Wanda's gone, it doesn't matter how long we're held up now.*

That's rubbish, she's still alive. Just.

"I have to go to Wanda." Shanifa's fingers groped in the half darkness for the door catch.

For one awful moment Max thought that Shanifa was about to open the door, get out and rush blindly into the wintry night, trying to find her way through the waiting vehicles.

His hand reached out, closing firmly over hers. "Darling, there's nothing anybody can do. We have to wait here along with everybody else. The hospital is a good two miles from here."

She did not reply, just sat there staring straight ahead of her, as though she might not even have heard him. Then he sensed her stiffen, start to tremble violently. It was as if she, too, shared his latest awful premonition.

In the weird artificial light he saw her expression change. Her eyes widened, her mouth opened as though to scream, but no sound came from her lips.

A look of sheer terror, pressing herself back in the seat, cringing from . . .

"*Oh, my God!*"

Max saw but seemed incapable of understanding, as if his reasoning had suddenly been blanked off, a film that had stopped, left just a still on the screen. That double line of approaching traffic, the twin snake with a thousand eyes stretching back into the misty darkness whence its lair lay, appeared to be arching its back as though casting off its winter skin. A jerking zigzag movement, a segment breaking free, scattering the rest. Powerful beams crisscrossed, elevated; a kaleidoscope of blinding light. The dazzling brightness was a spotlight focused on the hurtling giant that had torn itself away from the rest; a monster that slewed, bucked as its front wheels hit the central reservation, springboarded into the air, its heavy tail jackknifing and scuppering stationary cars as a child might scramble its toy models in a sudden tantrum.

A gargantuan robot bent on destruction, it bore down on the helpless Fiat, singled it out and demolished it instantly, crushing it into oblivion. Still ravenous, a steel dragon steaming with lust and fury, it saw the Fiesta with its blazing eyes.

Momentary hesitation, but its appetite was unsatiated, and it lurched forward again, scented its next prey amidst the carnage. And moved in for the kill.

Max said something stupid like, "It's all right, my darling."

A lie because it wasn't all right. They were both going to die like the occupants of the Fiat in front had. Like Wanda had just died. Holding on to each other, clinging to those last few precious seconds. So much to talk about but no time in which to say it, hearing the beast's killing cry, feeling it vibrate every nerve in their tortured bodies, smelling its foul, rubbery breath as it lowered its squat head to take them.

Darkness. Oblivion.

Then there was light again, a dazzling whiteness that seared the eyeballs, had Max screaming at it to go away, to leave them alone. He wanted to shield his eyes from it, but his arms were trapped; he was unable to lift them. He found that he could move his feet, but they did not seem to go anywhere. It was as if he had lost control of them.

Metal cutting metal, those awful earlier vibrations magnified a thousand times. Oh, God the creature was ripping at the car, biting its way in to its trapped human victims.

Shanifa! *Shanifa!*

He found her, thank God she was still all right. The roof and the sides of the Fiesta had been pushed inward, enclosing them in an igloo of ripped upholstery. The facia was gone, had disappeared somewhere beneath the *U* of the bent steering column. Alongside Max, lying facing him, staring quizzically at him through the trailing vines of her blond hair, was Shanifa. Her fingers clutched the gear lever; her shapely legs were somewhere down in the dark recess of the well along with his own. He tried to rub against them, but he was unable to locate them.

Max discovered that he could move his head, twist his neck just far enough so that his pouted lips kissed Shanifa's forehead reassuringly.

"It's all right, darling."

It clearly was not, but he had to lie to her. She did not reply, he did not expect her to. Everything came back to him with frightening clarity. There had been a multiple pileup on the opposite carriageway; a truck had hit the central reservation, jackknifed, and ploughed into the double line of stationary traffic.

The Fiat in front had been the penultimate victim, had probably acted as a buffer, just enough to slow the progress of the rampaging truck but not able to halt it. Max endeavored to work it all out; in all probability the car behind them had escaped unscathed.

"It could have been a lot worse." He wished that he could slip a comforting arm around Shanifa, hold her to him and kiss her. "As it is, we seem to have escaped injury." He wanted to laugh when he remembered how Taylor had dented the car door that morning: he didn't because he recalled with an eerie certainty that Wanda was dead. Right now Shanifa was probably grieving silently for her sister, so it was best to say nothing at all.

The screeching of the steel cutters goose pimpled his skin, made him tense, that same sensation he used to get when some of the boys at school scraped their fingernails along the sides of parked buses and cars. The noise was deafening; it would have been impossible to talk to Shanifa, anyway.

The rescue team was using powerful lights to enable them to see in the murky darkness. Max was blinded by them. He could no longer even discern Shanifa's silhouette. The firemen were starting to cut away the roof; it was the only way they could reach those trapped inside. Max ducked his head just in case they became careless in their haste. His new posture brought with it an aching neck.

"I expect they'll insist on taking us to the hospital for a checkup," he spoke during a lull in the cutting, just to let Shanifa know that he was still there. "I doubt they'll keep us in overnight, though, because there's a shortage of beds. They'll only detain emergency cases."

It was ironic. They had been on their way to the hospital; now they would be ferried by ambulance for the remainder of their journey. But the trip was all a waste of time because Wanda was dead. In all probability he and Shanifa would arrive back home sometime later tonight. He wanted to look at his watch but would be unable to do that until their rescuers freed his arms. He wondered what time it was. It could not be more than seven o'clock at the latest. Somewhere, not too far away, somebody was screaming. Poor bastard! He and Shanifa didn't have a lot to complain about.

He would have to cancel tomorrow's lessons, probably the day after's as well. At least, until he got a replacement car. Max tried to recall his bookings, but the names eluded him. They were all in the diary by the phone. He'd ring them first thing in the morning. Just so long as Mister bloody Les Taylor wasn't one of them! He laughed aloud at the thought.

He thought he heard Shanifa speaking, but the din had intensified so that he could not be sure. She was probably telling him how she, too, knew that Wanda had given up her fight for life. Max could not see Shanifa, just shooting, exploding lights before his eyes, the aurora borealis gone berserk. Jesus, his head was hurting now.

"They're almost through to us," he was shouting, but he could not even hear his own voice. "Another minute or two and we'll be out of here." Then you'll be able to see Wanda, her corpse stiff and

white. You'll have hysterics, cry for days like you
did when your mother died.

Yes, this was Number Three, all right.

The roof was nearly off now, being lifted up like
the lid of a box. The noise was much worse, engines
revving, people shouting. Somebody was still
screaming. Max gave up trying to talk to Shanifa,
but somehow he had to let her know that he was
still here, still okay. If he strained in his seat belt
he could just reach her, like the last time. God, it
was painful; his chest hurt most, steel bands that
clamped and tightened.

Lips pouted in readiness, he searched for that
shock of fallen hair. But there was nothing, not so
much as a trailing strand. He probed with an extended tongue.

Shanifa, where are you?

She couldn't have gone far; there was nowhere to
go. She was probably lying back in the extremity of
the space that trapped them; resting because the
trauma had exhausted her, crying softly to herself
because she knew that her sister was dead. Her grief
had already begun.

Arms were reaching down from the open roof,
fingers probing gently, faraway voices that talked
condescendingly, a patter of reassurance that had
been scripted and learned by heart for the benefit
of trapped and injured motorists.

"I'm all right," Max shouted up to them. "We're
both all right. Get my girlfriend out first."

They must have heard him, understood, because
he felt Shanifa being lifted out from beside him.
She had been all right, after all. Just resting.

His distorted vision caught a glimpse of her as they
hoisted her up through the roofless space above. A

silhouette hanging limply against the floodlit sky, her long hair awry and blowing in the sleety wind.

Then she was lost to his view, and they were reaching down for him, one of them clambering down beside him in order to cut through the twisted seat belt with a knife.

Max was relaxed now, drowsy by the time they pulled him up into the open. He was asleep as they bore him away from the flattened remnants of the Fiesta toward the waiting ambulance.

Two

It was late spring. Christmas was long gone. So too was Shanifa. And Wanda. Tragedy Number Three had been more than just a foreboding implanted in a superstitious mind. It had been a premonition of death.

Max was finished with crying; there were no more tears left by the time they discharged him from the hospital in late March, sent him home to an empty house. He had been instructed to attend the physiotherapy unit on Tuesdays and Thursdays. He probably wouldn't, there didn't seem much point.

Cracked ribs and pelvis, both legs and an arm broken, a hairline fracture of the skull; there had been a suspicion of brain damage, but it was unfounded. He had been unconscious for four days; after that it had been a slow and painful return to a near-complete recovery. The doctors warned him that unless he embarked upon a course of regular treatment he would always walk with a limp. Did it matter if he did?

His injuries bore a similarity to Wanda's. Fate was cruel; Wanda should have lived while Max died. He wished to God it had been that way round. At least then he and Shanifa would have been together, wherever she had gone. He had never been a religious man, but at times like these one tried to believe in something.

They had assured him that Shanifa had died instantly, painlessly, on impact. It was easy to say that; words were cheap. There were road deaths every day of the week. They were routine. For doctors and morticians.

Shanifa and Wanda had been buried three months ago while Max still lay in a coma. That was a relief. Mentally he could not have survived the dual burial in the suburban churchyard. Funerals were supposed to be a kind of therapy, the climax of your grief. Afterward you embarked upon a process of rehabilitation, existing rather than living, a continual state of disorientation. Time passed, you lost track of it.

The driving school was in limbo, temporarily suspended. Max's telephone answering machine informed all callers that "owing to ill health, no more pupils can be taken on at present. Please contact us again in a few weeks." The message would be left on indefinitely, until the tape wore out. In due course there would be an insurance payout, doubtless a considerable sum, but for the moment Max was not interested in money. His solicitor had left a message for him to call at the office in relation to this. Next week, perhaps.

Max had put the house up for sale, but it might be months before it sold. At a substantial reduction. It was a buyer's market; if you wanted a house on the Radnor Estate, there were fifty or more identical red brick boxes to choose from. There were no distinguishing features to tempt the discerning house hunter; you went for the cheapest. The view was the same whether you lived on Radnor North or Radnor South, row after row of mass-produced semis and four-bedroom detacheds, seventies style.

Max hated the house now that Shanifa was gone. Bleak and featureless, cold and inhospitable, it was just a roosting place for him at night. It was a tomb, the focal point of his tragedy. He slept there simply because he had nowhere else to sleep; not that he slept much these nights, tortured by his anguish until slivers of gray dawn crept in through the windows.

During the daytime he walked the city streets. Aimless rambles, sometimes he lost his way, wandered on until eventually some familiar landmark nagged at him, headed him homeward against his will.

The city was large with endless, sprawling suburbs. In area, if not in population, it might have been as big as the metropolis. A class system that was defined by boundaries, divisions that fuelled hatred and separated poverty from wealth. The affluent monopolized Southside with its commuter belt, controlled the Centre, the economic heart pumped by the new stock exchange. Northside was the working class stronghold, mighty warrens of council estates and rundown terraced houses. The DHSS had moved its offices to North Central; not for the convenience of the unemployed, it was rumored, but to keep the riffraff away from the executive sector.

The rich became richer, lived on estates that were a conglomeration of modern mansions set in landscaped gardens with fish ponds and swimming pools; several had solariums. Seldom was a "for sale" sign to be seen on Southside; properties were in constant demand and sold on the strength of a whisper in golf clubs or plush restaurants.

Once Max's wanderings had taken him down to

Southside, a maze of tree-lined avenues and cul-de-sacs, driveways with wrought iron gates and shrubberies that screened the houses from prying eyes. Mercedes and BMWs were parked where they could be seen by passersby, but he seldom caught a glimpse of the occupants, their status symbols on view while they indulged secretly in the pleasures of the rich that were denied to the masses.

He walked with a limp that would probably remain with him for the rest of his life. In his bitterness he relished the dull ache in his left leg, his punishment for being the survivor of that flattened Fiesta. His decision to spurn physiotherapy had been more than stubbornness; it was a deliberate decision to leave him with a physical reminder, his own body a shrine to the memory of Shanifa. A man who dragged his leg when he walked, his grief stamped on his deformity.

Once he had nearly phoned Janice. Just the once when temptation beckoned him in the loneliness of an empty house. One phone call could have solved a lot of mundane things: dusting the furniture, vaccing the carpets and cleaning the windows, a warm bed and a partner to copulate with when the physical urge took him. But it would not have replaced the love that he had shared with Shanifa; that was lost to him forever. He was not seeking a compromise, which was why he did not make that call even though his hand had reached out for the telephone.

Max walked up to Northside one gray, drizzly April afternoon in an attempt to cleanse himself after his foray into the yuppy stronghold. He needed to rid himself of that atmosphere of wealth and selfishness, a kind of evil, which had seeped into his system. He had to identify again with the class that had spawned him, a kind of subconscious apology for having envied the rich their luxurious lifestyle, for having trespassed in their lordly domain. More than that, he wanted to find his roots again, to breathe the aroma of frying from the takeaways and savor the smell of ale that permeated West Street which was famous for having more pubs than any other street in the city; to stand and watch the queues outside the bingo hall where housewives jostled one another in their haste to squander their family allowance; to sniff cigarette smoke instead of the heavier aroma of cigars. A way of purging himself, yet another tribute to Shanifa who, like himself, had come from these humble surroundings. But he would not go on up to the churchyard at the top of the hill. Not yet, anyway.

The area had changed. His disillusionment began the moment he emerged from the underpass that separated a divided city. The Cottager's Rest was closed, boarded up along with the other pubs. The demolition of West Street was imminent. Terraced houses, some still with their "for sale" signs leaning or blown down, had fallen prey to the developers from across the Ring Road. Maybe a hypermarket or blocks of luxury flats would rise like the phoenix as the yuppy army conquered yet another tract of enemy territory.

On all sides there was desolation where the unemployed had been driven still farther back, compacted into their last bastion. And even that might fall before long.

The tire factory was shut, corrugated iron sheets barricading the main entrance, its asbestos-roofed buildings inside the compound silent and unlit. A mountain of worn tires rose in an unsightly monument to the redundant work force; perhaps the synthetic rubber would be burned, its fumes a poisonous pall stretching across the council estates behind, a final insult to those who had created prosperity for their masters.

Max's walk was now a shambling, demoralized gait. He dragged himself on in spite of the pain in his leg. He did not want to see more, but he had to know what they had done to Northside while he had been away. A dowdy corner shop was making a gallant but futile effort to survive in the shadow of a new supermarket opposite, which was, according to the gaudy hoarding, scheduled to open in the summer. The tiny store would fight, but it would not win. The price war would determine its fate. Whatever your status, economy was the criteria; loyalty had no place in an age of price cutting. The rich sold cheaply, the poor purchased their wares out of a diminishing income.

Unlicensed cars were parked alongside the crumbling curbs, rusted bodywork that would ensure their eventual unroadworthiness. Yet, there was a neatness, a freshness, about some of the terraced houses that depicted pride in a way of life, a defiance of a new age. These people would hold on as long as possible.

The main shopping area was still unchanged, the sixties precinct allowed to remain for the time being. Shoppers window gazed, there was a queue inside the post office, a newsagent's counter was predominantly stacked with Easter eggs and cards, and in the doorway a news placard announced that the planners had won their battle to route the proposed bypass through Northside. The *coup-de-grace*.

Max tried not to see the Clock Cafe in case Shanifa should be back there serving tea and scones to middle-aged housewives whose climax to their afternoon's shopping was to catch up on the latest

gossip. But he found himself looking in through
the open doorway, felt his heart flip and step up a
beat at the sight of a shock of fair hair, a slim girl
collecting dirty crockery on a tray, her back toward
him so that he was unable to see her face.

Relief, his breathing reverting to normal because
the hair was too short, a shade too dark; the posture
was altogether wrong. All the same, it hurt, brought
back memories.

He hurried on past Cemetery Road in case he was
tempted, seduced in his mental and physical state of
exhaustion into going to the grave side. But there
was no point; Shanifa would not be there. Just a
hump of raised earth, a wooden marker with a number on it. Everybody was a number, alive or dead.

It was evening; the skies had cleared enough to
show the early stars against a saffron lining. The
raw dampness of the day had given way to mildness,
a spring warmth that tempted the walker to idle,
the completion of Nature's cycle that was about to
begin again. Max felt almost relaxed.

There was a haziness about the ensuing dusk, a
mist that might creep in later. He paused, and
thought about retracing his steps, going back over
ground that was no longer familiar. Another street
perhaps, he had come this far.

And, anyway, there was nothing beyond the old
wooden barriers that had designated the end of
Northside ever since he was a child. Ever since his
father was a child, maybe even his grandfather.

Nothing that was any good to anybody.

Max shivered uncontrollably, almost turned back.
Only curiosity held him, had him wondering if the
dereliction that lay on the other side of those ageing, rotting barricades still existed. Or whether the

developers had claimed that place that the locals called the Ghetto.

He almost shied from the thought. Childhood tales, legends of a working class community that had been told and retold so that mischievous children did not stray into dangerous and derelict places, so that they pulled the sheets up over their heads and went to sleep at night. A variation on the bogeyman theme, passed from generation to generation, embellished and exaggerated to the point of ridicule. Except that you did not ridicule the stories because, even in later life, you were still afraid of them.

Just as Max Frame was now.

But he was still curious how far the yuppies had gone in their quest for even greater wealth, if their greed had prevailed over their fear and they had conquered the terrible foe that supposedly grovelled in the gutters and tumbledown edifices of a landscape that had been derelict before the industrial revolution.

He had to know.

Standing there in the deepening dusk on the corner of that deserted street, he recalled his mother's words, could hear her husky voice even now as she sat on the end of his bed in the attic. She had not intended to scare him; she had no reason to, for he seldom played farther than the end of Chapel Street, and he was rarely troublesome at bedtime. She had simply told him for his own good, because it was only right that he should know what lay on the other side. So that he should never be tempted to venture there, even in later life. As far as she knew, nobody ever had.

Local people said that it was a sort of bogeyman's land where you went if you were bad. She didn't

believe that part of the legend, but she did not doubt
the existence of the *Downers*. They were the remnants
of the factory community, the slaves of a bygone era,
maybe the last of the Luddites who had shut themselves away and formed their own lower social strata.
Interbreeding had reduced them almost to animal
status, feared and despised by those who favored progress, left alone in their ghetto. Ostracized, they
never ventured forth, harmed none . . . unless you
were foolish enough to trespass in their domain.

Children *had* gone missing— Max's mother averted
her gaze— but that happened everywhere; there was
no evidence to support the rumors that they had
gone into the Ghetto.

"Maybe the Downers are still there, maybe they
ain't." She stood up and moved toward the door.
"All I'm saying is, don't go trying to find out for
yourself. I always say 'live and let live,' that way you
won't come to no harm."

Max was not going *into* the Ghetto, he promised
himself once again, nearly three decades later as he
stood on Chapel Street and squinted down past the
end houses, trying to make out the barriers. But it
was too dark to see them from here even if they
were still there. All he was going to do was to *look*.
And after that he would embark upon the weari-
some return journey to the house that he called
home.

Just a quick look, no more. He shuffled up to
the barrier, the top strut hung precariously at a
crazy angle; faded, almost illegible red lettering
warned of ROADWORKS. Max laughed aloud, that
was a bloody joke! In the half light it was just possible to discern where once a roadway had existed;
now it was a rutted area of potholes and rubble as
if repairs had once been started and then aban-

doned. Because nobody wanted to go that way anymore. *Because they were afraid.*

He peered between the boards and made out a
landscape that differed little from the demolition
that had already begun on Northside, shells of
houses standing eerily, defiantly, amidst a sea of
broken bricks and stones, tilted chimneys that had
weathered two centuries of gales. He shuddered at
sight of the atmosphere of decay rather than rede-
velopment clearance, a place that had been left to
die because nobody wanted to live there any longer.

Except the Downers.

In the distance, against the night skyline, buildings still stood, a clock tower and a church steeple,
lines of roofs that denoted streets. A haze that
might have been smoke.

It was as if the inhabitants of this ghost town had
retreated from the march of civilization, eked out
an existence of some kind rather than accept
change, still defied those who sought to destroy
their homes and build hideous edifices. But that
was stupid because nobody lived here.

Max might have turned away then and left, hurried away from this dreadful place where childhood
fears were spawned and people were afraid to venture, not even glanced back in case he was tempted
to pass through the dilapidated barricade to satisfy
a morbid curiosity.

Except that he saw the girl.

Had she been just any girl, then he might still
have departed, for it would have been none of his
business. A shadowy form on the opposite pavement, her footsteps tip-tapping and echoing in the
deserted street as if she was late for an appointment
or maybe feared to be out alone once darkness had
fallen. Though featureless, it was her silhouette that

knotted his stomach and sent shock waves through
his system.

At first he thought that it was the waitress from
the cafe, her chores done and eager to be home.
But her hair was too long; her posture familiar,
short steps, arms down by her side, head slightly
forward as if scrutinizing the ground in front of
her for anything that might cause her to stumble.
Unmistakable in every minute detail, she had him
recoiling, mouthing a name that would not come
because it was sacred to him.

Shanifa!

No, it was impossible, and yet even her clothing,
the way her thigh-length rainproof jacket swung in
time with her distinctive movements, implanted a
terrifying certainty in his still-doubting brain.

She passed through a narrow gap in the barriers
with scarcely a pause, a decisiveness about her, the
familiarity of one who walked a particular route frequently, negotiated the maze of puddles and ruts
unhesitatingly. Outlined now against the fading
light of the western sky, her litheness appeared to
Max, that shapely body which had given him such
pleasure before it had been cruelly snatched from
him.

Not understanding, not caring, his ecstasy frightening in case it was some trick of the light or a
cruel jest of a grieving mind, he staggered after
her. The pain in his leg was gone; his weariness
was evaporating along with the daylight.

He tried to call her back, but only a whispered
croak escaped his lips. Her footfalls were fainter
now; soon she would be lost to him. He found the
place where she had passed through, snagged his
anorak on a rusted nail, and tore it free in his
haste.

Hurrying, panicking, oblivious of the deep puddles of muddy water that filled his shoes and saturated his socks, dragging his deformed leg as he stumbled blindly, he followed in Shanifa's wake, for he had no doubt now that it was her, impossible as it was. He would not turn back, wherever she went, even if she led him into the bowels of this awful place which had been the hell of his early childhood.

Three

He had lost her.

Max stopped, listened, but the only sound was water dripping from the roof of a derelict house, a monotonous sound that fleetingly reminded him of the depressing regularity of windshield wipers, had him recalling that terrible night when life, for him, had ended.

The will-o'-the-wisp that had lured him into the Ghetto was nowhere to be seen, not so much as a fleeting shadow. Possibly it had never existed; he had imagined it, succumbed to a figment of a grief-stricken mind.

No, I saw her, she has to be here.

Where, then? She could be anywhere. Or nowhere.

It was fully dark now, but ahead of him, maybe a quarter of a mile away, there were streetlights, their glow permeating the gloom of deserted streets, casting shadows; creating silhouettes, weird shapes that came and went as though they were living entities seeking hiding places at his approach.

A feeling of being watched, his every step monitored by a host of hidden eyes.

If it had not been for his certainty that the girl he had glimpsed was Shanifa, he would have turned and fled.

It wasn't Shanifa, that is impossible.

It *is* her, I saw her.

Conflicting instincts confused him. He was afraid of the shadows, wanted to move away from them, walk in the middle of the rubble-strewn streets well away from the crumbling dwellings on either side. But if he pandered to his fears, then he would be easily seen.

By whom?

It was a disconcerting thought. He shrugged it off, told himself that there was nobody else here. Except Shanifa.

They were still watching him, whoever they were.

All right, he would keep to the shadows of the broken sidewalks until he reached the lighted area. There had to be people living there, ordinary folks like him, otherwise it would not be illuminated. This wasn't a shadowland, a bogeyland; it was just an extension of Northside where those who found themselves homeless, evicted because they were unable to pay rents or mortgages, had moved to live. Squatters. It was in the interests of the local authorities to provide basic services for them; it was cheaper than rehousing. Max felt easier now that he had reached a logical conclusion. An inhabited slum, in fact, hidden away here because if its existence was known, there would have been an outcry. The Ghetto was an embarrassment to the housing and social services departments. He had nothing to fear, after all.

The houses were less derelict now, shabby but intact, as far as he could ascertain in the half darkness. Here and there cars were parked alongside the crumbling curb, old models from the last two decades: a Cortina with a couple of flat tires, a rusting Mini Clubman estate that sat heavy on its springs, tilted to one side. Abandoned probably, the parts stripped from it to refurbish some identical old wreck. He shivered slightly. These vehicles gave the impression that they had . . . died.

He wondered why there were no lights showing in any of the houses, not even a paraffin lamp where the electricity supply had been disconnected. The occupants had moved on, deeper into the Ghetto, in search of somewhere more habitable. Just as the residents of Northside were retreating in the face of the developers. Driven back until there was no place left to go.

Yet he had the feeling that these houses were not deserted, sensed a presence behind the locked or barricaded doors; felt again those eyes following his shambling walk, more than just curiosity, burning into him like laser beams. Malevolent. That was because the inhabitants of this place resented strangers trespassing in their last retreat. They were suspicious of everybody outside their own kind: dropouts, drug addicts, meths drinkers. The scum of society. Max tried to feel sorry for them; they were the victims of the Southsiders. You could not blame them, only pity them in their terrible predicament.

He quickened his pace. The lighted area was surely no more than two streets away now, and undoubtedly that was where Shanifa had gone because she would not linger in these dark, hostile side streets.

Something grabbed his ankle, closed over it, gouged sharply into the flesh.

Max cried out in pain and terror, felt the clutching grip tighten still further and then lose its raking hold as he tore himself free. He heard an intake of breath in the deep shadows, a snarl that was akin to the frustration and anger of some nocturnal hunting beast whose prey had managed to extricate itself from its sharp claws.

Max staggered out into the street, then cast a frightened glance behind him. Shadows lined the pavements, some blacker than others. One moved, a hunched shape that might have been an extension of a flight of steps, drawing itself back until it merged with the rest and was gone whence it had come.

His ankle burned beneath the sodden fabric of his sock; he was probably bleeding. What in God's name had been lurking in the darkness? He needed a cigarette. Badly. His trembling fingers fumbled a crushed pack of Dunhills out of the pocket of his anorak, spilling a couple of white cylinders in the process. The flame of his lighter flickered uncontrollably, had difficulty in locating the tobacco.

The streetlights were close now, less than fifty yards away, and his initial thought was that he had completed a circular tour of Northside itself, traversed the slums and arrived back at the clock tower, not far from the cafe where the girl who had reminded him of Shanifa worked. Surely his distraught mind had played a cruel jest on him; it was the waitress whom he had mistakenly followed in the dusk, dogging her footsteps until he lost her. And somehow he had arrived back at his starting place.

No, this was definitely not Northside, similar in some aspects but markedly different in its dowdiness and aura of poverty that transcended an area of high unemployment. It had no place in Britain even in the depths of an economic recession. But for Max Frame it had the most welcoming feature of all right now— *light*.

He was standing on the edge of a market square,

in the center of which stood a statue, green with
moss and headless so that it was unrecognizable, a
stone effigy towering up out of weedy cobblestones;
even featureless it could not hide the evil in its
threatening posture. A Luddite, Max decided, judging from its stone-clad attire, urging those around
it to go forth and destroy. Inanimate but living, it
embodied hate and oppression; your instinct was to
cower from it.

There were people moving about, dejected forms
in drab clothing, mooching to and fro aimlessly,
staring forlornly into badly lighted, dirt-stained,
cracked shop windows. Some parked cars, again
makes and models of yesteryear, in conditions vary-
ing from shambolic to immovable wrecks, untidily
parked so that they created an obstruction to passing traffic. Only there were no mobile vehicles.

Max moved back into the shadow cast by a precarious overhead wooden canopy, first checking to ensure
that there was nothing crouched in the darkness. His
ankle was throbbing, the scratches smarted, and
blood oozed from the wounds. He felt its thick liquid
warmth.

Where in the name of God was he? What was
this place of utter dejection and cloying terror
which housed creatures that skulked in dark places
and clawed passersby? The Ghetto, of course, a forbidden hell that had no right to exist in any civilized society.

Max lit another cigarette with the butt of the
first. His priority was to find Shanifa and take her
away from here. It was a daunting prospect, and
only the remote hope of seeing again the girl who
had been lost to him forever prevented him from
fleeing in blind panic.

Perhaps Shanifa wasn't dead after all. Logically,

she could not be if it *was* she whom Max had glimpsed earlier. After all, he only had *their* word for it that she had died, doctors and police who were both manipulators of the System. He had been in a coma at the time, had no way of disproving the evidence presented to him except by exhuming Shanifa's body. Which would have been vetoed had he sought permission because it would have exposed their cruel deception.

Suppose Shanifa was brain damaged . . . that the Ghetto was some kind of communal asylum, a hospital of degradation where the insane were interned to live out the natural term of their lives. Secreted away from a society who would not want to know, would shun them, anyway. Oh, Jesus Christ, it was a possibility. . . .

So he had to find her quickly.

It was then that he noticed the cafe, squashed inconspicuously between a drapery store and a butcher's shop, a row of mangy-looking rodents, hares or rabbits, hanging above the doorway of the latter. His gaze switched back to the cafe. He tried to make out the worn sign, thought it said THE GRILL, but the lettering was too faded for him to be certain. It was just possible to see through the glass door in spite of the dirt smears. The interior was long and narrow, a counter on one side, rickety tables strewn with dirty crockery on the other. The majority of tables were empty; just two were occupied, the diners sitting with their backs toward him.

Obviously it was self-service. There were about half a dozen customers queuing at the counter, screening his view of the assistant. Max hesitated, took a long drag on his cigarette, and tossed it into the street in a shower of sparks. He had to start somewhere, and this was as good a place as any.

The unoiled hinges creaked loudly as he scraped the door open. Nobody looked round. The stench inside was overpowering, a combination of stale cooking and body odors, the walls shiny with condensation, or it might have been grease from the smoking frying pan on the hob.

Max's mouth was dry and filled with a sour taste. He needed a drink; the thought of food was nauseating. Especially here. He stole a glance at the others in the queue: two women of indeterminable age, frayed head scarves almost masking their faces, shabby brown coats tightly belted. A kind of uniform, almost, in keeping with the drabness of the Ghetto. They were engaged in a muttered conversation. It sounded as if they were complaining, commiserating, afraid that their shared grievances might be overheard by those around them.

The five men wore either caps or trilby hats, mufflers knotted and tucked inside oily dungarees or heavy dark coats. Shoddy footwear scraped on the gritty, filthy floor. Manual and office workers, this appeared to be their meeting place after work, the only respite available to them at the end of the day's gruelling labors. A workers' takeaway, or eat at one of the grubby tables if you've time to kill, Max thought. It was revolting. Anywhere else the department of health would have closed this establishment down immediately.

Except in the Ghetto.

One of the women slouched toward a table, slopping thick brown liquid out of a chipped mug on the way. It might have been cocoa, but Max decided it was probably overmashed tea. You had to listen carefully to detect a hum of conversation, a faint buzz of whispered, indecipherable words, the undertones of terror.

Dirty glass sandwich covers attempted to hide their wares: bread that furled at the edges, ham that was suspiciously dark in color, cress that had withered and yellowed. The pungent aroma was not quite so strong now, possibly because Max had become acclimatized to it.

"Yes?"

Until she spoke, Max had not noticed the girl serving behind the counter, the degradation of the cafe and its clientele having distracted his attention. He was jerked out of his depressing and frightening reverie by her husky voice. He stared at the long blond hair which straggled and matted, the slim figure which even the creased and stained gray overall failed to hide; the pert features with the soft red lips and the blue eyes which would have smiled a welcome anywhere else. They were fixed on him, but there was no hint of recognition in them. Expressionless, a job that had to be done and that was all there was to it,

"Can I help you?"

Max swayed, held on to the counter in case he fell, felt his feet threatening to slip on the torn linoleum floor, his legs unable to support his weight. Shock waves coursed through him as if he had touched a live electric wire. *Oh, God in Heaven, it was Shanifa!*

He tried to speak, a jumble of distorted words that became trapped in his throat. Staring at the girl for whom he had searched these past hours, he willed her to recognize him, but her expression remained blank.

"Shanifa!" At last the name bubbled from his quivering lips, a strangled grunt that was lost amidst the hubbub of muttered conversation from the tables.

Her expression altered; a shadow appeared to flit across her pallid features—a dimming of the overhead naked light bulb or it might have been a momentary spasm of fear. Her hand knocked against something on the shelf beneath her, sent it rolling and clinking. It fell to the floor and shattered.

It seemed an eternity before she spoke again, a note of uncertainty in her voice, a whisper that was not intended to be heard at the tables. "I . . . I think you must have made a mistake."

"No. No, I haven't. You know me . . . don't you?" Oh, please, you *have* to know me.

Her eyes told him that she did, that recognition was frightening, that she was trying desperately to will her customer to be anybody else in the world, in the Ghetto, other than Max Frame. Wanting him to go away, to walk back through that door and out into the Square, to vanish; never to have existed. She closed her eyes briefly, swayed, but when she opened them again he was still there, staring at her with pleading eyes.

"Max." It came out as a sob. She averted her gaze. "Max, why did you have to come here? Oh, *why*?"

"To find you, Shanifa."

There was silence except for the continual background whispering. Nobody seemed to have noticed the newcomer. Thank God!

"I'm afraid we only serve tea. We're out of coffee, awaiting a delivery. It should be here tomorrow."

She remembered that he always drank coffee, never tea. Maybe the cafe had been waiting for years for that coffee which would never arrive. Max fought to get himself under control, then spoke in a faltering voice. "I've come to . . . to take you

back home, Shanifa. So that we can be together
again."

She almost dropped the mug that she had taken
from below the counter, but grabbed it just in time.
"I'm afraid that's impossible. I have to stay here."

"But *why*, in God's name?" He raised his voice
in desperation, a terrible feeling of despair beginning to creep over him. He had never once envis-
aged that if he found her, she would refuse to
accompany him out of the Ghetto. Now his stomach
was balling as an awful thought struck him: *he had
spotted her beyond the boundary, in Northside; she could
have returned home then if that had been her wish.* Instead, she had gone back to this awful cafe. Was
there, indeed, something mentally wrong with her,
and those who manipulated the System had brainwashed her into remaining here, an inmate in a
psychological prison?

She slopped some of the thick tea as she poured
it, then looked up. "I can't leave, Max, and that's
that. But *how* did you get here? *Did you die in the
accident, too?*"

She was crazy, after all. Her words struck him
with the force of a physical blow, and that icy prickling was back again at the base of his spine, starting
to travel upward. Yet, sane or insane, he meant to
take her back home. If this was the System's way
of disposing of their mentally sick patients, then he
would expose it, sell his story to the sensational tab-
loids, blow the lid right off.

"Look"— she pushed the mug across to him, spilling another puddle of the mahogany-colored brew
on the way— "just go back home, Max, and forget
that you ever came here. You aren't helping me . . .
you could get me into an awful lot of trouble."

Max sensed heads turning behind him, was afraid

to turn round in case he saw the faces beneath those caps and head scarves. He shivered. It was icy cold in here. Maybe the door didn't fit properly.

"I . . . I don't know if I can remember the way, Shanifa." The prospect of that maze of unlit streets was frightening. His ankle throbbed as if to remind him of the unknown horrors that lay between here and the safety of Northside.

"Oh, God!" There was despair in her expression as she entwined her fingers the way she used to do when she was agitated. She glanced over his shoulder at the other customers, then looked back at him. "I can't talk to you much longer, Max. *Please* go, for your own sake as well as mine." She was trembling, close to tears. "Go out of here, turn left, take the next street on your right . . . if only it wasn't dark. . . . By daylight, though, the police might pick you up . . ." Her twisted fingers were whitening in her dilemma. "But you'll have to take your chance; there isn't any other way. *But after dark there's Downers crawling out of every manhole, cellar, anywhere else they hide up by day!*"

"Downers?" Max tasted bile, fought against panic. No, it was a myth, the old legend mothers told their kids; it had gone on so long that everybody believed it. Dropouts, winos, that's all they were. Not pleasant, maybe even dangerous, but they weren't bogeymen. His inflamed ankle tried to tell him otherwise.

"You wouldn't understand." She was wiping up the spilled tea, speaking so quietly that he could barely hear her, her eyes darting furtively from side to side. "The bottom rung of the social ladder here, the dregs. Dropouts, only much, much worse. It's still early, though; they often don't emerge until well into the night, so you might be lucky. I pray that you will be. There's no other advice I can give you except to go and keep going—don't stop until you reach the Northside exit."

Max's ankle was throbbing painfully, an awful reminder of that creature, whatever it was, that had made a grab for him out of the shadows. A wave of dizziness hit him, and the counter tilted, taking Shanifa with it. And when it had steadied she was whispering again, even more furtively so that he had to lean forward to catch her words.

"I don't know how you got here, Max. I doubt if you do, either." Her words were anguished, but he sensed that she did not want him to go in spite of her repeated requests for him to leave. "But I want you to go, this very minute. Just slip away, and I'll be praying every second that you make it. Just . . . just remember me as I used to be."

"All right." I'm going to go home and get this bloody mess sorted out, but I'll be back. If necessary, next time I'll bring the police with me, Max vowed silently. "I'll go, if that's what you really want."

She nodded, tried to smile, but her trembling lips stopped her, her glistening blue eyes revealing an inner agony that she was unable, or afraid, to put into words. "Just keep walking and don't stop, whatever you do."

Max did not look back, went right out through that warped door. The Square was deserted; the window-shoppers and loiterers were gone, just the cars and that hideous headless statue left. Over on the far side a couple of stray dogs slunk into an alley at his approach. His brain was confused. He had difficulty in remembering Shanifa's directions; turn left . . . take the first street on your right. . . . He hoped he had got it right.

He stepped into total darkness the moment he

turned out of the lighted shopping area, shied from the impenetrable blackness which engulfed him, stood still and hoped that his vision would adjust. Afraid even to feel his way along some leaning railings in case. . . .

After a few minutes he found that he could discern the silhouettes of houses on either side of the street that led on into an awful abyss of black nothingness. He fought against panic, the urge to flee back to the light, to Shanifa. He recalled that she had mentioned the police, her fear in case they picked him up. Well, he was not afraid of the law; he had nothing to hide. Perhaps they would escort him out of the Ghetto. And yet there had been an undertone of terror in the way she had referred to them that was disquieting. Perhaps it was better if he did not come across a policeman. Or the Downers.

Had it not been for that vicious attack on his ankle, he would have dismissed the whole thing as pure fantasy. He was prepared to accept that there was something terribly wrong with Shanifa, that she was in need of psychiatric treatment, that she had been banished to this slum for a purpose. So it was not surprising that she believed the legends. But the agony in his ankle was stark reality, and that was where his escalating terror began. He had no choice but to run the gauntlet of whatever horrors lurked in the Ghetto.

Twenty minutes later Max was certain that there was no street leading off to the right, yet equally sure that he had not missed it. His route seemed to be turning back on itself in a vague horseshoe, and his greatest worry was that he might arrive back in the Square.

Don't stop, keep going, whatever you do.

He came to a fork and decided upon the right in preference to the left. Perhaps this was the road to which Shanifa had referred. He craved another cigarette but resisted the urge since the flame of his lighter might attract unwanted attention, giving him away to the prowling dropouts and muggers. The whole area was a dreadful slum; even that shopping precinct would not be acceptable to the working class residents of Northside. Maybe fifty years ago they might have tolerated it, certainly not nowadays.

The silence was unnerving him. He took to walking on tiptoe, an exceedingly painful posture after a short while. His injured foot ached, gnawed right up into his thigh, throbbed incessantly. It might be infected. He had no idea who or what his attacker had been. It felt swollen. Tomorrow he would let a doctor look at it.

Tomorrow . . .

A sudden cry shattered the cloying stillness, seemed to hasten the clouds up above on their way to shut out the stars, to hide from mankind whatever it was that had uttered that awful sound. Max stopped, pressed himself up against a stone wall, and tried to determine from which direction that unearthly noise had come. A kind of scream, the anguish of a tortured soul cut off before it reached its climax, the night air vibrating long after it had died away.

He was sure that it had come from up ahead, thankfully some distance away. He wanted to turn back, but that was out of the question. Listening, bracing himself in case it came again, he heard in his terror fast padded footfalls heading down the street toward him. *Coming for him.* But it was only his own palpitations that he heard.

The sound had probably been a scavenging cur, one of those mongrels that he had seen skulking in the Square. The place appeared to be infested with them.

Or a fox. The city was supposedly plagued by urban foxes. There had been a piece in the local newspapers a few weeks ago about how the council pest control officers were trying to combat the menace. Vixens screamed to attract a mate, an eerie, spine-chilling sound. So the article had claimed. . . .

It was a fox, then. He had nothing to worry about.

He continued on his way, always keeping to the right; this was his third right turn. Or was it the fourth? He wished that he had studied astronomy; then perhaps the stars amidst the scudding white clouds would have been an aid to direction. But, logically, if he just kept going, then he would come out *somewhere* eventually. He hoped that it would not be back at the Square.

Exhaustion was beginning to take its toll; he was having to drag his wounded leg along with him. The sky had cleared, and Max was able to discern his surroundings more clearly in the starlight. Some patches of shadow were blacker than others; he skirted them fearfully.

He was being watched again.

The feeling was stronger, more positive than his fear of the dark. Again he sensed the hidden watchers, tried to quicken his pace, but continued to slow down.

It was as if the unseen watchers were observing his progress, monitoring it, reporting it from one to another by means of some kind of weird telepathy, a host of evil eyes peering out of boarded-up windows and rotting doors. See him, follow him. *He is lost.*

They were following him now; he was certain of it, turning to look behind him, fearful of what he might see. But there was nobody in sight. Just shadows, dark indefinable shapes that froze in case he spotted them moving. Trying to run, staggering back to a walk, Max fought the urge to lie down and give up. It was some kind of sadistic game that they were playing with him; they could have taken him any time they wanted. Just as they had taken that poor creature whose death cry still rang in his ears.

No, it had just been a vixen calling for a mate.

Suddenly, he found himself on open, rubble-strewn ground. Sheer relief filled him. Here there were no shadows, nowhere for stalking creatures to lie in wait for him, just piles of soil and stones. The area was vaguely familiar. He told himself that it had to be that stretch of desolation that fringed Northside. Somewhere, not far away, were those dilapidated barriers, the boundary between madness and sanity.

Max called upon his last reserves, traversed the maze of rain-filled potholes, and stepped across deep trenches, afraid in case he slipped and fell into some bottomless abyss. The sky had clouded over. He was unable to see any recognizable landmarks, not the distant clock tower or the church. Or even the glow of the city lights. There was nothing except unending darkness.

He came upon an insurmountable mound of earth with dead weeds sprouting from it. He had not the strength to clamber up it; there seemed no way round it. It was as if an army of bulldozers had levelled this stretch of ground, pushed all the surplus rubble into one mighty mountain. Like a sort of Berlin Wall, Max thought, to stop people from getting in or out of the Ghetto.

They had let him get so far, those watchers knowing all along that there was no escape for their prey. Give him hope, dash it, let exhaustion render him a helpless victim for when they were ready.

Then he saw the small hut standing crazily on uneven ground, its rusted, corrugated sheets somehow hanging on, offering scant shelter.

Once, long ago, it might have been an ageing night watchman's hut, a refuge from the bitterly cold nights, a brazier glowing outside. Just as a shipwrecked mariner might have grabbed a length of flotsam, so Max Frame crawled inside its cramped interior. It creaked, grated a metallic protest at this intrusion, but, miraculously, it held firm.

It stank of urine, a sharp, sour odor which had somehow defied the cleansing winds that swept through this bleak inner-city desert. The earthen floor was dry and dusty in spite of the recent rain.

Max sank down, testing a wall with his back. It leaned but held. His head was beginning to ache; he might have a migraine before morning.

Morning. Did morning ever come to the Ghetto or was there only eternal night? He didn't know. Right now he didn't care.

If those Downers, as Shanifa called them, wanted him, he would not fight them. He had had enough.

But if daylight did come, then he would surely find his way back to the city he knew. Whichever it was to be, he would accept his fate.

Somewhere, a long way away, he heard that awesome scream again. This time it was not cut off, just lingered and grew faint like a mountain echo dying away. The killing cry of a wild beast that had run its prey to ground.

In a strange way the cry came as a relief to Max. For he was not the victim, the hunter had caught and killed and perhaps its bloodlust would be satisfied for this night. He had given up trying to convince himself that it was a fox.

Four

Morning *did* come to the Ghetto, after all. Max stared out from his rickety tin edifice across the gray, featureless wasteland. Lowering skies, a fast drizzle that reduced visibility to less than a hundred yards, obliterated the Northside skyline for which he searched.

He stretched his stiff and aching limbs. Even in the fog he should, by perseverance, be able to find his way out of here. No city suburb, no slum, was *that* big. Was it?

His socks and sneakers were still damp, and his ankle was throbbing. He knew he ought to examine that wound in the daylight, just in case it was starting to fester. It was a disconcerting prospect, and he didn't want to look at it. The thought itself was repulsive. Perhaps it was better to start looking for a means of escape, have it checked later by a doctor or a nurse at the hospital casualty ward. There wasn't much he could do about it here, whatever his findings. He did not have access to a first aid kit, not so much as a bottle of TCP. All the same— he shuddered at the thought— he would risk a quick peep.

Ugh! Max recoiled from the sight of the four red scratches across his ankle, which were pulsing visibly as if they went deep enough to score the bone.

They had bled and congealed into scabs, the flesh adjacent to them an unhealthy-looking pink. They might have started to go septic already.

Clawmarks, without a doubt, but what the Christ was capable of inflicting such a hideous injury in a suburban slum? Fox, cur, feline . . . Downer? Whatever, it had left its mark upon him. He would be scarred for a long time to come because of some unspeakable nocturnal fiend. He tried not to think about what might have happened to him had he not dragged himself free.

He looked at his watch. It had stopped. Damn, it had never done that in all the time he had owned it, an anniversary present from Janice eight years ago. 19.15. PM, of course, otherwise the twenty-four-hour digits would have read 7.15. That uneasy shiver returned to his cold and cramped body. *It was about quarter past seven yesterday evening when he had entered the Ghetto in pursuit of Shanifa.*

He was hungry, but that would have to wait because he wasn't likely to find any food until he got out of this hellhole. Escape from this place of degradation was his priority, and now time was on his side. He had all day in which to locate an exit, approximately twelve hours of daylight ahead of him, and, logically, if he just kept walking, he had to emerge somewhere.

Everywhere was muddy, a thick sucking mire, and within minutes his sneakers resembled heavy clogs. At every step he had to extricate his feet from the quagmire, stirring up foul vapors that nauseated him, had him retching. The stench of decay, the foul smell of decomposing matter as though this was some nightmarish graveyard and he was releasing the odor of rotting corpses that were buried just below the surface. His left leg was aching again, worse than yesterday, that dull throbbing spreading up into his thigh. Max knew that he could not keep going indefinitely.

He wondered why there was nobody about, not that one expected to meet anybody on a tract of derelict ground; but the Ghetto was definitely inhabited, so the chances were that he would meet somebody sooner or later. Shanifa's warning that the police might pick him up still nagged him. In which case he would explain his predicament to them. All the same, he would rather not meet anybody. The so-called Downers were reputed to be nocturnal creatures, so he didn't have to worry about them. At least for another twelve hours. . . .

It was drizzling now, thickening the fog, decreasing visibility to twenty yards or less. He could taste the dirty, gray vapor like stagnant algae-flavored water on his palate, tried to spit it out. A film of filth adhered to the shiny surface of his anorak, adulterated the fawn to a dirty gray. An old-fashioned smog, he had vague memories of their demise in his boyhood, how they rolled down the streets, spawned their own monsters out of everyday landmarks. You could get lost a couple of streets from home. . . .

Max stopped. He *was* lost, had been ever since he left the cafe last night. He had not the slightest idea in which direction he was heading. If only the skies had been clear, he would have been able to glean an idea from the position of the morning sun. But there would be no sun today, that was a certainty. Just thickening fog and unrelenting mud. For all he knew he might be travelling in a circle, and end up back at that tin shanty just as darkness was falling. Or worse.

He came upon the man unexpectedly. Max's initial

reaction was to turn back, sludge his way, hopefully
unnoticed, back into this vile mist. The other was
clearly unaware of Max's presence, sitting on a broken wooden beam in the same way that he might
have relaxed on a park bench on a summer's day,
arms folded, staring in the opposite direction, engrossed in his thoughts, whatever they might have
been.

Max noted the thick, curly black hair, the green
and red woollen sweater, tight-fitting Levis and
thick-soled boots caked with this accursed clay soil.
Casual smartness, frightening when you encountered it in the middle of a hateful no-man's-land.
Had the other been hurrying, going somewhere,
then Max could have accepted it with some degree
of normality. But nobody, by choice, would rest
awhile in this stinking morass. Yet clearly they
would, and did, for the man appeared to be doing
just that.

Max stood there undecided. It would have been
easy to obey his instincts and creep away; yet if he
pandered to his fears, he might wander here, hope-
lessly lost, until nightfall. Night, the time of the
Downers, when chilling cries were heard and unseen watchers observed you, followed you; when
your secret phobias turned to reality and you became a beast of the chase.

Max cleared his throat, a meaningful sound designed to announce his presence here. I say, I'm
sorry to disturb you, but I wondered if. . . .

The stranger turned around slowly, almost reluctantly, and Max saw that he was of Caribbean origin,
his skin dark brown, his features swarthy. But it was
the lack of expression that had Max squelching back
a pace, reminding him of his meeting with Shanifa
before her fear had manifested itself. Neither sur-

prise nor annoyance at having his reverie disturbed, just an acceptance that he was no longer alone. Staring, not speaking, not so much as a nod to signal a chance meeting.

Max swallowed. "Good morning."

No reply. Those eyes saw, but there was no curiosity in them. At any second the other might turn back, return to his own cocoon of oblivion. Perhaps it was some kind of meditation, Max decided.

"I don't want to disturb you." I do, I already have.

"That's all right," the thick lips spoke in a monotone, the face still devoid of expression. Words because they were expected of him, they carried no meaning.

Max waited, but there was nothing more forthcoming. It was all right to be disturbed and there was nothing else to say.

"I wonder . . ." Max felt in his pockets for his cigarettes. "That is . . . do you think . . . you could tell me in which direction the city lies?"

"That way." A half turn from the waist, an arm extended, a finger jabbing behind him into the mist. He turned slowly back. He had answered the question; he had nothing more to add.

The city lay over there, obliquely to Max's left. He noticed a well-trodden, mud-compressed track leading off in the direction indicated. Obviously others walked that way, a primitive thoroughfare, possibly a shortcut. And this was as far as they came, their destination a half-rotted beam on which to sit and enjoy the foul, lung-coating vapors at their leisure.

"Cigarette?" Max extended the crumpled packet.

The stranger regarded it steadily, almost as if he did not comprehend. Then a faint movement of his head might have signalled either an acceptance or a refusal. The fact that he turned away, resumed his original posture, obviously meant that he had declined the offer to smoke.

Ignorant bastard! Max forced himself to be angry because anger kept fear at bay. He drew the tobacco smoke deep down into his lungs, then expelled it slowly in twin streams from his nostrils. At least something had been achieved from this unexpected meeting; he was a giant step nearer to finding a way out of the Ghetto than he had been since leaving the cafe last night. The city lay over there, how far or near he had no idea, but if he set off right away, he was certain to reach it before too long. At least, this time, he had a defined route to follow. The man had come that way, obviously, so Max would return by the same path.

The going was easier now. Max was forced to stop less frequently to dislodge the mud balls from his feet. In places the clay was compacted as though many feet had trodden it to a firm surface. The fog was not thinning, but it was not getting any thicker either. One was entitled to a little optimism; Max felt more confident now. At least he appeared to be heading somewhere instead of nowhere.

The cigarette tasted sour, but it was preferable to the fog's flavor, pollution at its worst, all the foulness of a forgotten slum seeping up out of the ground, permeating your system, contaminating you. Just as it had contaminated this place and its weird inhabitants.

One moment Max was walking on mud, beginning to despair once again of ever emerging from the fog, the next he was standing on a hard concrete surface; a pavement, people and traffic hurrying past him. The sudden transformation of his surroundings had him leaning up against a wall, trying to adjust to his new surroundings, a wave of dizziness sweeping over him. Not understanding, for the moment not wanting to. Suffice that the fog had cleared, that he had at last emerged from that dreadful urban marshland— *if* it had ever existed. Standing here on a busy city street, he had his doubts. A glance down at his muddied footwear assured him that it had been no nightmarish hallucination, no mirage of that foul fog. It had been reality, all right.

He clawed another cigarette out of the pack. Maybe it would help to dispel the sourness in his mouth once and for all, but, more important, it was something *normal* with which to occupy himself while he attempted to adjust. He needed to work all this out for the sake of his own sanity, to reason, to reach some kind of an acceptable conclusion.

One: he had wandered into the city's slums, lost himself into the bargain.

Two: Shanifa was alive and living there.

Three: he had to return home, bathe and change before he caught pneumonia, then consult a doctor about his ankle.

Four: he had to return and rescue Shanifa. If necessary, he would go to the police.

An uneasy feeling crept into his already disturbed mind. Something was dreadfully wrong, but he could not quite place it. He had found his way back into the city, but despite having lived here all his life, instructing driving pupils through virtually every street, *he was totally ignorant of his present surroundings*.

He drew hard on his cigarette, eyed passersby surreptitiously. Multiracial features, everybody hurrying, nobody lingering. *Nobody talking.*

He let that shiver have full rein, allowed it to rush right up his spine, into his neck, and tingle his scalp. The stranger in the mist had been correct in the directions that he had given. That muddy track had led right into the city.

But where and what on God's earth was this city?

Directly opposite stood a department store, seven or eight floors high, adjacent to a hotel. No name, just HOTEL. People were going in and coming out of both buildings, a milling throng, but all had one feature in common that was emphasized by the line of stretch limousines parked outside— *affluence.* More than that, an arrogance, a contempt for the other walkers, pushing rudely past them in their efforts to reach their plush vehicles or their hotel accommodation. A class distinction that was . . . *evil.* In a way they were far more frightening than the nocturnal inhabitants of the Ghetto, Max thought, because their malevolence transcended a bestial existence. They had *power.* They flaunted it over a lower class.

Max could have convinced himself that by some strange means he had been transported back in time to an eastern bloc country before the fall of the Berlin Wall, a totalitarian state, where these people he observed ruled cruelly, while at the lower end of the echelon the peasants had been driven to live in degradation in the subways and sewers. And somewhere Shanifa was caught up in it all.

Which was all sheer bloody nonsense, he tried to assert to himself. This was Britain approaching the twenty-first century; such divisions did not exist. He had flipped his brain, a direct result of the car accident. He needed help, treatment, and not just for his ankle.

Max ground out his cigarette beneath the mud-caked sole of his sneaker. He could not stand here indefinitely. He had to talk to somebody, find out just what the hell was going on. *If* he could find anybody who conversed.

The wailing of a siren interrupted his thoughts, had him cowering back against the wall as a black sedan, a flashing blue light on its roof, squealed its tires round the main traffic island beyond the hotel. He saw white lettering on the car's side, a stark POLICE.

It slewed its way through the congested traffic, caught the wing of an old green Renault, and ploughed on. Coming this way. . . .

Bile scorched Max's throat. He wanted to run, but his legs would not move. His intestines were knotting like a nest of poisonous snakes intent on throttling one another. Shanifa had warned him to beware of the police, and now it appeared that the hurtling, braking patrol car had smelled him out, was bearing down upon him, bumping the curb as it skidded to a halt directly alongside him.

Somebody had broken away from the crowd, running, a figure in a gaudy green and red sweater, skin-tight Levis and mud-caked boots padding on the sidewalk. Panic-stricken flight. Where earlier those swarthy West Indian features had been expressionless, they were now contorted into a mask of sheer terror.

Max savored a moment of selfish relief because these policemen were not after him; they had already singled out their prey.

Now they had him.

An elasticized figure on the end of a full-

stretched sweater was being hauled in, a fish fighting a nylon line all the way. Vicious grunting, the
police were pulling him in, a forest of batons poised
to strike.

A kneecap cracked with a pistollike report as
wood shattered bone. The fugitive would have fallen
but for the tautness of his garment, a farmer's
scarecrow crucified, held aloft, legs dangling bro-
kenly.

A single protest before they smashed his mouth.
"Motherfuckers!"

Bloodied features hid the agony from the crowd
of onlookers, brown awash with crimson. The victim
was no longer struggling.

One of the uniformed officers thrust with his
weapon, took the prisoner full in the genitals; had
him writhing like a string puppet dancing a wild
jig. More blows rained down.

Max turned his head, retched; on a full stomach
he would have vomited. Sheer brutality for the sake
of it was being perpetrated by those elected to
maintain law and order.

Some of the watchers had slunk up to Max,
crowded him, featureless figures in fawn macs with
caps or trilbys. The women wore head scarves,
folded so that they resembled Easterners who were
forbidden to reveal their faces. Angry but demoralized, none of them would go to the wretched man's
aid. Even crowd courage, it seemed, did not exist
here.

Max found his gaze meeting with that of an adjacent bystander, eyes that flickered their terror under the lowered hat brim, bloodless lips compressed.

"What's he done?" Max whispered. "Why are
they doing this to him?"

"He came back." The reply was a wheezed whis-

per as though the speaker suffered with bronchitis
or some other chest ailment.

"Back? From where?"

"From the Waste." The other's voice was so low
that it was scarcely audible, those eyes shifting from
side to side, fearful in case he was overheard. "Once
you are condemned to the Waste, you do not return. See for yourself what happens if you do!"

Then the man had moved on, carried along by
the trickle of frightened observers who were now
leaving, afraid to remain any longer. There was
nothing to stay for now. It was all over.

Three policemen were dragging the huddled,
bloodied form toward their car, lifting him by his
smashed arms and legs, swinging him up into the
open boot. There was a thud as he landed; a leg
that draped lifelessly over the side was kicked back
in, the lid slammed shut.

One of the officers regarded the retreating crowd,
his baton cradled in the crook of his arm in the
manner of a sporting gun. Arrogance and bestiality
in his posture, mutely challenging them, willing
them to rush him. He and his colleagues had tasted
blood; they craved more.

Max followed the crowd, limped along with them,
going wherever they were going because there was
nowhere else to go. But there was no safety in numbers, just companionship in fear and misery.

Jesus, how the hell did this place come to exist;
why had nobody ever found it? They must know
about it outside. It was all a big cover-up like he had
first supposed. The Ghetto was more than just a
slum; it was a city within a city, somehow hidden
away from prying eyes, allowed to fester in its own
evil, affluence and poverty living side by side, beset

with terror and violence, and creatures that screamed their bloodlust under cover of darkness.

Everybody had gone. Max realized that he was alone, standing in a street with houses on either side but not a soul in sight. He wanted to shout for that tramping crowd, yell for them to come back. He would have followed except that he had no idea where they had gone. One moment they were all around him, the next they had disappeared. Please, don't leave me here alone. A surge of panic, he found himself cowering in case a police car roared into view, skidded to a halt alongside him, and uniformed officers spilled out with their batons ready to break his bones and pulp his flesh to a bloody mulch. But even they were no longer to be seen.

Something was different, and once again the sudden change in his surroundings brought with it a sense of vertigo. It took his confused mind several seconds to recognize what it was. The bleakness was gone; the houses, neat semis, exuded a lived-in warmth, a welcome to a lonely and frightened wanderer even though there was no sign of their occupants.

The pavements were swept clean of litter. Alongside lay tidy front gardens with closely mown lawns and flower borders dug over in readiness for spring planting, bulbs pushing up out of the soil. The cars were modern and rustless, shining from a recent wash. Close by a bird was singing; Max did not know whether it was a blackbird or a thrush. It did not matter, suffice that it was a bird and it was singing.

He checked his surge of sheer relief, his euphoria, in case it was yet another fiendish trick of the Ghetto. You see it, now you don't.

He clutched at a gatepost, hung on with grim

determination. He wasn't going anywhere except here. He would cling on here forever.

Gradually, in stages, Max brought himself back under control. Somehow, miraculously, accidentally, he had escaped from the Ghetto, stepped right back on to Northside. He could even smell the aroma of the fish and chip shop on Queen Street. He had found his way back to the city.

Only one thing marred his ecstasy, the reminder that he had left Shanifa back in the Ghetto. He promised himself that one way or another, he would go back for her.

Five

Doctor Stackpool was not renowned amongst his patients for his bedside manner. Often abrupt, his personality was virtually nonexistent, his expression stoic so that it was impossible to guess the outcome of a diagnosis by studying his features. He might, or might not, reveal his findings. If he decided to break the news, good or bad, then he told you the plain facts. Usually he just scribbled out a prescription, tore it off the pad and thrust it at you, left you in no doubt that the consultation was at an end. A clearing of the throat discouraged any questions that might be asked. The button on his desk was pushed; a buzzer sounded at the far end of the corridor, and a neon sign in the waiting room announced "next patient."

At fifty John Stackpool was still hopeful of a partnership in a rural practice somewhere, preferably in Wales because the scenic landscape appealed to him, although he had never confided this to anybody. An aura of mystique was an integral part of a GP's status.

Max Frame had hoped to obtain an appointment with one of the two younger doctors. It was significant of Doctor Stackpool's popularity that he was the only one of the three who was available on that day.

He consulted Max's file, then asked what the

problem was in a tone that obviously anticipated a request for tranquilizers or sleeping tablets. It would have been the easy way out for both of them.

"This." Max pulled up his left trouser leg and rolled the sock down. "I'm worried in case it's infected."

With not so much as a pursing of his lips, Doctor Stackpool examined the wound; pressed with his fingertips so that Max winced and gasped. He let the trouser fall back; he had seen enough. The doctor straightened up and turned away.

For Christ's sake ask me how I got it; *tell me what did it!* Max was taut, angry at the medic's nonchalance. The bastard wasn't interested, didn't give a shit. Maybe he supposed that his patient had scraped his foot with a gardening tool; more likely he didn't suppose at all. It was just a nasty wound. He worked by the book and knew what he had to do.

Stackpool reached for a syringe in the cupboard, then turned away to fill it. A tetanus booster, without a doubt. Max tensed, closed his eyes. It was going to bloody hurt. It was intended to. It did.

Max watched the other scribbling something on a pad, snatching at the perforation so that it tore unevenly.

"Er . . . thank you." Max accepted the square of paper, but did not bother to try to read it because the writing would be illegible, anyway. He wanted to ask, "It'll be all right, won't it?" or "It isn't infected, is it?" But that aura of superiority over nonmedical folk which the doctor had created, a barrier against questions that he either could not or did not want to answer, held Max back. You've had your injection, now go and get your pills and don't bother me again.

The buzzer sounded far away. Max hesitated momentarily in the doorway, gave the doctor one last chance to put that question to him. Go on, ask me what species of animal attacked me. Because I've got my story ready, a feral cat that's been hanging around the estate for weeks. But Doctor Stackpool did not look up; he was busily, too busily, shuffling the next patient's file. He had prescribed the required antibiotics; it wasn't his problem anymore. Piss off.

The police station was an even more harrowing experience for Max. An attitude of disinterest that bordered on hostility began at the reception desk, a dour uniformed sergeant with a built-in grievance that stemmed from his lack of promotion prospects.

"Yes?" I don't want to help you because I'm too bloody busy, but I'll go through the motions because I have to. A sigh, get it over quick and get out.

"I'd like a word with the chief superintendent." Max tried to sound self-confident, went for the top rank in the hope that he might be fobbed off with the assistant chief superintendent.

"The . . . chief . . . superintendent?" An admonishment for daring to ask to see the chief, incredulity that had been perfected with practice, was designed to discourage and overawe. Eyes wide, forehead furrowed, tapping the desk with the top of his ballpoint.

"That's right." Max smiled, lodged an elbow on the shelf. "My name is— "

"The chief superintendent only sees people by appointment"— belligerent, challenging— "by written request, addressed to this station." Haughty, assumed indignation that came over as rudeness. "If you really wish to see him, sir, please make your application in writing, stating your reason, together with your name and address. If that reason is good enough, then the chief superintendent will reply to you making an appointment for you to call. But it is an exception rather than the rule, sir."

Jesus in a wheelchair! Write a letter, post it first class and in all probability it wouldn't arrive until next week. Allow another week, ten days, for a reply, an appointment fixed for the week after that, provided the reason was good enough. And throughout all this procrastination Shanifa was trapped in that hellish slum hole. Bureaucracy in motion, dragging its heels in the hope that you would give up and forget it. A parallel with Wanda's fatal accident; the guy had been charged with causing death by drunken driving, fined £400 and banned for three years. The police had not even taken a statement from her husband, who had been the only witness, a botch-up from the start. The System determined who received justice and who went without it. You can't see the chief, sir, in case you ask awkward questions and cause the force embarrassment.

"What about the *assistant* chief superintendent?" Drop a rank.

"I'm sorry, sir, he's currently on a fortnight's leave."

Shit, the pecking order was diminishing by default, descending upon . . .

"Can *I* help you, sir?" I won't if I can avoid it, but I'll do my damnedest to get rid of you and hope you don't come back.

"Perhaps the chief inspector can help me. *If* he's available."

The sergeant turned away abruptly and walked back across the main office toward the switchboard. Slowly. He dialled an extension number, spoke into the mouthpiece, and came back to reception. "Can I have your name, sir?"

"Frame. Max Frame."

A further delay, the sergeant's expression had changed because he was, presumably, speaking to the chief inspector. He replaced the receiver, then came back. "If you would like to take a seat over there, sir, the chief inspector will see you in a few minutes."

Delaying tactics, playing the waiting game. All part of the conditioning process, kept waiting like a naughty schoolboy sent to the headmaster by his form teacher. By the time the head eventually saw you, all you wanted to do was blurt out your confession to some misdemeanor, whether you were innocent or guilty, and get the punishment over as quickly as possible. It was twenty-five minutes before Max was escorted by a rookie constable to the chief inspector's office.

"And what can I do for you, Mister Frame?" Chief Inspector Horlick was in his late thirties, wavy brown hair and an alert expression, a whiz kid who might one day make it to chief constable, Max decided. Maybe even to a top rank in the metropolitan force. His friendliness was a facade. Those keen gray eyes searched Max out, looked for flaws, weaknesses whereby he could be broken down if the necessity arose. "Do sit down, Mister Frame, and tell me what's bothering you."

"The Ghetto!" Max blurted it out, shock tactics in the hope of a reaction. His ankle was throbbing mercilessly; the antibiotics had not yet had time to work. He was tense, angry; the long wait had not helped.

"The . . . *Ghetto?* Oh, you mean *Pace Park!*"

"Yes." So that was what they called it nowadays,

a touch of pseudo respectability that was possibly intended to detract from any racist implications.

"It's just a derelict slum, nothing more." The chief inspector's eyes flickered briefly beneath lowered lids, his tone of voice almost a banter. A dismissal, the big play-down." Nobody ever goes there except a few dropouts and drug addicts. I can't for the life of me see why it should bother you. The council have barricaded up all the possible places of entry to keep the public out. For their own good. There's nothing there to interest anybody, nothing to see. One day it will probably be redeveloped, an industrial site, factory units and the like, I expect. How on earth can it be a problem to you?" A sudden sharpening of the voice, a veiled reprimand.

"Because . . ." Max met the other's gaze, held it— "my girlfriend is living in there. Working in a cafe."

Horlick's expression was meant to say "you're crazy." Then he averted his eyes, consulted some typewritten notes on his desk, flipped a page, and flash-read it. Doctor Stackpool's aura of mystique had obviously spread to the police force, Max thought. He's got a bloody file on me; Big Brother doesn't miss a trick, answers scripted in advance to meet any eventuality.

"What is your girlfriend's name, Mister Frame?"

"Shanifa. Shanifa Smith." You bastard, you've got it written down there in front of you. A trick question, catch him out if you can.

When Horlick spoke again his tone was terse, matter-of-fact; the pseudo friendliness had evaporated. "That's impossible; she was killed in a car accident on December 23 last."

"*I* don't think that she was."

"I can assure you, Mister Frame"— irritation, a

tightening of the thin lips—"that Shanifa Smith is dead. A death certificate, a funeral on December 30. We can't argue with that. I think you've made a mistake."

"No, I haven't." Dig your heels in, don't be brainwashed. This is the big cover-up, and I'm not going to let you bloody well get away with it.

"A case of mistaken identity, perhaps." Condescending, smirking with it. "Everybody has a near-double somewhere, Mister Frame. A chance glimpse, possibly in uncertain light, coupled with emotional stress, you know."

"I tell you, I saw her. I *spoke* to her. She's working in a grotty cafe in the . . . in Pace Park."

"There are no cafes in Pace Park, Mister Frame. Nothing except ruined buildings and wasteland. And, anyway, how did *you* come to be there?"

Max sighed. You stonewalling, lying bastard! Next thing you'll be trying to convince me I'm . . .

"You were seriously injured in that same car accident, Mister Frame." Back to the sympathy line, a softening of the voice, the head inclined slightly to one side. "You were in a coma, on the critical list, three months in the hospital. A suspected hairline fracture of the skull. I believe you're still receiving treatment." Because I think it has affected your sanity.

"No."

"Oh . . . I understood that you were."

Christ, your minions have sure done your homework for you, medical records on tap at the touch of a computer switch, transferred to police files. It was probably an amalgamation of reports on the big pileup that night; they were still investigating it. Delaying because there would be no conclusive outcome. Just one of those things. Like him. "I was supposed to attend a physiotherapy clinic but I declined."

"Who's your doctor?"

"Doctor Stackpool." As if you haven't got that on your printout, too. "I saw him this morning, as a matter of fact."

"But you said you were no longer receiving treatment, Mister Frame?" A glib catch question, those eyes accusing, seizing an opportunity to prove that the other was lying. Small lies led to big lies. You're making the whole thing up, wasting police time, Mister Frame.

"That was for something else. *This!*" Max pulled up a Levi leg, pushed the sock down, and displayed his scabbed clawmarks. Now, you tell me, Inspector!

"Nasty." No revulsion; policemen were hardened to physical injuries. "Where did you get that?"

"In Pace Park."

Chief Inspector Horlick rose to his feet, walked over to the window and stood looking out, his back toward Max. He seemed tense, disturbed, but there was no way of knowing without seeing his face and he made sure that Max did not glimpse his expression.

"Mister Frame"— it was maybe half a minute before he spoke again— "you've been under a lot of stress, a bereavement. The mind can play strange tricks in such circumstances. If I may, I'd like to offer you some advice. Go back to Doctor Stackpool, tell him what you've just told me. I'm sure he'll be able to advise you."

"No." A hoarse whisper that embodied frustration and despair, the agonized croak of the hopeless. "The doctor can't do anything to help me. Just some pills to stop my wound from becoming infected."

"Very well, then." The policeman turned round, and there was no mistaking the anger in his expression. "Please yourself. See a doctor, or don't, as you wish. But I'm telling you here and now, Shanifa Smith is dead, and if you persist in thinking otherwise, then that's up to you. But don't come wasting police time with your crazy notions!"

"Thank you." Max moved toward the door. "To be perfectly honest, I half guessed you might say that. At least I know where I stand now."

"Before you go." The clipped command halted Max's departure. "Just a word of warning. Don't get going back to Pace Park, or the Ghetto, as you call it. Because you won't find her there, that I can promise you. You are sick, you've been hallucinating. But should you be foolish enough to disregard my advice, then I'm afraid that you might find yourself in trouble with the police. Pace Park is council land, strictly out of bounds to the public because its terrain is hazardous. A building might collapse and bury you or you might fall into an exposed sewer. A thousand and one mishaps could befall you. You take my advice, Mister Frame, go back to Doctor Stackpool; he'll sort your problems out for you. But whatever you decide to do, *stay away from Pace Park!*"

Max slammed the door behind him as he left.

Six

There was probably nobody else in the whole world, except Shanifa, to whom Max would have answered the front doorbell. Except Nat Bonner.

Max had gone upstairs to lie on the bed around midday. The tablets seemed to be working; his leg felt much less painful. Sheer exhaustion was beginning to take its toll of him; he might sleep a full cycle. Somewhere in the depths of his slumber he heard the chimes, tossed restlessly. They came again; he stirred. Whoever it was could carry on ringing; eventually they would give up and go away. If it was the solicitor, he would surely telephone later, leave a message on the answering machine. Max just wanted to be left alone. Nevertheless, curiosity lured him from his bed, had him padding barefooted across to the window. A quick peep, just to satisfy himself, then he would go back to sleep.

Nat Bonner had been seventeen last September. The week following his birthday his father had paid for him to have a course of driving lessons; they were both expecting too much, Max thought. One needed more than basic driving skills to pass a test. Experience, for a start. Patience, too, which the youth lacked and probably never would acquire. But it was business, money which could not be refused in lean times. With luck, combined with a lenient examiner,

Nat *might* just have passed. His test had been scheduled for January 6. An awful lot had happened in
the meantime. Max had forgotten all about it until
now.

Possibly Nat had phoned, left a message on the
answering machine; if so, it was still there waiting
to be played back. Max experienced a moment of
guilt, then began pulling on his clothes and rushed
downstairs. He owed it to Nat to enquire how the
test had gone, at least.

"Nat!"

Nat had given up, was walking back down the
driveway, shoulders hunched, head hung low, a lithe
but powerful figure in T-shirt and cords, his scuffed
trainers crunching on the gravel.

"Nat, wait!"

But there was no way the boy was going to hear
him. Because Nat was deaf.

A touch on the arm, Nat started, whirled round.

"Hi, Nat, it's good to see you . . ." Max's voice
trailed off. There was a sudden sinking sensation
in his stomach. The greeting was not reciprocated;
that wide smile, the effervescent personality that
even a disability failed to dampen, was nonexistent.
Blue eyes that normally glinted with the sheer joy
of living were shiny with tears, red-rimmed and
pouched. The lips trembled, struggled to stiffen.
The fair hair was awry, matted, had not been
combed recently. Despair, dejection, it might not
have been Nat Bonner who stood there in the
spring sunshine, instead some vague lookalike.

"Nat, what's the matter? You failed your test?"

"No. I passed, Max."

"Congratulations." It sounded trite, seizing on a
way of hiding his embarrassment. Something was
terribly wrong; it transcended trivialities like driving

tests. Max gestured toward the open front door.
"Would you . . . like to come inside?"

The youth hesitated, then looked back down the
drive, perhaps regretting having come here. Finally
he nodded, swallowed.

Max led the way through to the kitchen and
switched the kettle on. This wasn't going to be easy;
he was in no frame of mind to enter into one of
those you-cry-on-my-shoulder-and-I'll-cry-on-yours
situations. But now that Nat was here it was best
to let him tell him whatever it was in his own time.

A remarkable kid, you had to admire him. Officially designated as "partial hearing," Nat had been
rendered deaf when he was three, possibly due to
meningitis. But he had fought all the way, knew
sign language but relied on lipreading most of the
time. He watched you speak, understood you, and
conversed in a near-normal voice; you might suspect
that he had a slight impediment of speech if you
were a stranger, but you didn't notice it after the
first couple of sentences, forgot about it.

Max and Nat had struck up a kind of camaraderie
after that first lesson; not because Nat was an excep-
tional learner, but because he was a one hundred
percent trier. If he did not master something at the
first attempt, he persevered until he did. Deafness
was no real disadvantage where driving was concerned; you did not even have to declare it on your
license application form. Car drivers listening to ra-
dios or cassette players shared an equal handicap.
Nat had learned to coordinate gear changes by the
engine's vibrations rather than trying to listen to the
revs. He had mastered it better than most hearing
students. He was ready to take a test after ten lessons,
Max had decided. He had been proved right.

"I'm pleased you passed your test, Nat." Max

tried to make small talk; the silence was awkward, embarrassing.

There was no reply. Damn, he had forgotten again; Nat had to be able to see your lips when you spoke. Max turned round to face his visitor. "I'm glad you passed, Nat."

"Thanks." An instant reply coupled with an attempt to smile; he almost made it. "I heard about . . . I'm sorry, Max. I called at the hospital, but they said no visitors. I came here once, but you weren't at home. And then . . ."

Nat was close to breaking down. This was no time to press the issue, whatever it was. Max slid a mug of coffee across the table. It had to be small talk for a while yet.

"I would've phoned if I could, Max, but you know I can't hear on the phone."

Max nodded. Nat did not have much of a home life. His mother had died when he was eight, and his father had been left to bring him up alone. Sid Bonner spent most of his life at the ironmongery in Northside Central, six days a week and often had to catch up on lawn mower maintenance on Sundays. The stalwart of the firm, he had worked there since leaving school, and he would retire from there.

"Max . . ." Nat was staring at the steaming coffee as though right now it was the most important thing in the whole world to him. His lips were moving, but had difficulty in forming the words that he was trying to say. "Max . . . my father's . . . *dead!*"

"Oh! I'm . . . I'm terribly sorry, Nat." Embarrassed, Max tried to share grief over someone he had never met, only heard mentioned in conversation. A name, another number in the System; he was sorry for Nat, wished somehow he could feel sorry for his father. Somebody died somewhere every minute of every day. Death was commonplace, all part of living, until it happened to somebody close to you. Max deliberately switched his thoughts to Shanifa in an attempt to generate grief within himself. It didn't work. Because Shanifa wasn't dead.

"Three weeks ago." Nat sipped his coffee. His cheeks were wet; it might have been from the steam. "They buried him a fortnight ago yesterday."

The small talk was done with; from now on it was up to Nat to tell what he had come here to tell. Another awkward silence. Max fixed his attention on the clock on the èlectric cooker. The Belling had not been used since last December, there was a cobweb across the top oven door, but that timepiece was still going. Bloody incredible when you thought about it, five months of trauma for himself but that clock had never faltered, not by so much as a second. A shiver pricked the nape of his neck. His watch had stopped, though. In the Ghetto. There had been nothing wrong with it; by the time he had returned home it was going again, had caught up where it had left off. Like that night had never existed.

"A heart attack." Nat let it out in a rush as though it had been trapped inside him for the past three weeks. "A massive one. He was servicing a lawn mower, collapsed on top of it. Gone instantly. I guess it's the best way to go. Oh, God, I'm sorry, Max, I didn't realize. I wasn't thinking."

"It's all right." Max smiled reassuringly. "You're right, it's better than lingering on for weeks in pain or in a coma."

Another silence and then, "You're sure you don't mind me telling you all this, Max?"

"No, of course not."

Max sensed that there was more to follow, saw how Nat was nervously picking his nails, the way he

used to do when he was being tested on the High-
way Code. The youth was trying to muster the courage to say what he had come here to say, fearful
of making a fool of himself and being ridiculed.
His father's death was just the starting point.

"Something else you want to tell me, Nat?" A cue
if it was needed, a nudge. "I think we know each
other well enough by now to say anything we want
to say, don't you? There's something I'd like to talk
to you about as well. Afterward."

"Thanks, Max." There was genuine gratitude in
the other's tear-filled eyes, but it was more than
just grief causing those tears, Max decided. Some
kind of inner anguish that went much deeper than
the death of a loved one.

"My father's gone to hell, Max."

Shit, this was really over the top. "I'm sure he
hasn't, Nat. Your father was a good man." I didn't
even know him, but any guy who will slave six days
a week, sometimes seven, to bring up his son can't
be bad. "I guess he's gone to heaven where all good
people go."

"I would like to think so, but I *know* different!"
Nat's face was screwed up with the agony that raged
inside him. "He's in hell."

Had it been anybody else but Nat, Max would have
dismissed it as overemotional ramblings brought
about by stress and grief. But he recalled a couple
of instances during those first few lessons when Nat
seemed to possess an incredible sense of anticipation
that bordered on foresight, more so than most experienced drivers, including himself. Once the youth
had sensed that an elderly motorist was about to pull
out of a line of parked cars without signalling, and
had swerved in time to avoid a crunch. On another
occasion a dog had darted out into the road. Nat

could not possibly have stopped in time unless he had known what was about to happen *before* the animal came into view. He had slammed on his brakes with inches to spare. Uncanny. Almost . . . *psychic*.

Max believed what the other was saying, that Sid Bonner was in hell. It was illogical, crazy. It was also very frightening. He found himself wishing that Nat had stayed away, or that he had not answered the door to him. No, that would not have solved anything.

"Hell isn't what you think it is, like they tell you in church." Nat was calmer now, speaking in a low voice. "It's not eternal fire and all that crap. It's just a place, and not as far away as we might think."

Max's flesh was covering with goose pimples.

"In fact, I think it's quite close to here." There was a terrifying naivete about the youth that made Max believe him even though his logic screamed at him not to. "Maybe so close that we don't recognize it for what it really is."

Max's vision blurred. He found himself clutching at the edge of the table in case the room started to gyrate; it threatened to but steadied. There was a roaring in his ears, his temples were throbbing.

"It's the city of the dead," Nat went on, staring fixedly at the coffee mug as he talked, perhaps afraid to look at his companion in case he saw doubt and scorn in his expression. "You know, drab, featureless, but awful. The people exist there in hopelessness, tormented because they know it will go on forever. A slum, but there are rich folks there as well; there has to be because somebody has to make life intolerable for everybody else. But the rich are in purgatory, too, because they are just another part of the System, fighting one another to gain power. Like a communist regime, if you see what I mean. But everybody ends up there when they die, Max. There was an alternative once, a heaven, but not any longer. God has punished the human race for allowing this decadent society of ours to flourish. I think that He wants them to suffer in the pit of their own corruption. However good you might have been in life, you'll still go to hell. Like my father has."

"How do you know all this?" There was a sincerity about the question, a hesitancy because he feared the answer. It was like listening to the gibberish beliefs of some weird religious sect, but he did not doubt Nat. He wished to God that he did.

"Because I have been there!"

Max swallowed. That sour taste was back in his mouth, reminding him of the foul mist that had rolled across the Waste and the inhabitants of the Ghetto.

"I prefer to think of my visits as dreams, terrible nightmares, but they were more than that. It was as though my soul left my body while I slept and ventured to this hell and back. It happened again only last night, and that was the worst of all, the reason I am here now, telling you. Because if I don't tell somebody I shall go mad. I was there, standing in this street, almost suffocated by the vile stench of the place, when on the opposite side of the road I saw this line of warders making their way toward the prison for their morning shift. Oh, Max, you should have seen the expressions on their faces, the sheer cruelty as they lusted for their prisoners, talking and laughing about the sadistic tortures they were going to inflict on them! But, Max—" Nat's face was a mask of terror, drained of every vestige of color, shaking so that he could barely speak— *"my father was amongst them, one of them, an animal!"* He slumped forward on the table, his fingers scrabbling on the Formica surface like a trapped rat trying to claw its way out of a trap, sobbing uncontrollably.

Max looked away. Consolation was futile; the boy had to get it out of his system in the only way he knew how. Nat had been bottling it up inside him; letting it out had hurt but it was the only way.

Nat raised his head. His eyes seemed to have shrunk back into their sockets; his quivering lips were bloodless. "I'm sorry, Max." His voice was like the last whisperings of an echo. "I can't expect you to believe me. I shouldn't have come, I'm sorry."

"I believe you, Nat." Max reached across and squeezed the boy's hand, a father who had gone to his son's bedroom in the night to soothe away the trauma of a nightmare. Only this time it was reality. *"I know you are speaking the truth because I've been to this hell of yours, too. Not in my dreams but in reality."*

There was a flicker of disbelief in the other's expression, but it was gone as soon as it came. "Tell me about it, Max. *Please!*"

Max told him. About Shanifa, and the Ghetto police, how they beat up those who dared to return from the Waste. He talked for almost half an hour by the cooker clock, relived those hellish night hours, retraced in his agonized mind his whole journey from the time he first spotted Shanifa on Northside to his return to the city of the living.

"That is the place, all right," Nat said when his friend had finished. "You've described things which I thought only I knew. One day we shall surely both go there, as will everybody else when they die. Terrible as it is to contemplate, I wish that I could die right now so that I could be with my father to comfort him in his wretchedness, maybe prevent him

from doing the terrible things which they make him
do."

They sat in silence, each with his own thoughts
of the Ghetto and loved ones who suffered there.
A thought crossed Max's mind, hit him with such
force that the headache that had been threatening
began to hammer his temples. An idea so terrifying
in its conception that he had no right to put it to
Nat, even to suggest it. Had it not been for the
other's grieving, he would not have done so. At
least, that was the sop that he cast to his own conscience, for Max's motive was a selfish one. Right
now he cared only for Shanifa.

"Nat"— another squeeze of the trembling hand—
"how . . . *how about if you and I went to the Ghetto
together?*"

Nat recoiled and snatched his fingers away as his
complexion went a shade paler. He mouthed words,
but had to wait before they became sounds. "You
mean . . . we should *die* together?"

"No!" Oh, God, the boy had misunderstood. "I
mean that we should walk in through those barriers
on Northside, just like I did when I followed
Shanifa. We'd go together, find your father and
Shanifa, and bring them back with us."

"That's impossible, the dead cannot escape from
hell!"

"Shanifa did."

"Maybe *she* isn't dead. But my father is."

"Can you be sure, though?"

"I went to his funeral."

"Did you actually . . . see him?"

"No." There was a glimmer of uncertainty, doubt,
in those eyes.

"I think it's all a big cover-up by the authorities,
a convenient way of getting rid of those who are

either mentally ill or a nuisance to the System. Criminals, even. A gigantic hospital-cum-prison."

"It's hell." A stubbornness that defied any who dared to question his belief that the Ghetto was the place of the dead.

"All right, we won't argue over it. Suffice that there's a hellish slum just the other side of North-side in which there are two people whom we both want back. I *know* it's possible to rescue them; it will undoubtedly be difficult. I have been to the police. We can expect no help from them, just the opposite, in fact. Whatever you decide, I intend to go back into the Ghetto. Two of us might stand a better chance than one. I've no idea how or if we're going to be able to pull it off. I'm not asking you to come with me, Nat, but I'd be pleased to have you along if you decide to join me."

Max got up from the table, walked across to the window and stood looking out, his back toward his visitor. You bastard, Max Frame, he thought. You selfish fucking bastard!

"I would sooner die and join my father that way," Nat said.

"And waste your life? My way, Nat, you have two chances. We'll either rescue them or die in the attempt. We'll be with them again, one way or the other."

It seemed for a moment that Nat Bonner might break down again, but he shook it off with an effort and slurped his cold coffee.

"All right," he said, "like you say, I've got nothing to lose. When do we start?"

Seven

There was furtiveness, guilt, in the way Roxy Burgoin climbed the long flight of ill-lit concrete steps in the apartment block. Her feet rustled litter, sent an empty drink can rolling and bouncing all the way down to the floor below, its metallic clinking magnified by the bare surroundings, announcing to any of the occupants who heard it that Roxy was late home again.

She paused on the third floor, held on to the broken rail, her shoulder-length jet black hair in stark contrast to the whiteness of her finely molded features. Expensive clothing, a brown two-piece suit, a diamond ring struggling to sparkle in the dim light.

She looked around her as though she was afraid that a mugger or a rapist lurked in the shadows, satisfied herself that they were empty of everything except spilled garbage from uncollected waste bags, then started at the scuttling of a disturbed rat. Reluctantly, she moved on toward the next flight, her unwillingness to return home apparent by the way she looked upward and licked her dry lips. She paused, thought about turning back but changed her mind.

She wondered if Ed was home yet. Maybe, maybe not, it did not really matter these days, but it was easier for her if he wasn't. In the beginning she had been afraid, a constant nagging fear that he would find out that she was having an affair. That had been almost a year ago. Now they were both cheating on each other, pretending that they weren't, maintaining a pointless facade in an atmosphere of tension.

Her husband guessed, of course, but surprisingly he had never once commented upon her comings and goings or made excuses for his own. They told no lies; they did not have to, but it could not go on like this indefinitely. Sooner or later one of them had to make the break that they both secretly wanted. Each was waiting for the other to do it.

They had been drifting apart for the last two years, a gradual process of marital erosion, sharing a bed because there was nowhere to sleep separately in their cramped quarters. They prepared their own food or else ate out, a pizza from the takeaway consumed on the walk home. Conversation was almost nonexistent between them; they had said everything they had to say to each other years ago. It was a relief not to have to talk. They had adopted a routine of near silence, communicating in monosyllables only when it was absolutely necessary to speak.

Of course, it was all Roxy's fault; she had recently given up blaming her husband for her childlessness. In the beginning it could have been either of them, they had tried hard enough. It had been fun then, nights of wild passion in which there was always the possibility that she would conceive. If not this month, then next; or the one after that. It was a long time before she gave up hope. At least, hope of having a baby by Ed.

So she had seduced Rick, the manager of the department store where she worked. Their torrid relationship had lasted three months. When Roxy still was not pregnant, she had tried Lang. And three or four others, a path of fornication that had led her to Stu Merrick. Stu was still full of surprises six months later, even if he had not succeeded in making a baby for her. That would have been a bonus; at the moment she was content to carry on the way they were. Because her lover was Stu, for no other reason.

Stu Merrick had worked his way up the governmental power structure by any means that presented itself to him. An opportunist, he rode roughshod over any who stood in the way of his ultimate goal.

He would be running for mayor at the next election; he had whispered it in her ear tonight with such conviction just as she neared her climax. Consequently, she had had three orgasms.

Stu stood six feet, four inches and weighed two hundred ten pounds. Fully clothed, you assumed that he was solid muscle; unclothed, you discovered that he wasn't. He was an expert at disguising surplus flesh. A rugged, lived-in face, he could not have been termed handsome, but he had an appeal to the opposite sex. He knew how to please a woman, and his partners learned to reciprocate. He had no inhibitions, and he did not expect them to have any either. Roxy did everything he wanted and did it well; her ring and the necklace she wore were proof of that. If Stu *was* going places, then she wanted to go with him, to share the power that would be his, the luxuries that would replace the drudgery of life with Ed Burgoin in an apartment.

Roxy had known at the outset that Stu ran the Ghetto's prostitution racket, headed the faction that rivalled Ruben Quiles' drug empire. Whoever won the election would control both. She consoled herself that there would always be drugs and whores in the Ghetto, so it was irrelevant who ran them. Except when you shared Stu Merrick's bed. It was a case of being practical, not moralizing.

She thought Stu would win. His manifesto had a greater appeal; the public would buy it. "Safety for Citizens" was his slogan, and that was something most people would be happy to pay for. Sure, it would raise taxes, but it promised that your apartment wouldn't be burned down, nor would you be mugged in the street. There was no *guarantee* of personal safety, but at least there was hope, and compensation if you were one of the unfortunate ones.

Stu vowed to exterminate the Downers. That guaranteed him votes, except those of the Downers. He had incorporated it in his Safety for Citizens promise. Okay, it'll cost you more, but at least you'll be able to sleep safe in your beds *or* go out after dark. "Your homes will be safe, your streets will be safe, and YOU will be safe." Nobody would object then to a few whores on the streets.

Quiles made no such promises. He needed the Downers, their votes to put him in power, their addiction to boost his drug racket. He hinted at free crack, a kind of introductory offer if he came to power. The Downers *could* tilt the balance in his favor, and he was gambling on it. His law enforcement officers would be sympathetic toward the lower classes.

Only government files held the Downer population figure, and no party in power was going to reveal *that*. The numbers game, that would be the criteria in the ensuing weeks.

Luis Diogene was no real threat to the mayoral struggle. A pretender, he played on public fear in a different way, but he had no real backing when it came to the polls. Luis had been executioner at the big prison for over a decade; when his picture appeared in the paper it was half-shadowed, an illusion of Death looking at you. *He* wasn't God, the Law and Order Committee filled that role. They decided who lived and who hanged. Diogene was their puppet; they pulled the strings, he pulled the lever.

He was ripping off Stu with his "I'll Hang the Downers" slogan. Roxy despised him for that. He would execute them, all right . . . after Stu's police had rounded them up! Luis wouldn't be able to handle that part of it. And he wouldn't poll votes, because if he won, he would not be particular whom he hanged.

So it came down to a two-horse race, Stu Merrick and Ruben Quiles. The Downers would determine the outcome, one way or the other. It would be close, whoever won.

Roxy moved up another floor. One more to go. It was crazy. She was scared of confronting Ed; yet in another month she might well be copulating in the mayoral suite, and she wouldn't give a shit about a baby then. Right now her only worries were Ed Burgoin and the Downer population census that had never been made public. Ed could go screw himself, and the Downers wouldn't exist any longer if everything worked out the way she prayed it would.

Ed was sitting by the heater, his back toward her, when she entered the partitioned living room. He gave no indication that he had heard her come in; only the cigarette smoke eddying up told her that he was not asleep. On occasions he slept in that wooden armchair, maybe because he didn't like sharing the bed with a wife who had come back from fucking with someone else.

The room was too damned warm; you struggled to breathe in it. If Ed had been out tonight, then he had left the heating on while he was away. That was wasteful.

This place was an even worse shithole each time she came back to it. The strawboard walls were peeling, the carpet was frayed. The only place of reasonable comfort was the bed, and Roxy hoped that Ed would not join her in it tonight.

She threw her coat over a chair, her jacket followed. Her breasts were small and firm inside the thin cotton blouse. She lit a cigarette, thought about a drink before retiring. She was half-drunk already; another would not make much difference. Except that she might sleep tonight.

"Roxy?"

Fuck, we don't *have* to talk, do we?

"Yes?" She tensed, wondering if she could get past him and into the bedroom before she had to answer that goddamned question, whatever it was. Roxy, you've been with another man, haven't you? Oh, Christ, don't lie, don't start crawling. She began to tremble again. Damn it, get it over and done with now. Yes, Ed, I've been screwing with other men for a long time now. Just tell me that you've been shagging other women, and it'll make me feel a whole lot better.

The silence was knotting her guts. She wanted to rush past him, not to the bedroom, but to the lavatory, and get on her knees and vomit as hard as she could into the filthy bowl.

"Roxy, there's something I have to tell you." He did not look round, but she saw him in her mind as clearly as if he had. Angular features that had once bordered on good-looking, but he had let himself go: his cheeks were hollowed; his dark eyes seemed to have shrunk into their sockets. Troubled, haunted. He didn't bother to shave, even when he went out. This woman of his had to be a right slut; most of the women in the Ghetto were.

"Go on."

Silence. He was taking his time, building himself up, going to let rip the way she had only once known him to do. Uncontrolled rage, that tightrope between verbal abuse and physical violence. She braced herself for it.

"Roxy . . . you're not going to like this. . . ."

"Try me and see." Her breathing had gone very shallow.

"Roxy . . . I'm having an affair, I've got somebody else."

It took several seconds for Roxy to grasp the meaning of his words. Her brain, her logic, rejected them. Not Ed. She must have misheard, misunderstood him.

"You've . . . what?"

"I—"

She heard him swallow.

"I'm having a relationship. I'm sorry, Roxy, but I've fallen in love with this girl. You see . . ."

Oh, thank God! Roxy checked the urge to shout her exuberance aloud, to kiss her husband in a way that she had never kissed him before. Oh, thank you, Ed, you've made me so happy. Instead, she said in a shaking voice, "Thank you for telling me, Ed. I appreciate it. I hope you'll both be very happy."

She thought she heard him sigh his relief aloud; it might have been her own release of pent-up tension. An awful lot of problems had been solved in a few seconds. Amicably.

"I'll be moving out shortly," he continued. "You'll be all right, won't you?"

"I'll be fine." She was shaking for a different reason now. "Don't you worry about me, Ed."

Months of anguish were over for her. She had been worrying unnecessarily all along. It was difficult to imagine Ed having a girlfriend. Roxy wondered who she was, if she knew her, what she looked like, but to have asked might have started off a round of awkward questions.

There was going to be an awful lot of changes in the Ghetto before long. For better or for worse.

Eight

Max knew that Nat was scared. Scared to hell, like he was himself. They both had to be crazy to come back to the Ghetto.

Finding the way in through the barriers on Northside had been the easy part; then they had followed the winding track until they reached the first row of ruined houses. So far, so good, but from then onward their surroundings had seemed somehow different, as far as Max could recall. The desolation, the degradation were much the same. It was difficult to be certain in the darkness, but he had the gut feeling that they were walking unfamiliar streets. In other words, he thought, we're bloody lost already! But he would not confide his worst fears to Nat, not yet, anyway, because the other was holding on to his arm so tightly that it was beginning to restrict the circulation. It would have been heartless to have thrust Nat from him, only made matters worse.

With hindsight they should have come in daylight, not left it until dusk. That was the crass stupidity of characters in vampire and werewolf films, delaying until sunset before going up to the dreaded castle.

Max had decided that they stood a better chance of travelling unseen in the dark. Except by those . . .

he tried not to think about the nocturnal inhabitants of the Ghetto. Once they reached that lighted area they would be reasonably safe. Their destination was the cafe where Shanifa worked; selfishly he had ignored the problem of locating Nat's father. Afterward, maybe. That could wait until morning; they could watch out for the prison warders going on early shift. Shanifa was a priority. For himself.

"How much further?" Nat whispered yet again.

"Not far now." His tone lacked conviction, embodied that hopelessness that he had experienced the last time. He could not even see the glow of the Square in the night sky, and that in itself was disconcerting. Possibly it was because the night was cloudy and overcast. More likely, they were heading in the wrong direction, had been doing so for the past hour.

Max's watch had stopped again.

Nat was the lucky one; he was spared the night sounds. Right now, though, there was only silence, not even a rustle of windblown garbage in the gutters. The stillness was as terrifying as . . . Max tried not to think about it.

Nat grunted to attract his attention. Max peered, but it was too dark to lip-read, so he gave his companion a reassuring squeeze; a lie, but it would not help matters to admit that they had lost their way. It was all Max's fault; he had had no right to persuade Nat to accompany him on this foolhardy, impossible mission. He tried to console himself with another lie, that if he had not brought Nat with him, then the boy would probably have taken his own life. That was unlikely. But the stark fact remained that they were here in the Ghetto whether they liked it or not.

Max motioned to his companion to stop for a

minute. The boy was too bloody impatient for his own good. Like himself.

The row of derelict houses that they had been following seemed to have petered out. Max felt for the wall that should have been on his left, but there was nothing except emptiness within his reach. His uneasiness was mounting by the second; there was an awful thought nagging him. Perhaps they should turn around, hurry back the way they had come, endeavor to locate the barricades again and squeeze through that narrow gap on to the safety of Chapel Street.

His mouth was dry, that familiar sour taste back on his palate, and he smelled again the putrescence of an open graveyard. No, it could not be, they had not come far enough. . . .

The sky was clearing; the cloud formation that had persisted all day was beginning to break up. One star. Two. Max thought he recognized the top of the Plow. Its ethereal light slanted down, a spotlight trying to focus on the principal, unwilling actors on an otherwise empty stage. Just a silvery glow, enough to see by, to recognize the rubble, the rutted terrain, an evening mist seeping up from those rain-filled potholes.

Max's worst fears were confirmed— *they were back on the Waste.*

There was no point in trying to reason how it was they had found their way onto the Ghetto's stinking area of dereliction; they were here and there was nothing that they could do about it.

"Are we . . . all right?" Nat was mouthing his uneasiness in the starlight, pathetically gaunt in his black leather jacket and matching jeans. He sensed his friend's shocked surprise, clutched at him. "Max, where are we?"

"I know this place." Max tried to sound confident. "I've been here before. We just have to keep going . . . that way." He pointed on up ahead; it would have been all the same if he had suggested going back. On the Waste all directions led nowhere. He could only hope that eventually they would emerge somewhere. One way was as good as another.

The mud began to build up on their feet, huge glutinous clods which they had to stop and dislodge every so often, holding on to each other to keep their balance while they scraped one foot against the other.

The mist would doubtless thicken into that awful permeating fog before morning. At the moment it was patchy. They walked into a swirling stinking bank of it, came out on the other side into clear starlight. But wherever they looked there was only mud and more mud.

Max's leg ached, but that was the result of the accident, something with which he would have to live for the rest of his life. The wound on his ankle no longer troubled him, the antibiotics which Doctor Stackpool had prescribed were obviously working. That was the one minuscule consolation amidst their traumas; he was fitter now to face whatever lay ahead of them.

Into the fog; out of it again. Another vague sense of familiarity had him peering around until he glimpsed that precarious tin shanty up ahead of them. A moment of relief for, spartan and damp as it was, it offered some form of shelter for the night, a refuge until the foggy dawn when surely they must find a way out of here.

"Nat . . ." Max's fingers gripped the shiny leather sleeve, tugging the boy back, that fleeting feeling of hope instantly dashed as only the Ghetto knew how to destroy it. He fought against the panic that flooded over him, that urge to flee from the scene that greeted his tired eyes, to flounder blindly through the mud before those up ahead spotted them.

A brazier, perhaps the corroded remnants of that same one that a succession of night watchmen had used to cheer their lonely vigils half a century or more ago, was burning, smoke spiralling up from it. An iron pot was suspended over the glowing coals, cooking something that gave off a pungent, nauseating aroma, mingling with the foulness of the fog. Max smelled it, tasted it, but it was not from that alone that he recoiled in revulsion.

Silhouetted around the fire, huddled together, were three deformed figures. They were visible only in outline against the firelight, but that was enough to bring an inarticulate grunt of terror from Nat Bonner. Scrawny ragbag figures, they were only vaguely human in shape; hunched shoulders on twisted bodies, tattered clothing ribboned from their near-skeletal frames, their heads thrust forward in a posture of ravenous lust as they waited to vent their appetites on the contents of the cook pot.

Uncut hair fell in tangled masses from their out-size heads, their straggling beards in danger of singeing or catching fire as they leaned over the brazier. Seemingly immune to the intense heat, one of them stirred the pot with a broken stick, releasing yet another waft of that sickening stench.

Max was aware how Nat shook, how they trembled together, compelled to stand and watch as that unholy trio fished chunks of the vile-smelling, steaming food out of the cauldron with mud-caked sticks, grasped and tore hungrily at the offering, slurping noisily as they ate.

Jesus Alive!

Nat was whimpering. Max backed away a step, almost lost his balance as his foot stuck in the cloying mire. Thankfully those dreadful ragbags were so engrossed in their repulsive repast that they were oblivious of everything else.

He looked away in case the glow from the fire might reveal their features, a sight that might snap the mind of the beholder. Their faces were too awful even to visualize.

"What . . . who . . ." Nat was mouthing his terror, his teeth chattering like distant machine-gun fire.

Max made no attempt to explain; there was no explanation that he could give. They had seen, pray God that they never looked upon that sight again! Anyway, it would have been impossible for the other to lip-read him in the smoky half light.

It was too dangerous to linger here. They held on to each other for support, looked back apprehensively as their feet squelched loudly in the sucking mud, but there was no pursuit.

They were Downers, Max had no doubt about that, the night dwellers, the scum of the Ghetto. Last time he had only heard them; tonight he had seen them. Winos, tramps, dropouts, call them what you will, every slum in the world was infested with them. Drugged or drunk on meths, they survived on gutter food, human scavengers. Christ, what the hell were they eating? It was meat of some kind, rotten and rancid; its smell reminded him vaguely of pork. Scraps from the dustbins, most likely. Their wretched, diseased bodies were doubtless immune to bacteria that would have killed a civilized person.

These Downers lived and died in filth, cancerous creatures of the night condemned to a life of near-starvation. Max tried to pity them; he failed, and retched at the taste of their cooking that still lingered in his mouth. He needed a cigarette, but he had forgotten to bring any with him, yet another oversight on this ill-prepared quest for the impossible.

Nat stumbled, lurched as his foot caught against something in the mud, almost fell and took his companion with him. The youth cursed beneath his breath; it sounded to Max like "fushinell."

"Probably a piece of wood or a stone." Nat would not hear, but Max was unwilling to waste time discovering the cause of their near-fall. "Come on, hurry!"

At that moment Nat Bonner screamed, hung on to Max, buried his face against him and sobbed uncontrollably.

"It's all right, Nat, we're well clear of them now. There's nothing to be afraid of—"

There was. Max saw and almost vomited as the bile burned his throat. A shaft of starlight cruelly revealed the cause of Nat's stumble, played on the bloody mulch lying there on the ground. *There was no way that it could have been anything other than a heap of human remains, a trunk from which the limbs and head had been hacked away, severed sinews trailing, offal spilling from the sliced belly.*

Max held Nat while they both spewed. Miraculously they did not faint. The youth was saying something, talking gibberish, but Max understood, all right. There was no way in which the mutilated corpse could be misinterpreted, for without any doubt it was the prey of the Downers, a victim of their own kind who had been slain, the flesh ripped away for the cook pot. *That nocturnal repast on the Waste had been a cannibalistic feast!*

Holding on to each other, Max and Nat sludged on their way, not caring in which direction they travelled as long as it took them as far as possible from this vile deed and its perpetrators.

"Max!" Nat stopped suddenly, gripped his companion with an even greater intensity, and almost toppled them both into the mud.

Oh, Jesus Alive, what now!

"Max," Nat spoke in a tone that somehow overcame the terror of the last half hour, embodied both exuberance and disbelief so that he was barely able to speak coherently. "Max, I . . . I . . ."

Max held him. The boy's mind had snapped; those inhuman fiends out there had taken his sanity just as surely as they would have taken his flesh. They had rendered him a mindless idiot. A flood of guilt because he should not have persuaded Nat to come here. Christ, it's all my fault!

"Nat, it's all right." It wasn't all right, it never would be.

"Max." The boy was shaking, mouthing soundless words in the half darkness until at last he managed to get them out. "Max . . . *I heard them out there!*"

Max doubted his own sanity now. This was impossible, a cruel trick played on a terror-blasted brain. Vibrations, perhaps, but not *sounds*. No way.

"Nat . . . can you hear *me?*"

"Sort of." The youth was calmer, still trembling. "More than I could before but not clearly. But I tell you I heard them, Max, every noise as clearly as you did. I've only just realized!"

It was not altogether an impossibility. Max recalled reading in a newspaper during his lengthy spell in the hospital how a deaf girl had fallen,

banged her head and her hearing had been re-
stored. Not totally, but an eighty-five percent improvement on her previous condition. If sheer
terror had done the same for Nat, then that was
absolutely marvellous. Selfishly, Max thought that
some good had come from his bringing him here.
It eased his troubled conscience.

"I'm delighted for you, Nat. We'll have to see how
your hearing goes on. But in the meantime, we
can't hang around here."

Surprisingly the queue in the foyer of the Employment Office was relatively sparse, just four men
and two women. They reminded Max of those cafe
customers, head scarves and caps; not talking, studying faded posters on the wall while they waited as
if deliberately using them as an excuse to hide their
features. Hollow coughs from time to time echoed
with a pneumonic hollowness in the sparse building.
There was an atmosphere of hopelessness that differed from that of the Job Centre in Northside Central. There you slouched away because there was no
work available; here, it seemed, the applicants were
successful. Every one of them. Yet they bowed their
heads and hunched their shoulders, disillusioned.

A pen holder vibrated every time the silent clerk
on the other side of the grill banged a rubber
stamp on some official documents. The scratching
of his pen was like mice gnawing electric wiring in
the attic. No interviews, no conversation, a proce-
dure that was executed with depressing efficiency.

"We'll have to try and find work, for the time
being at any rate," Max had told Nat when, with
no small amount of relief, dawn had found them
in the main part of the Ghetto; their route had

taken them along a road that filtered on to the big
traffic island beyond the Hotel. They were exhausted, damp from the mist which, amazingly, had
not thickened to the expected fog. "We need money,
a base of some sort." He scrutinized the early
morning, mooching window gazers. "Let's face it,
we don't look any different from that lot, do we?
Who's to know?"

Apparently nobody did. Or cared. The odd passing glance, eyes turned away immediately. You did
not converse with strangers in the Ghetto, thank
God!

There was a box of Work & Accommodation forms
just inside the Employment Centre entrance. Max
took a couple, handed one to Nat; dog-eared, dirty
brown leaflets, faded print on cheap paper. Some
basic questions had to be answered by applicants:
name, address, if applicable, if not then you ticked
the "applied for" box. Age. Type of work required.

Max doubted the existence of a driving school,
yet he marked the appropriate box— "driving."
Commercial, public transport, anything would be acceptable. No signature or proof of identity, it
seemed, was necessary.

Nat pondered. The ink smudged as he printed
his name, absorbed into the paper. Work required . . . he was currently taking an art course
at college, so he scratched "art and design," then
returned the pen to its socket.

They were kept waiting less than ten minutes.
The clerk did not so much as glance up at them,
merely stretched out a hand for the form and scrutinized it.

Max's pulses were racing; he knew now how a spy
travelling with a forged passport felt. One small

oversight. . . . Will you hold on a minute, sir? Step into the office, please.

The balding head was bent toward him, that hand groped for the official stamp. A thud, then the pen was scratching its shaky handwriting again. Perforation rasped as a gray form was torn from a pad.

"Next."

The duplicator had run short of ink or perhaps economy was a priority in the Ghetto's officialdom. The form was headed up "Work Permit." There were just two boxes this time:

> Employment: City Taxis, New Street.
> Accommodation: 417F. Block 18.

Nat's application was being stamped, and there was a rustle of paper. The street door opened and closed; another job seeker had come in.

Max's first reaction was one of sheer relief at the ease with which everything had been finalized. They had work, a roof over their heads, a headquarters in this alien city. He waited until they were outside before he examined his companion's permit.

> Employment: City Posters, New Street.
> Accommodation: 418F. Block 18.

"Well, at least we're neighbors"— Max laughed softly— "working and living next door. Come on, we'd better check our digs first."

"What about finding my father? And Shanifa?"

"One thing at a time." Max folded his permit, pocketed it. "First, this is the main part of the Ghetto, and I'm not sure where the Square is from here. But taxi driving will be a distinct advantage;

I'll be able to case the whole place out. If we rush it, we could well end up in that prison where your father works. Or else get beaten up by the police. Neither of which will help us, to say the least. At the moment we're one of *them*." He shuddered involuntarily at the thought. "We need a systematic plan of action. First, our HQ. Second, a job and a chance to look around. After that we'll work out our little plan. Right?"

Nat nodded reluctantly. Max was grateful for his selfishness in bringing the other along; right now he needed him. They had to try to forget the horrors that they had witnessed last night. The Downers were not their problem; in all probability they would not encounter them again because they lived on the outskirts and on the Waste, far from here.

Apartment 417F was reminiscent of an up-market henhouse, Max decided. A single room with an adjoining toilet, chipboard walls, a gauze ventilator because there were no windows. A table and two chairs, you were obviously not expected to entertain more than one visitor at a time. A camp bed was pushed up against the wall, worn linoleum covered the floor, and the electric heater and cooking ring were metered. That was it, everything provided for you to exist at basic level.

Nat's quarters were identical. Doubtless so were the other 416 and however many the numbering went up to.

They boiled the kettle, and found a damp packet of instant coffee and a tin of powdered milk on the unit shelf, courtesy of the System, a moving-in present. They shared it, insipid liquid that had a stale taste. Max's watch was still not working, but it had to be around midday by now, surely.

"We'd best get our jobs fixed up"— Max put the empty mugs in the sink—"because our priority is some money. We won't get far without it here, any more than we would elsewhere."

The taxi firm was situated in a basement garage beneath one of the many apartment blocks, an oily floor, garbage piled up in a corner, the shabbiness in complete contrast to the line of polished stretch limos. A brown-uniformed official stood outside a glass cubicle office, fleshy featured and glowering from beneath bushy eyebrows. *You* can't afford to hire one of *our* cars. Piss off!

Max handed him the work permit, waited. Another ripple of nervousness, his luck had surely held for too long. But the other barely glanced at the piece of paper; there was no hint of suspicion, only disinterest. Boredom, even.

A sudden disconcerting thought had Max's fingernails gouging his palms. His driving license was back home on the sideboard; this guy would most certainly demand to see it. Oh, shit!

"Get yourself a uniform from the changing room." A thumb jerked in the direction of a half-open door. "You new around here?"

"Yes."

"You'll need a street plan, then. Take one off the table." The man turned away, making no attempt to return the job document; obviously the employer retained it, kept a rein on his work force. The interview was over; get your uniform and start driving. It was as simple as that.

The small room was suffocatingly overpowering with a mixture of odors, the predominant one being that of unwashed bodies and the smell of the adjacent uncleaned toilet. A dozen or so rumpled brown uniforms sagged on a line of coat hooks. Max moved along them, searched for one that might fit him. They were all secondhand, came with the job; you handed them back when you left. They stank, too, as if the previous wearers had never taken them off, lived in them, perhaps even slept in them.

Jesus! He lifted one down and held it at arm's length. The flat cap was greasy; whoever had worn it last had used some brand of pungent hair cream. But Max had to go through with this deception for Shanifa's sake; he would not have done it for anybody else.

The tunic hung awkwardly on him. The trousers were too large around the waist; he used his own belt to hold them up. He had to tilt the hat back on his head to prevent the peak from obscuring his vision. It was the best he could do. The other uniforms would not have been much of an improvement; they had either stretched with wear or else shrunk, probably in the rain. He doubted if they had ever been washed.

The street map was hand-drawn and photocopied; a jumble of intersecting roads with their names scrawled on them. He needed to study the plan, to commit parts of it to memory. It was like a maze that somebody had created, an afternoon's entertainment for the family, expressly designed to ensure that they did not find a shortcut out of it.

There were no boundaries marked, the streets all turned back on themselves, and it was impossible even to hazard a guess on which side Northside lay. He flipped over another page, found what he was searching for—the Square. They even called it that, and in the center was a circled cross marked "monument." Max's forefinger shook as it traced a likely looking route from the Employment Centre to that area where Shanifa worked. Simple, really, two right turns and a left brought you straight to it. If only the map had had a scale marked on it, he would have been able to work out how far it was.

So far, so good. He wondered about Nat, how he was getting on.

In the street up above Max heard the wailing of a police siren. Tires screeched.

Somebody began to scream.

Nine

Yolanda Morrison had been on Death Row for a long time. She could not remember exactly how long. Time was judged by daylight and darkness in the big prison; calendars and watches were forbidden. The penalty for being found in possession of either was severe, solitary and near-starvation for an indeterminable period. After the first few weeks time ceased to matter; you conditioned yourself to a robotlike existence akin to divorcing your body from your mind. It was the only way to survive.

The prison stood on the edge of the Waste, a decrepit stone edifice that sprawled within the high gray walls topped with broken glass. It was reputed to be an ancient fortress that had been partly renovated for the purpose of depriving the more unfortunate inhabitants of the Ghetto of their freedom. A sprinkling of criminals, mostly they were condemned to live out on the Waste itself, but the majority of inmates were those who had been found guilty of treason against the Establishment. Many were still awaiting trial after years of confinement. Appeals were a farce, a procrastination of any justice that might have existed, for hearings were invariably postponed until the next, a succession of adjournments that merged into permanent incarceration so that eventually the accused served a term far in excess of any sentence that might have been passed for the original offense.

The male and female blocks faced each other across the extensive exercise yard. Sometimes the prisoners indulged in shouted conversations with each other, generally a release of sexual frustration which the authorities allowed to go unchecked. Perhaps the listening warders derived some kind of bawdy titillation from it. Indeed, there were times when they appeared actively to encourage this daily tirade of obscenities. Corporal punishment was meted out within this arena-style enclosure to the delight of a sadistic audience watching from the barred windows of their cells.

Invariably it was a flogging, the victim, male or female, led to a central dais which afforded an unrestricted view from every angle. The spectators judged the severity of the offense by the number of strokes that were administered. The victim was always naked, whichever sex, draped head downward over the single rail. It was an unhurried process, obviously savored by the warder whose duty it was to wield the birches or the whip. Each stroke was decisive with a lengthy pause in between, inflicting red welts on back and buttocks, examining his handiwork at intervals.

If the unfortunate recipient struggled, then he or she was held forcibly in place by two assisting uniformed men. In the case of a fainting, the unconscious body was draped double over the railing and the flogging proceeded as before.

There was no mistaking the enjoyment that the watchers derived from these occasions. Whistles, coarse encouragement to he who might be chastising any one of them next time, cries of disappointment if the victim lost consciousness. They spat their disgust from their small windows if their pleasure was too brief.

Yolanda had been flogged once. She would never forget that awful morning even if she had forgotten the reason for her punishment. She had been escorted down from her cell on the fifth landing, then ordered to strip in the interrogation room. It had been damnably cold; it always was. Her huge stature disguised some of her surplus fat even when naked, and her bright auburn hair matched her complexion. Not embarrassment. She faced the male warders with hands on hips, legs slightly apart. Look if you want to, it doesn't bother me, towering over them like some female Gulliver rendered helpless by her Lilliput torturers. Angry because they could treat her this way.

It had been foggy outside in the yard; Yolanda doubted whether the watchers all around could discern more than her vague outline. As she stepped up onto the platform, she turned toward the male block in one brief gesture of defiance, cupped her voluminous breasts in her large hands and lifted them provocatively. The warders grabbed her wrists instantly and threw her across the rail.

They whacked her buttocks that morning because they knew that would hurt her most, not physically but the pain was that much greater because of her degradation. Whether or not the other prisoners could discern her wrinkly flesh through the swirling mist, they cheered each *thwack,* and the cry of "dirty whore" echoed in her ears long after the warders had dragged her back to her cell. Somehow she had fought off her tears until after it was dark. The bastards had humiliated her, but she would not let them break her. Since that day she had not stood at her window to watch the floggings.

Neither did she watch the executions. They were now a distinct reality that infiltrated the bad dreams that she had from time to time. Of course, they were performed in the yard down below for the benefit of those confined on Death Row, Yolanda had no doubt about that. Occasionally, Luis Diogene, the hangman, went on a walkabout in the corridors of the condemned, a squat, gloating figure whose black attire was worn to instill terror in his prospective victims, his thick lips stretched in a leer of lusting anticipation. If he had a god, then it was Power; if he dreamed, then it was of the day when the polls favored him. The gallows were both his love and his manifesto.

There was an arrogance about his waddle from the prison to the gallows at the rear of the execution procession. The mask was only donned after an ungainly turn of 360 degrees; look upon my features, gaze upon Death.

He took his time adjusting the noose, stroked the hemp lovingly with his soft, fat fingers. A whisper in the ear of the doomed, a smile that was neither sympathy nor regret. Just a love of hanging. The occasion was one to be savored, his fleshy hand resting on the lever for several seconds before he finally pulled it, plunging the body down into the pit below.

The onlookers waited in silence, listened for the crack of a snapping neck. Some of the long-serving prisoners remembered that morning when Luis Diogene had had to have the body hauled back up onto the platform and had hanged it a second time because for some reason death had cheated him. The victim had kicked for several minutes before eventually succumbing to the inevitable. Incompetence on behalf of the executioner, but you dared not so much as whisper it to your most trusted friend for fear that you might yourself become a victim of that same deliberate cruelty that ensured a slow and terrible death.

The gallows were a permanent structure; the prisoners exercised around it. Sometimes, during "organized activities" they were forced to run up the steps, then jump down into the yard from the platform; a kind of bizarre vaulting horse. An enforced familiarity, an acclimatization. A mental torture.

Diogene checked and serviced his beloved instrument of death with regularity in the manner in which an obsessional hobbyist might maintain his beloved vintage car. He always wore his black robes; he was never seen without them. A weighted dummy on the noose, that same savored anticipation in his expression and posture as he toyed with the fatal lever. Most afternoons when exercise sessions had finished he was out there in the yard, reliving the morning's execution or enacting the morrow's. Finally he would stand, and allow his gaze to move slowly along the barred apertures of Death Row as though singling out his prey for the following day. For if it was your turn to be hanged, you were only advised of your fate within minutes of the hanging.

But they would not hang her. Yet. It was the first time for a long time that Yolanda had thought about her predicament. In a twisted sort of way it gave her a feeling of satisfaction, almost of power. Because she was a vital pawn in the Ghetto's political game. It would be easier for those concerned if she was dead, but her execution could cause considerable embarrassment both for Stu Merrick and Ruben Quiles.

Quiles would not hang her in the twilight of his current mayoral reign; he needed to keep things ticking over, win the votes he needed. Afterward, it was a different matter. Merrick would ensure that she had the quick drop, eliminating her with a swiftness that might even entail one of those surreptitious nocturnal executions. A lethal injection, her body disposed of secretly.

She remembered the days when she had shared Merrick's luxury apartment, strutted proudly in and out of the Hotel, a mistress who was always at his side. But Stu did not have absolute power then, an up-and-coming contender for Ruben's growing dictatorship, a feud that was responsible for many of the pawns being removed to the Waste. Yolanda's position had been precarious, but throughout she had never suspected that her greatest danger came from her lover. Until the day he tired of her.

The bombshell came without warning. One night she was sharing his bed, the next she was soliciting on the streets with the rest of his army of whores on a ten percent commission basis. You had a weekly target, and if you didn't achieve it, you could expect a roughing up at the very least. Once, during a spell of bitter weather when the streets were deserted, she had chipped in some of her own meager savings in order to spare herself.

At the time Quiles' law enforcement officers were having a purge on prostitution, cleaning up Merrick's girls so that he could replace them with his own. Doubtless, Yolanda had been singled out as a target; Merrick's ex-mistress in prison was quite a coup for the opposition. A trumped-up charge and a sham trial to ensure that she stayed there. A guy had been knifed, and they produced "conclusive" evidence that had Yolanda on Death Row within a week. But nothing was going to happen until after the forthcoming election. Either way she was on a loser.

Stu would dispose of her quietly; Ruben would use her execution to show his electorate that he meant business, that he was going to clear the streets of whores. Mass hangings, probably, a cleanup of Merrick's streetwalkers before he replaced them gradually with his own prostitutes. What better way to start the purge than with Yolanda's execution? She had long ago resigned herself to her fate.

Luis Diogene came to her cell on average once a week. God, how she loathed the fat bastard; he reminded her of a slug on a wet night! Smirking, lusting for her voluminous body but not in the way the other male warders lusted for it. Sadistic, savoring, estimating her weight, the tension on the rope, in his mind stroking her dead flesh before he lowered her to the ground. He didn't talk much, just ran his eyes up and down her. If, by some quirk of fate, he polled the most votes, then he'd execute her, all right. There would be carnage in the Ghetto, hangings day after day.

"When your time comes, I'll make it as easy as I can for you," he spoke with a slight lisp. "It will be very quick, you won't feel a thing. Just like *that!*" He snapped his fleshy fingers, and they made a kind of squelching sound.

"I *might* get a reprieve," Yolanda snapped. "I've been here four, perhaps five, years and they haven't hanged me yet!"

"They will," he assured her with a thick-lipped smile. "Make no mistake about that. For you, the sooner the better. What is the point of clinging to life in here? Far better to get it over and done with."

She resisted the temptation to slap his face. She would do just that if he ever tried to feel her up. But he wouldn't because he didn't get his kicks in

any normal way. And when the time came and he
stepped up onto the platform alongside her, she
promised herself that she would spit right in his
repulsive, gloating features.

There were more male warders than female these
days; the balance had swung appreciably in the last
year. Yolanda suspected that the women officials
spent most of their time over in the men's block;
corruption was no longer clandestine. Tobacco and
drugs were freely available. If you had what the
warders wanted, you could trade it for almost anything. Except freedom.

Possibly outside these prison walls Yolanda
wouldn't have spared Sid a second glance. At fifty-
seven his hair was gray and thinning, his shoulders
were stooped and his crumpled uniform hung
loosely on his lean frame. A sparse moustache
adorned his upper lip, and he seldom smiled, a
typical example of the Ghetto's working class, who,
outside the prison service, would have worn a greasy
navy blue overcoat, knotted muffler and either a
trilby hat or a cap. An asthmatic, his lungs wheezed
their protest at the cigarette that habitually smol-
dered in the center of his thin lips. But he had one
attribute that separated him from the rest, a tenderness that was reflected in his gray eyes, a sadness
that watered them at times.

Yolanda wished that Sid could have been permanently on the night shift. He still visited her when
he was on days, but there was no privacy then; there
was always somebody passing to and fro in the corridor outside, stopping to stare into the cells like
zookeepers checking on their animals.

She didn't think that her relationship with Sid
would have gone beyond a platonic friendship if she
hadn't made a positive move to seduce him. Even

then it hadn't been easy, and he hadn't been able to make it the first time. It was sordid at best, a removal of only those garments that were absolutely necessary, and both parties were tense throughout. Her vitriolic tongue had kept the other warders off her. They retaliated with contempt, some of them exposing themselves to her and laughing coarsely at the abuse that she showered on them. Which was, possibly, why she wanted Sid. She closed her eyes when he entered her, found herself fantasizing about Stu Merrick. Stu was a bastard, she hated him, but as a lover there was none better.

Sid gave her what she needed, and if, in her erotic imagination, it was Stu, then she was using both of them for her own pleasure. After all, both would see her hang, so she was entitled to something in return. And she didn't think that Sid was screwing with any of the other female inmates, which was an added bonus.

"What will they do with me if they don't hang me?" she asked Sid one night after he had done his best to satisfy her.

"I'm not sure." He found his cigarettes, lit one and talked through it.

"Let me go free, pardon me?"

"No." A spasm of coughing shook him. "They won't do that."

"Keep me in for life?" Yolanda couldn't recall any lifers. Neither could she remember anybody ever having died here except on the gallows.

"No." He was looking away, trying to camouflage his evasiveness with another bout of coughing.

"What, then? Come on, Sid, I want to know."

He was still averting his gaze. She could see that he was trembling now. After a few moments he said,

"If they don't execute you, they'll send you to the Waste."

Oh, God! Yolanda had half guessed that that was what might happen to her, but this was the first time her fears had been put into words. Sid's gnarled fingers found hers, squeezed them as if to comfort her. "But, with any luck, you'll hang one of these days."

"I see." She didn't really, it all seemed so point-less. Her trial had been so farcical that anywhere else the charge would have been thrown out of court. She had an alibi for the time of the killing: Loren, the banker. But he had denied their asso-ciation, and the court, such as it was, had refused to investigate further. Bankers did not associate with prostitutes. So Loren's name was cleared and Yolanda went on to Death Row.

"I'd like to die," Sid said at length.

After that they had not mentioned it again, and after Sid had done a spell on the day shift, he ap-peared to have forgotten their conversation.

Discipline was slack amongst the warders. They could smoke, drink, do what they liked on duty just as long as they fed, exercised and locked their charges away again. They meted out their own brand of punishment that might range from star-vation to a flogging in the exercise yard. Only death was reserved for a higher judgment.

Yolanda wished that she could stop thinking about Stu Merrick. He was no better, no worse, than any of the others who might aspire to mayor. Ex-cept that she had loved him and that was what hurt most. If he had jilted her for some woman in the Ghetto's ruling class, Yolanda could have under-stood it, maybe accepted it in time. But he hadn't. He had plucked a serving wench out of a downtown eating house, set her up on a pedestal and thrown Yolanda back into the gutter.

Stu wouldn't learn, but that jumped-up slut would. When he had tired of her slim young body, he would sell it on the streets, give her a ten percent cut until she was only fit to crawl out onto the Waste and let the Downers have her in return for decomposed food scraps. Or else eat her when they were starving.

Yolanda conditioned herself to believe that the gallows was the best way out, after all.

Ten

The art and design studio was merely an extension of the adjacent packaging warehouse, a long, low building with an asbestos skylighted roof. Makeshift desks of warped chipboard, supported on uneven trestles, lined the four walls, the central desks being occupied by stoic supervisors wearing dirty gray smocks.

There was just one rusted, iron radiator to heat the entire workplace. Nat Bonner concluded after the first hour that it did not work, and kept his leather jacket on. It was damnably cold in here, but none of the others appeared to notice. Men and women pored over drawing boards, relying upon old-fashioned wooden rulers to draw straight lines. Nobody spoke, nobody looked up. Whatever they were doing, they appeared to be executing it with a pedestrian pace and efficiency.

Nat flipped through his loose-leaf folder of basic designs. He had no idea for what purpose they were intended; instead he had the feeling of sitting in an examination room with an approved crib sheet in front of him. You drew what you liked, copied, and left the finished design in a wire tray which, at some stage, would be collected. There was no screen printing here, he was certain of that; it was just a case of putting in the time. Maybe at the end

of the day the designs were thrown away and tomorrow you started on another batch. Utterly pointless.

From time to time he glanced surreptitiously at
his colleagues. They had one common factor, an air
of hopelessness about the way they dressed and
worked. A couple of teenage girls wore clothes that
might have been fashionable in the fifties or sixties.
Nat wasn't sure; his awareness of fashion only went
back as far as the seventies. Short skirts that might
have been acceptable had they not been too large,
blouses of faded colors like hand-me-downs or jumble sale purchases. A youth, who was certainly no
more than a couple of years older than Nat, wore
an outsize checked sports jacket and baggy jeans.
Anywhere else except in the Ghetto Nat might have
laughed. Here, there was no humor. The drabness
was frightening.

There was silence except for the scratching of
pencils on paper. No colors, not even basic crayons,
everything was drawn in black and white.

Around midday a trolley loaded with mugs and
cardboard trays of sandwiches was wheeled in by an
apron-clad woman. Nat joined the queue and took
a drink and two sandwiches back to his desk. He
grimaced at the strength of the tea, dark brown,
tepid liquid that was oversweet; the bread was stale
and curling at the corners, the filling some kind of
bland paste.

Still nobody spoke. Either talking at work was forbidden or else there was nothing to talk about. The
afternoon wore on, the baskets filling with strange,
futile design work. Tomorrow it would be the same,
and every day after that; Nat knew that there would
be no variation in routine here.

It was with a sense of acute relief that Nat heard

a bell ring in an adjoining room, and saw this silent work force rise from their chairs as one, leave their desks and file toward the doorway. Only the smocked supervisors remained seated; perhaps they slept here.

Out in the street Nat stood and waited to get his bearings. Everywhere was so drab that one street was much the same as another; it would be only too easy to get lost. Every building seemed to be either a shuttered shop or a warehouse with closed doors; people were trudging somewhere but going nowhere, the products of an aimless lifestyle.

The sky was overcast. There was a mistiness about this godforsaken environment that hinted of fog by nightfall; you smelled and tasted the encroaching murk. Nat got his bearings, knew that if he crossed the road and turned into the next street, it would bring him to the apartment block. As he walked he wondered what time Max would be home. He hoped his friend would not be late. A feeling that was more than loneliness, a kind of abandonment that bordered on terror. He almost believed that he would never see his friend again, be forced to spend the rest of his life in this city of his nightmares that had suddenly become frightening reality. They should not have come here; they had pandered to grief in the depths of their despair. Far better to have taken his own life rather than succumbed to *this*.

There was no traffic in this side street, and the pedestrians had thinned to a trickle. It was as Nat crossed the road that a figure on the opposite pavement attracted his attention. No more than a silhouette, but the posture, the walk, was so familiar that his heart missed a beat. He stopped, stared, broke into a run.

"*Dad!*" A hoarse shout, one that embodied fear and hope, disbelief.

The uniformed, stooped figure halted, turned. *And in the smoky gray light of late afternoon Nat Bonner recognized the face that undoubtedly belonged to his father.*

Sid Bonner's expression was momentarily one of shock, a widening of the gray eyes, the mouth starting to open. Then it closed into an uncompromising thin line, a stoic stubbornness that had Nat backing off a pace, the irritation of one accosted by an unwanted street collector. The rejection of a loving son by a once doting father.

"Dad . . ." Nat's voice trailed off.

"You must be mistaken." The voice was gruff but still that of Sid Bonner, who had collapsed with a heart attack over the lawn mower he was repairing. "I'm not . . . your father." There was uncertainty in his tone now, a tremor of guilt because he lied.

"Dad . . . Daddy!" A ten-year-old's cry of anguish, pleading. "I *know* you are."

The older man tried to mouth a denial, but it refused to come; so he turned his head away and might have continued on his way had not his wrist been grasped in desperation. He made a feeble effort to shrug off the hand that held him, then shook his head in resignation.

"You shouldn't be here, Nat." His voice was low, his eyes flicking furtively from side to side in case he was overheard by a passerby. "How did you get here? What *happened* to you?" Now his tone was insistent, tinged with fear.

"Nothing has happened to me, Dad. I came here with Max Frame. You remember Max, the chap who taught me to drive? He's here, too, looking for his girlfriend. We've come to take you both back home."

"No, that is impossible! We can't go back!"

"We can. Max knows the way back out onto North-side."

"Look, Nat"— Sid Bonner's face was thrust close to that of his son, his words a trembling whisper— "there is no way back from the Ghetto. Once you are here, it is forever. Now, I must go, it is dangerous to linger on the street. Go back to your friend."

Nat let his father tug himself free, then stood there dejectedly as the other hastened away, turned down a side street and was lost from his view. The youth made no attempt to follow, realizing the futility of pursuit, and gave way to a flood of tears. Just as Shanifa had refused to return with Max, so was his father insistent on remaining in this place of degradation and hopelessness.

Max was not in his apartment when Nat arrived back. The youth fought against the wave of panic that threatened to surge over him. Oh, Max, hurry back, *please*. I need you more than ever now.

Max whiled away the seemingly endless hours by browsing his street plan of the Ghetto. Its symmetry reminded him of New York, not that he had ever been to the States, but he had looked at a guide once that belonged to Janice. Roadways and avenues that were dead straight, intersecting with others that had not so much as a slight curve in them, as if the place had been designed by a lazy architect. But it made life easy, that was one consolation.

He began to wonder if this taxi firm ever did any business. Four stretch limos stood idle; no vehicle had left or come in the whole time he had been here. There was no sign of any other drivers; even

the uniformed manager, if that was his title, had
gone off somewhere. The entire setup was like some
sick joke except that it was too eerie to laugh at.
You've got a job, mate, but you don't have to do
anything other than put the time in; you're a taxi
driver only you won't have to drive. Just sit around
until it's time to go home.

Max was satisfied that he had got the general gist
of the map. He knew how to get to the Square and
that was all that mattered. He began to fidget,
walked up and down, but his footsteps echoed and
made him nervous; so he sat in one of the cars
with the door open, listening to the rumble of passing traffic in the street up above. At least *somebody*
was going somewhere.

He didn't even know what time his shift ended.
Did they work a nine-till-five routine here or were
there three eight-hour shifts? It wasn't likely there
was a night shift, if nobody wanted cars in the day,
they weren't likely to at night.

His thoughts returned to Shanifa. She wasn't
likely to welcome his return any more than she had
his first visit. Christ, he'd balled it up, rushed headlong back into the Ghetto, right back to the proverbial square one. An ill-planned expedition, no
better than the last time. But he'd had no choice.
The police wouldn't listen, and there was nobody
else to turn to for help. Except Nat. They'd have
to talk it through tonight, formulate some kind of
plan of action. If Shanifa refused to go back with
them, then they would have to kidnap her. Max
groaned; this whole business was becoming more
fanciful by the hour.

"Grub."

Max started, banged his elbow on the door. He
hadn't heard the manager's approach. It was as if

the fellow had deliberately crept up on him, maybe hoping to catch him doing something he shouldn't be doing.

The other was holding out a plate on which two rolls lay soaking in some spilled tea from the precariously balanced paper cup.

"Oh . . . thanks." Max took the plate, slopped some more tea.

"There's a job for you at three, a pickup at the Hotel. He'll tell you where he wants to go." Expressionless, an order conveyed in the same tone in which the food had been offered. Eyes that watched but gave nothing away.

"Oh, right." Max bit on a roll. The soggy bread was undoubtedly stale, the filling meat of some kind, possibly ham. "I'll be there."

"You'd better be. Mister Merrick doesn't like to be kept waiting. He'll be the next mayor. And a good 'un!"

The uniformed man made no move to go away. His presence made Max uneasy. He took another bite, and decided that the best way to avoid conversation was to keep his mouth full.

"Things'll be a lot better then," the man went on in that same monotone, like a recitation that had been learned by heart, some kind of political propaganda to be spread by word of mouth. "The streets'll be safer, there'll be law and order. And he's going to round up the Downers."

"That's a good idea." From Max's previous brief encounters with the lower echelon of the Ghetto, that was good news by any standards. "Why's it been left till now? Couldn't the present mayor do it?"

"Ruben Quiles?" The voice became a whisper,

those piercing eyes narrowed, flickered with suspicion. "You're not a Quiles man, are you?"

"Oh, no!" Obviously it was policy here not to be a supporter of the reigning mayor. "Not at all, I just wondered why he didn't round them up."

"Because he don't want to. It ain't in his interests. They'll vote for him, try to keep him in office so they'll get free drugs, be left unmolested to prey on any that happen to fall into their clutches. But I'm forgetting, you're new here, you wouldn't understand. I should've warned you."

"About what?" Max's spine tingled, and he had difficulty in swallowing.

"About when you're on nights and get a call out. Don't stop for nobody, and if they stand in the road and try to force you to stop, run the bastards over, leave 'em where they fall. We lost a driver to 'em some time back. Worst part was they got the car, set it on fire. We can't afford to lose cars."

"When . . . when will I be on nights?"

"Depends." The heavy lips pursed beneath the moustache. "Might be tomorrow, maybe not till next week. All depends."

"On what?"

"On whether you're needed. We're short of drivers right now. Maybe they'll send some down from the Centre, maybe not. What did you do . . . *before*?"

Max tensed. The stale bread roll seemed to have balled in his intestines. He took a drink of tea; it was barely lukewarm. Those eyes were searching him out. This was some kind of devious interrogation.

"I . . . I taught people to drive."

"Well, well, that's handy, it really is. Most of them as are sent down here can't drive properly. And we can't afford to have the cars dented. Only a week or two back we had a crunch. Costly business, can't afford no more. So you reckon you can drive a bit, eh?"

"A little." Jesus, this was like a bloody madhouse! They gave you a job, whatever you asked, didn't even check you out.

"Good. You'll be handy, chap. Mostly I've had to do whatever driving there is myself. Any others they send us, if I don't think they can drive, I get them washing down the cars, sweeping the place out. Nice easy jobs where they can't do no harm. Get me?"

Max nodded.

"You'll be useful, chap." The manager's gruffness had relaxed a little. Max thought that before long he might even permit himself a smile. "You can pick up Mister Merrick at three, like I told you. Just concentrate on your driving; he ain't interested in talking to the likes of you. And I'll have a little bet with you, chap, as to what he's got in mind." The words were almost inaudible now, and Max had to lean forward to catch them. "It'll be a woman you'll have to go and pick up. He's like that is Mister Merrick. If he fancies a bit of crumpet, he has her, no matter if she just scrubs the steps at the Hotel. You'll see for yourself. But don't let him see that you've seen!"

"I won't, don't worry." Max tossed the empty cup into a litter bin. "I'll let you know how I get on."

The traffic was heavy. Max recalled how it had been that day when he had stood and watched from the pavement opposite the Hotel. Driving here was much the same as anywhere else, stop-start, other drivers cut you up, blared their horns. He was constantly alert for police cars, but there did not seem to be any about today. If there were, then maybe an official taxi and his uniform would give him immunity.

The big island was in a state of chaos, vehicles jostling for position, Klaxons sounding impatiently. Max edged into the nearside lane, and spotted the Hotel down the street on his left. It looked just the same as when he had last seen it, people entering and leaving, forcing their way through the flow of pedestrians. His mouth was dry. He wished he had been sent to another destination, anywhere else but here.

There were several other limousines parked outside, maybe belonging to a rival taxi firm or else out on private hire. Uniformed chauffeurs stood beside them, an air of servility in their posture, waiting to open the doors the moment their passengers emerged from the entrance.

Max spotted an empty parking space, glided into it, and switched off the engine. His nervousness bordered on fear. He had no idea what Stu Merrick looked like; perhaps the man would recognize the car. The guy sounded a bastard. He couldn't take any chances. He got out, and stood by the car.

It might be foggy later; there was a haziness in the atmosphere that threatened to thicken with the approach of evening. But by then he would be back in his apartment with Nat; it wouldn't worry him.

The moment he saw the big man coming through the revolving doors Max knew instinctively that it was Merrick. Features that had hardened with arrogance, a brusqueness that had a porter touching the peak of his cap, passersby halting to let him pass. Power that strained the buttons of an expensive suit that was a size too small, a veritable god who inspired awe amongst the lesser beings in a city that was divided so starkly between wealth and poverty.

Max opened a rear door and held it as the other approached. He saw the contempt in the man's expression, eyes that searched for a vestige of fear and would not be satisfied until they had found it. He sensed evil, smelled it in the cigar smoke and the pungent aftershave, almost felt pity for the wretched Downers, who would suffer at the hands of this man when he came to power. As he surely would, for there was no mistaking the sheer ruthlessness that bordered on invincibility.

Max stalled the car, heard the grunt of impatience from his passenger in the rear, and found himself muttering an apology for his clumsiness.

They were back in the flow of traffic before Merrick grunted his destination, a clipped, husky order that crackled the intercom. "The Square."

Max heard, understood. Stiffened. That ham roll was heavy in his guts again; his palms were sweaty on the wheel. He nodded because he knew that he was expected to acknowledge, tried to concentrate on his driving. A van blew its horn because he had strayed over toward the offside lane. He glanced in his rear mirror, but Merrick wasn't watching him, appeared to be deep in thought.

The Square was congested with badly parked, rusting cars, the way it always was, symbols of a lower status of tradesmen and residents, a backwater of working class outcasts. Max looked for a parking space, then eased onto the cobblestones alongside the headless statue. He was creating an obstruction, but it did not matter because his passenger was Stu Merrick.

"Wait here." Merrick made no move to get out; the implication was that he would not.

Max stared at the remnants of the statue because he did not want to look elsewhere. The cafe was to

his rear; it would have meant turning his head,
maybe inadvertently meeting the gaze of the man
behind him. Another time, after he had talked with
Nat. In the meantime he did not want to see. The
glass door would be stained with dirt, its filthy
opaqueness hiding the girl who served stewed tea
and apologized to her customers because the expected delivery of coffee had still not arrived.

They waited.

Max heard the rear door open, then click smoothly
shut. He caught a faint whiff of perfume mingling
with the cigar smoke.

"Bontoft Avenue, driver."

A name, an avenue that Max remembered from
the street plan. Uptown, the capitalist area, just one
block away from the mayoral suite, the penultimate
step to dictatorship. Merrick would make it all the
way, Max had no doubt about that.

The glance in his rearview smoky interior mirror
was instinctive, habitual for one who drove Fiestas
and taught his pupils the importance of mirror use.
But it was enough to cause him to swerve so that he
came within inches of clipping the wing of an overtaking truck, invoking a horn blast from the irate
driver— enough to chill the damp sweat on his body.

Framed in the oblong of glass, Max had seen the
face of his female passenger for one brief second
before it was hidden from him in Stu Merrick's embrace; the soft lips upturned, the blue eyes shining
as they had once shone for him.

And with recognition came the awful realization
that Merrick's latest mistress was none other than
Shanifa.

Eleven

"I tell you, I saw him, Max, I *spoke* to him!"

"All right, all right, I believe you." Max stood with his back against the door, still wore his driver's uniform. He had been in his apartment for at least twenty minutes, but the small entrance hall was the farthest he had progressed. Nat had been there when he had arrived, had let himself in with the spare key which Max had given him, a distraught youth on the verge of breaking down, devastated by his meeting with his father.

It was like a bad dream, Max thought, everything happening all at once and you're praying that in a second you'll wake up and everything will be fine. But there was no chance of that. This was stark, terrifying surrealism that blended with awful reality.

"Let's go into the living room, Nat. We can talk there." He thought the boy was going to refuse, bar his way, but Nat turned round and slouched into the sparse room ahead of him.

Christ, this was all he needed after his own recent experience. It had taken a determined effort to drive the limo back to base and check out. He had been trembling, ashen with shock, but the manager had not appeared to notice.

"There's a job for you first thing in the morning." You've done well, chap, better than I expected; now I'm really going to put you to the test. "You've got to pick up Mister Diogene at seven sharp. Not a minute later. Because tomorrow's Wednesday, and we all know what Mister Diogene goes up to the prison for on Wednesday mornings." Smirking, gloating.

"I'm sorry." Max had difficulty in concentrating. "As you know, I'm new here."

"Oh, yes, I was forgetting." The lips were drawn back, exposing a double row of broken, yellowed teeth, had Max recoiling from the soured breath. "I don't suppose you even know who Luis Diogene is, chap." A mild admonishment, the lips pouted. "Well, Mister Diogene is the *executioner;* he's been hanging the scum of this place for the last ten years. Does a real good job, too. Wednesdays are always hanging days. Might be one, perhaps half a dozen, you can never tell. But we have a contract job to drive him up to the prison, wait for him to do what he has to do, and then take him back home. It might be just an hour, could be three or four, depending on how many he's got to do."

"Oh . . . I see."

"If you're lucky, he might let you."

"I beg your pardon."

"I said, if you're lucky he might let you see, allow you to go inside with him and *watch!*"

Max's stomach threatened to eject that undigested ham roll; his throat scorched, but somehow he kept it down.

"If you get the chance, chap, you go and take a look. I've watched a couple of times and, believe me, it's well worth it. Murderers and the like, they're not so brave once they're up on the platform and Mister Diogene puts the rope round their necks, believe me. Sometimes they scream and struggle, but it makes no difference. Every one that goes down through that trapdoor makes this a better place for the likes of you and me. All the other prisoners watch from the windows of their cells. Does 'em more good than ten years inside 'cause they know it might be them next if they don't behave themselves. Get me?"

"Uh-huh." Max nodded again.

"A bit nerve-racking the first time you watch, but after the first one's had his neck stretched, you'll get to enjoy it. But whatever you do"— a warning finger shook within an inch of Max's face— "don't refuse to go in if Mister Diogene asks you, because you can't afford to offend him. He puts a lot of business our way, regular weekly journeys which are useful when times are slack. Besides, he *might* just be the next mayor. It ain't likely 'cause it's mostly between Merrick and Quiles, but there's always a chance that an outsider might surprise everybody. And if Luis Diogene gets to be mayor, then there'll be more necks stretched than this place has seen for twenty years."

Right now, though, Max's recent trip overshadowed anything that might happen on the morrow. God, it was unbelievable, nauseating, what had gone on in the taxi that afternoon. Max tried to tell himself that his imagination was playing tricks on him, that the slim blond girl whom Stu Merrick had kissed and fondled was somebody else. Anybody but Shanifa. But it was Shanifa, all right, as fresh and as lovely as she had been the last time Max had taken her in his arms. He wanted to believe that she was necking with that arrogant bastard because she didn't have any choice; when a bureaucrat singled out a working class girl she submitted to his lust for fear of what might befall her if she refused. There wasn't any other explanation. There couldn't be.

And now he had Nat's troubles to contend with. It was his own selfish fault for bringing the boy along with him, burdening himself with an additional, unnecessary problem.

"Just as I knew in my dreams, my father's a prison warder, Max. I'm going to go to him. If necessary, I'll get myself put in prison!"

"You stupid bastard!" Max grabbed him by the lapels of his jacket, thrust his face close. "I don't know what the hell's going on in this place, but I do know that if you go to jail, you might well find yourself being hanged. Because the guy who's the executioner here hangs 'em right, left and center!"

"How do you know that?" Sullen defiance, *you're lying just to frighten me.*

"Because tomorrow I've got to drive this despicable fucker to do his work, and there's just a chance that he might invite me in to watch. And if he does, then I've got to go, even though I'll keep my eyes tightly shut the whole time." Max released his hold, and Nat sank down into a chair.

"Then I'm going to the prison with you, Max." *Why don't I keep my bloody big mouth shut!* "You can't, Nat. You've got a job of your own, and there's no way I can take you along."

"I'm not going to the studio again. It's awful. You don't do anything except sit in a draughty warehouse and draw things that nobody wants, anyway."

"You don't have any choice, no more than I do tomorrow. At least you won't have to watch people being hanged!"

"It won't make any difference to them if they are hanged, Max."

"What the hell are you talking about?"

"Because everybody here is dead except you and me, Max. This is hell. Shanifa's dead, so is my father. We can't take them back. The only thing we can do is join them, and I'm going to my father whether you like it or not!"

Max sat down in the other chair. He tried not to believe, but there was no other explanation. The only hope he clung to was that he had seen Shanifa on Northside that evening. If she was dead, then she could not have left here. That hope was fading fast. All right, then, everybody else in the Ghetto was dead except Shanifa. And himself and Nat, of course.

"Look, Nat." It was some moments before Max could trust himself to speak again. "If you want to go to your father, any way you choose, then that's up to you. But I can't take you up to the prison, and I'm not going to try. All right?"

"All right," the reply came sulkily. Nat was staring at the worn linoleum. "I guess we'll just have to go our own separate ways, Max. Thanks for bringing me along, at least."

Max watched Nat let himself out, heard him bang the door of the neighboring apartment. Some time later he thought he heard the youth sobbing on the other side of the thin partitioned wall.

Nat Bonner awoke sometime during the night hours. A dream, a bad one, had disturbed his restless sleep, but it had vanished without trace as he stirred into consciousness. He groaned, sat up, and reached for the light switch. It took him several seconds to locate it in his unfamiliar surroundings.

The nightmare, whatever it was, had left him shaken, the sweat chilling on his trembling body in the cold room. He almost called out for Max, but stopped himself just in time. He wasn't a kid shouting for his parents because he was scared in the middle of the night; he was an adult. And, anyway, Max wouldn't help him. All he was interested in was finding his girlfriend. He didn't give a shit about Nat's father.

The dream had been like the others, he was sure of that, his father trapped in this everlasting hell, crying out for help. The only difference this time was that Max was here with him. He had to go to his father.

Furtively, he left his bed, and began pulling on his clothes. He stopped to listen, then breathed a sigh of relief when he heard shallow, rhythmic breathing from the other side of the thin wall. Max was asleep; he must be careful not to wake him.

The landing was in darkness. Nat groped until he found the iron stair rail, then began to follow it downward. His foot kicked against something, sent it rolling on ahead of him down the steps, a plastic throwaway cup by the sound of it. Litter rustled; something crunched beneath his feet.

Only when he reached the ground floor did he pause, reflecting for a moment on the rashness and hopelessness of his mission. He did not even know where his father lodged; their meeting had been a chance in a million. He considered turning back. Maybe he should hang around in the proximity of the prison in the daylight, wait for his father going to work. No, his father needed him. The rejection yesterday had been a sham brought on by the fear of being seen, perhaps afraid that he might endanger his son by exposing him as a living being in this place of the dead. At least Nat had to *try*. He owed his father that much.

Nat stepped out into the dimly lit street. The lighting was reduced to one lamp every hundred yards or so, an eerie half light that struggled to penetrate a thick fog, cast disconcerting shadows. He stood listening, but there was no sound, not even the sighing of the night breeze. Utter silence all around.

He smelled the fog, tasted it like marsh gasses seeping up from some foul bog. Nat knew that he had to follow the pavement to the right, the way that led to the art and design studio. It was along there where he had glimpsed his father. Warehouses and more warehouses, interspersed with the odd shuttered shop that had probably not opened for business for years, an endless desolation; he might have been in any one of the Ghetto's streets. Suddenly he came upon a street that turned sharply to the right. He was certain that that was the one along which his father had hurried away from him. If not, then the next one was probably identical. He turned, walked faster now, keeping to the wall all the way.

A scream shattered the stillness, shrieked like a train hurtling from a tunnel, a night force that vibrated the pavements and buildings, reluctant to disperse as though the fog trapped it in this narrow street.

Nat cowered, peered into the gloom, but nothing moved. Slowly the silence seeped back as though it had never been broken. He wanted to flee, to run blindly back to the safety of his dowdy apartment, to wake Max. Except that whoever, whatever, had screamed might be lurking behind him. Or in front of him. It was impossible to tell from which direction that hellish sound had come.

And in that instant Nat knew that it was that same scream that had awoken him. Real or dreamed, it had trespassed in his sleep, the anguished cry of the damned or perhaps some nocturnal beast that roamed the Ghetto streets in search of prey.

He accepted the futility of trying to find his father; in an empty maze of streets it was difficult enough, but with terrible creatures that defied the imagination on the prowl, it was impossible.

In which case he had to return to his apartment. He thought he could find it again without too much trouble, a left turn and then straight on until. . . .

Something materialized out of the foggy shadows.

It was a human being, at least it stood upright on two legs, and a pair of long arms dangled by its side. The orange murkiness of the sparse streetlights prevented Nat from discerning more than a silhouette, brought with it a vague feeling of relief because it wasn't some monstrous four-legged brute, which he had associated with that cry.

The other had seen him, there was no doubt about that, the head thrust forward in an attempt to peer into the shadows, a shuffle forward as though to obtain a better view.

"Er . . . good evening." Nat licked his lips. It sounded bloody stupid in the empty streets; it would maybe have been preferable to hurry on past the stranger. A golden rule when in doubtful surroundings, always seem to be in a hurry and appear to know exactly where you are going. That way you did not invite unwanted attention.

He could have crossed over the road, walked at a fast pace, prepared to break into a run if necessary. His impression of the other was that he was old,

maybe a tramp, a scrounger on the lookout for a
handout. Frail and starved, no threat, just a bloody
nuisance. He should not have spoken, just ignored
him.

A shaft of misty light slanted down onto the
other's features, showed them to be near-skeletal
with wisps of gray hair sprouting from the cheeks
and chin. The cavernous mouth was agape in an
unmistakable snarl, the teeth broken or malformed,
saliva stringing from the wasted lips. The body was
clad in ribboned rags that scarcely hid its deformed
obscenity, the feet twisted, toes curled and growing
under. Hands that were filthy talons reached out,
the figure staggered forward with unbelievable agil-
ity for one so wretched, and the open mouth emitted that ghastly shriek for a second time.

Nat had turned to run, but his terror robbed him
of his mobility, a momentary form of paralysis that
froze him into a posture of recoil. That scream was
deafening, jarred his brain. He tried to scream in
unison, but if any sound came from his own lips,
it was drowned in that bestial cry.

The other was close to him now; Nat could see the
features in terrifying detail, smelled the fetid breath
and body odors, a suffocating stench that was a combination of sweat and urine and unimaginable filth.
The odor of the lair of a beast that inhabited sewers
and underground haunts, emerged only when the occupants of the upper city had retired for the night,
lay in wait for an unwary traveller.

They stood there regarding each other, the sunken
eyes glinting with unmistakable lust, fingers with
black and ragged nails reaching out as though to
stroke the flesh of their victim.

Nat wanted to faint. There was no escape; his legs
were threatening to buckle beneath him. He had

already accepted his fate, a ghastly death, his clothes ripped from his corpse, searched for anything that might be of any value. It happened in every city— London, New York— the Ghetto was no different.

And just when it seemed that those scrawny hands were about to take him, their owner sprung away and uttered what might have been a muttered curse, a grunt of frustration. Slipping away, merging with the fog and the shadows, gone as though it had been a figment of nightmarish hallucination, another bad dream of the Ghetto.

Nat fell to the ground, lay weak and shaking on the cold, rough concrete, shied from the shadows in case it had been just a cruel trick and that creature was waiting to pounce as a cat might tantalize a mouse with pseudo freedom.

Suddenly the light was brighter, dazzling whiteness where previously there had been a hazy orange glow. Through the echoes of the scream that still vibrated in his brain, Nat became aware of another sound. Rhythmic, metallic, it was some seconds before his frightened and confused mind recognized the familiar ticking-over of a motor engine.

The car had stopped in front of him; another two or three yards and it might have run him over. Its headlights were full on, blinding him, playing on the warehouse wall at the rear, dispersing the shadows and revealing that nothing untoward lurked where they had been. Doors were flung open. Heavy boots scraped on the loose gravel.

"Well, we've got one of 'em!" somebody said.

Nat's arms were gripped, strong fingers that dug cruelly into his flesh, pulled him upright with a force that might have dislocated a joint. Beyond the light he glimpsed flat caps, uniformed men who seemed giants by comparison with his own stature.

They hauled him to his feet, held him; shook him with frightening intensity.

"You filthy scum! We heard your cry, you didn't get away this time. Slipped and fell, eh! Well, you'll drop again—from the gallows when Stu Merrick gets to be mayor. All of you, every fucking last one of you!"

"I . . . I was . . . attacked!" Nat would have pointed in the direction in which his ragbag assailant had fled had his arms been free.

"Like fuck, you were!" A flat hand struck him across the face, jerked his head back. He tasted blood. He cried out, but a knee in his groin silenced him.

"One of the young ones," a deep voice from behind stated. "A cub learning to hunt. No matter, we won't go home empty-handed tonight. Quiles ain't protecting 'em now; he won't ever again unless he wins the election. Listen, you young bastard, you'd better pray in your cell every night that Ruben Quiles gets back to be mayor, 'cause if he don't, you'll be one of the first Downers to get his neck stretched. Okay, you guys, put him in and we'll take him back right away."

Nat was bundled into the back of the patrol car. He smelled the faded upholstery as he was held face downward, the swaying of the moving vehicle threatening to make him throw up. Oh, God, he had blown his last chance of ever seeing his father again now!

Twelve

Roxy Burgoin always kept to the vicinity of the Square after darkness. Most of the prostitutes did likewise, which rather condensed the competition into a restricted red-light area, but it was the only way by which safety was assured.

The police patrolled that part of the Ghetto constantly throughout the night hours. Prostitutes were left unmolested by the law, Quiles recognized that it was in his interests to allow the oldest profession to flourish even though his closest rival was organizing the racket. Even the Downers were kept away, odd ones arrested to show that "Citizen Protection" was not solely in Merrick's manifesto. But whatever the sham, if you were selling your body, you offered it within the realms of safety.

Roxy sheltered in a warehouse doorway and lit another cigarette. Trade was bad tonight, the worst she had ever known, and Stu didn't accept excuses lightly. If necessary, she would hand over some of her own money in the morning, try to make it up another night. There was another whore a hundred yards farther down. Roxy glimpsed her beneath the foggy streetlight. Any guy coming from that direction would see the other first. Charges were uniform; it wasn't a case of looking for a cheaper screw, rather which girl you fancied. Roxy backed her own looks, but age might be the deciding factor. Men often went for younger girls, twenty-year-olds being preferred to more mature, experienced hookers. She sighed, drew hard on her cigarette, and then picked up the sound of approaching footsteps. She tensed with expectancy; they came from the opposite direction.

Her bitterness toward Stu still lingered. She realized now that the only attraction his bed had held for her was the luxurious lifestyle that had gone with it. It had lasted less than two months; he had spotted that tart at the cafe, and Roxy had been thrown out onto the street. She smiled whimsically to herself; Stu's latest wench would be soliciting before the year was out, she would lay a bet with herself on that. It was a fact of life in the Ghetto; you rode the rough with the smooth, enjoyed the latter while it lasted. At least the money was good, apart from tonight, better than eking out a bare existence with Ed. Those footfalls were louder, nearer. She stepped out onto the pavement in full view of the approaching stranger.

There was a vague familiarity about the man who strode out of the fog that even the outsize overcoat and pulled-down cap could not disguise. Roxy caught her breath as she peered with a sense of mounting unease. He had seen her, was hurrying toward her. She stiffened, moved back into a patch of shadow, and checked again to see if the prostitute down the street was still within calling distance. Not that anybody went to help anybody in the Ghetto. If you had any sense, you didn't hear or see anything that was not your personal concern.

Roxy drew hard on her cigarette. A fiver in the alley just behind; ten if you come back to my place. Anything out of the ordinary is extra.

"Roxy?"

"Don't pester me, Ed!" Her tone was harsh. "If you want me, you'll have to pay, but I'd rather you didn't."

"Roxy." It was Ed Burgoin, all right, an expression of anguish on his features. "Roxy, let's go somewhere and talk."

"There's no talking left to do, Ed. Why don't you go back to your girlfriend?"

"I don't have a girlfriend any longer, Roxy. It was all a mistake. I'm sorry . . . for everything. Look, I know you couldn't help what you did; any woman in the Ghetto who turned down Stu Merrick would be crazy. Except that most of them end up like this. Okay, we're both to blame, but can't we go and talk, see if we can get everything back together, the way it used to be?"

"Ed." She took a deep breath, let it out slowly. "I don't want things to be like they were. I've had my fill of living in a cardboard henhouse, barely enough money to buy food, and even when you've got money there's no guarantee that there'll be food to buy. I make a reasonable living; Stu looks after his girls. Leave it at that, will you?"

"Roxy!" Despair now, he was reaching out for her as though to claim her back physically.

"Piss off, Ed!"

"I . . ."

The headlights of a car which had turned the street corner played on them, twin spotlights of dazzling white, blinding them momentarily. Brakes screeched as it slewed to a halt, one wheel on the pavement.

"Police!" Ed Burgoin threw up an arm as though to ward off an attack. He had committed no crime, there was no curfew in force at present, but patrolling officers were an unknown quantity, a law unto themselves. If they'd had an uneventful night, were bored, then they might pull just anybody in to break the monotony.

It wasn't the police. Roxy recognized the battered sedan in spite of its glaring headlights. It was one of Stu Merrick's unofficial patrols, vigilantes ensuring that his whores, his investment in flesh, were safe. After the election these men would automatically step into the role of official police. But in the dark hours, in a deserted street, there was no difference.

"You all right, baby?" The question was addressed to Roxy, the leading "patrolman" an awe-inspiring figure in dungarees and a taxi-driver's hat that was intended to convey an impression of officialdom in the half light. "This bum bothering you?"

"No, not at all," Roxy answered, an attempt to protect Ed because of what had once existed between them, a final act of loyalty. "Everything's fine, I've just got a client. Now if you gentlemen would—"

"Get in!" A hand grasped Ed's arm, twisted it up behind his back. "It's okay, miss, he won't bother you no more."

"He isn't . . ." Roxy's words died away. Christ, what was the use? These thugs had been touring the streets looking for Ed, knew that they could effect under cover of darkness that which might have attracted the attention of Quiles' policemen by day. They had been tipped off that Ed Burgoin was searching for his wife, feared lest he might learn from her things that were better left unknown to the masses. Stu never let his girls go back into public life; it was too dangerous. You whored until you were spent and then. . . .

Ed Burgoin was trying to struggle, the last throw of a desperate man who guessed his fate once his attackers had him in their car. A hand was clapped over his mouth to stifle the shout for help; a boot in his testicles rendered him helpless, had him writhing in the grasp of his captors as they lifted him into the rear of the car.

Roxy melted back into the shadows. There was nothing more that she could have done to help. A further intervention might have invited punishment for herself. Ed was nothing to her now, he never really had been. She lit another cigarette with the butt of the first one and watched the patrol car do a U-turn and head back down the street. Whatever they had in mind to do to him, he had brought it on himself.

She thought she heard another prospective customer coming along the pavement.

Ed Burgoin was incapable of speech; the pain in his lower abdomen had him groaning when he wanted to be screaming. He thought his arm might be broken, too. These bastards weren't police; they were Merrick's hirelings acting on the orders of their boss to ensure that Roxy's whoring was not interrupted. Husbands had a habit of causing trouble; they had to be removed, quickly and quietly.

The car was travelling at speed, hurtling along poorly lit, deserted streets, squealing its tires on every corner. The driver was obviously in no doubt concerning his intended destination.

It would not be the prison, Ed was certain of that, because even the Ghetto's corrupt internment organization would not accept inmates from Stu Merrick's officers until he became mayor officially. In which case there was only one possible alternative. The driver was beginning to slow down.

"Here we are, pal!" Ed was pulled up into a sitting position, saw through the windshield where the headlights cut a swathe into unending blackness. No buildings, just mud and rubble, gutters filled with rainwater and a perpetual fog doing its best to hide the shame of this feared place of no return.

The Waste.

"No, please . . ."

"Get out!" The man beside him released his hold, pushed and sent Ed Burgoin sliding headlong out of the vehicle. He landed in a puddle; some of the foul water splashed up into his mouth and made him heave. The car shot away, squirting him with mud from its tires, its taillights fireflies vanishing into the night.

Ed did not pick himself up right away; there was no point. Condemned to wander in this hellish wasteland forever, there was no hurry. He noted the direction in which the car had gone. Logically it should have been possible to follow in its wake until one reached the outskirts of the built-up area. But it did not work like that. Ed had heard too many stories of the Waste, a desert of mud, enshrouded in fog from which there was no escape. Occasionally somebody stumbled upon a way out, but if you were caught, then your fate was too terrible to contemplate, for you were an outcast, one who had walked in the lair of the Downers, maybe carried one of their terrible diseases or, at best, had developed a taste for human flesh in times of starvation. There was no reintegration; you were either cast back whence you had escaped or else put down like a rabid cur.

Somewhere out in that darkened wilderness Ed Burgoin heard a scream, a cry that embodied hopelessness and lust, the shriek of a creature of prey that stalked this barren land in search of food for its shrunken belly.

Thirteen

Luis Diogene was much as Max had expected to find him. A caricatured priest from some wayout religious sect, short and fat so that his black robes trailed around his feet as he walked, his flabby features shaded by the brim of his fedora, jowls that wobbled when he talked. And in spite of his profession of death, he was a talkative man.

"You're new here!" Almost an accusation, Max wondered if he had some distinctive, giveaway feature.

"Yes." It would have been foolish to deny it, the man only had to check with the Employment Office.

"You'll like it here"—a mirthless chuckle—"we have hangings twice weekly, three sometimes. You'll be able to drive the route blindfolded after a week or two. I go up to the prison most mornings. Today's special, though."

Max tried to concentrate on his driving, wished that the sliding window that separated the driver from his passenger had been closed. Diogene would most likely have opened it, though. The hangman loved to talk; maybe he did not look for answers. Just nod and grunt, let him ramble on.

"I said today's special."

"Oh." The other obviously did expect a reply, at least an acknowledgment. "As you said, I'm new."

"A woman who's been on Death Row for years." In his rear mirror Max saw Diogene sitting with his hands clasped on his protruding stomach, an expression of glib anticipation on his squat features. "A political pawn, in fact. A murderer, all the same, tried and found guilty, one of Merrick's ex-mistresses . . . and there are plenty of those around!"

"I see."

"No, you don't. At least, not until I tell you!" An admonishment, the guy was shrewd but crazy, had no time for polite conversation. "If you're new here, how can you know?"

"I'm sorry, just a way of speaking."

"If Merrick won the election, then she'd be the first up on the gallows, the very next day, before he started rounding up these blasted Downers. Quiles was content to let her stop on Death Row indefinitely, it seems. Me—and I tell you, driver, I shall win the election in spite of all these forecasts, which don't give me a chance, because I've got an ace up my sleeve— I'd hang the bitch, too. I've been waiting to get my noose round her neck for years. Now, suddenly, Ruben Quiles has signed the execution warrant. Just like that!" A snap of fleshy fingers. "There's a lot of speculation as to why, but I'll tell you why . . ."

"Why?" The other's pause was a cue for the question.

"Because he wants to deprive Merrick of the pleasure of revenge on this woman, that's why. One up on his rival, see what I mean?" Diogene was leaning forward, face close to the window. "She'll be a beauty to hang. I weighed her yesterday. Almost two hundred pounds, that's some weight for a woman!"

Max felt sick. He had always been in favor of the death penalty, but now he wasn't so sure. This was bizarre, brutal.

"Some weight, eh, driver?"

"Sure."

"They'll all be watching. A full house!" Another weird laugh sent prickles up Max's neck into his scalp.

"Who?"

"The inmates, of course. Every one of them will be at their cell windows. Oh, I was forgetting, you're new here. The cell blocks overlook the execution yard; there isn't a window from which the hangings can't be seen. As I told you, today's something special."

"So it seems." You fucking morbid bastard!

"Would *you* like to come in and watch, driver?"

Max's intestines balled. The horn of an overtaking truck blared because he threatened to veer out into its path. He was trembling.

"Did you hear me, driver?"

"Oh, yes, sure."

"Good. I'm sure you'll enjoy it. Will it be the first execution you've witnessed?"

"Er . . . no, you got me wrong. I said 'yes' because I'd heard you. No, thanks, I'd rather not watch the hanging."

"You don't want to watch?"

Max swallowed as he detected surprise and anger in his passenger's tone. The refusal had been taken as an insult. "Er, thanks all the same, perhaps next time."

"No, not at all, it'll do you good, particularly as you're new here, let you see what might happen to you if you commit a serious breach of the law. I tell you, when I'm mayor, there'll be a flush of hangings to begin with and then it'll taper off. There's no better deterrent than the rope, but you have to show 'em that you're prepared to use it. I insist that you are a spectator to the most talked about execution of the year, driver."

"All right." Ultimately, I have no option, better to accept gracefully.

"Good. You'll be glad afterward that you accepted my invitation."

Max was sweating heavily. He consoled himself that he could always close his eyes, turn his head away. But it was the prospect of that inevitable atmosphere of barbaric death that disgusted him most. Nothing could shut that out.

"Here we are!" There was a note of excitement in Luis Diogene's voice as the gray walls of the prison loomed up ahead of them. "Straight through the main entrance, driver, park up by the governor's office. I'll delegate a warder to look after you. A ringside seat, eh!" Shrill, piping laughter, manic sadism that foretold death in the halls of the dead.

Yolanda Morrison did not really believe that her execution would go ahead. It had been on-off, start-stop for so many years that she had become immune to the tantalizations. They had weighed her on at least half a dozen previous occasions. Possibly Diogene obtained some sick thrill from viewing her naked. There would be a reprieve about an hour before the scheduled time of the hanging.

Sid had let himself into her cell sometime in the early hours. There had been a distinct air of unease about him, and when he spoke his whisper shook. She thought that he might be close to tears.

"They mean it this time," he said.

"Crap!"

"No, honest." The hand that found hers was shaking. "Quiles has signed the warrant."

"Who says?"

"I've seen it, pinned up on the notice board. They've never gone that far before, not with you, anyway."

She was silent for a moment, and then, "Well, at least it'll get it over, deprive Stu of the satisfaction of hanging me. Come on, Sid, you'd better make it good for me the last time."

But tonight Sid Bonner couldn't make it at all. And it was the first time that Yolanda had seen him cry.

Nat was flung roughly into a darkened cell. He lay there on the stone floor, heard the door slam behind him and the key grate in the lock. The stench of excrement and urine was sickly overpowering. He retched, and it was only then that he sensed a movement close by and realized that he was not the only occupant of this cramped place.

He tried to move away, but came up against a rough stone wall that was cold and slimy to his touch, realizing then just how small this cell was. So dark, too. If there was a window anywhere, then it was not even visible against the night sky outside. Fear knotted his stomach; he had no idea with whom he was imprisoned, male or female, young or old.

Something touched his hand. He snatched it away with a gasp, found himself in a corner. Trapped.

"Hey!" It sounded weak, frightened. "Who . . . who are you?"

No answer. Just an intake of breath, lungs that

rasped as though they were filled with phlegm. The hand came again, feeling, probing, found Nat's thigh and scraped its way along it.

"Get away, you dirty bastard!"

The other laughed, a chilling sound. "We'd better get used to each other, friend. We're likely to be together a long time." The searching fingers were withdrawn, but Nat sensed the other's closeness, smelled his stale, warm breath.

"Who are you, friend?" The voice was coarse but young, maybe Nat's own age.

"Nat . . . Nat Bonner."

"How'd you get caught?"

"I was minding my own business when a police car came along. They beat me up, threw me in here."

"We all mind our own business, but they still pull us in. It'll be worse when Merrick's mayor. They'll hang us all then. You and me, they'll keep us locked in here, eating out of the same bowl, shitting in the same bucket, until the way's clear to hang us. You see if I'm not right."

Nat was shivering with cold and terror. There was something sinister about his companion. He wished it was daylight. Or perhaps it was better not to see.

"You from the Waste?"

"No. I'm new here."

"Oh, that explains it. Well, you'll learn. Some they throw back onto the Waste, others they imprison. No logic, no way of knowing which they'll do. My guess is that they're rounding up a few so they can have a real rope party when Stu Merrick gets to power."

"What's your name?" Nat was curious. Revolted as he was by the smell and his mental image of his cell mate, he was relieved to find the other friendly.

Maybe there had been no devious motive behind the fingers that had felt for him.

"Jez. Hey, lookout, there's somebody coming. Lie on the floor, pretend to be asleep!"

Slow, dragging footsteps halted outside the cell door; a torch beam flashed through the iron grill. Nat was dazzled even behind his closed eyelids; feigning sleep was not easy.

"That's the one they brought in last night." A sneering voice, the beam trained on Nat's face. "Don't look a bad kid, better than the other fucker, eh!"

"Let's have a look at him." The second voice was familiar, but in his terror Nat was unable to place it. "Come on, open up a minute."

"What's the fucking point? Waste of time."

All the same, a key grated in the lock and the door creaked and rattled as it swung inward.

"Come on, Jez, we know you ain't a-bloody sleep. Shift yer bleedin' self!" There was the sound of a boot thudding on something soft, a grunt of pain. "That's better, get out the way!"

Nat opened his eyes; it was futile to pretend to be asleep any longer. The tiny cell was lit up. The first thing he saw was his companion's features, and it was all Nat could do to hold back his cry of horror. Certainly the other was young, no more than twenty at the most, but his features were malformed to the point of grotesqueness. The skull might have been a trainee sculptor's first effort, perhaps a mold that had slipped so that the jaw bone was elongated, twisted to one side, taking the narrow mouth with it. Eyes that were too close together, the nose might have been broken in childhood and not reset. The flesh was pallid, sprouted hair in places like a carelessly sown lawn. Ragged clothing failed to hide the misshapen body, arms that were too long, legs too short. A product of interbreeding that had stunted and mocked the human form.

But the warders were not interested in Jez; they were peering, blinding Nat with their torch beam.

"What's the matter?" The one was obviously impatient, eager to be out of this stinking cell. "Just a kid, they don't all have to be from the Waste."

In that instant Nat's eyesight adjusted to the brightness. He saw the second warder's face as the first one swung the torch to one side, and yet again it was all he could do to prevent himself from crying out.

"Come on, Sid, you've seen all there is to see. A kid and a Downer locked up together, nothing special."

"I guess not." The other's voice was a shaking whisper. "You're right, let's go."

The door clanged shut, was locked again. The heavy boots scraped their way on up the corridor, and the darkness filtered back.

Nat sat on the floor, shook uncontrollably. The shock of having his companion's features revealed was forgotten by comparison with the face he had looked upon beneath that peaked prison cap. For his own father had looked upon him, recognized him and abandoned his son to his fate.

Nat started to sob, cried unashamedly until the early light of dawn found its way in through the slitted window. Oh, God, how he despised his own father. And how he hated Max Frame for persuading him to come here, luring him to this living death amongst the dead. Hang me, and at least let me be as they are!

* * *

"You're a fat sow." Luis Diogene stalked arrogantly around the naked Yolanda Morrison in the interrogation room, hands clasped behind his back, savoring this moment or two of gloating before the customary walk across the yard to the gallows. "I'd swear you're even fatter than you were yesterday when I weighed you!"

She drew herself up to her full height, her breasts hung heavy like over filled beanbags. Her cheeks were flushed with anger, a mass of freckles. She eased her legs apart, stood like some female colossus, defiant to the very end.

"Thank God I'm spared the sight of you without your clothes, Luis." A string of dangling spittle lodged in her cleavage. "When did you last see your feet?"

"Quiet, woman!" The executioner reacted angrily. "You will sing a different tune when you feel the noose around your neck. And remember, there will be a face at every cell window. Every prisoner in this jail will hoot with laughter at the sight of your wizened belly. It's like a forgotten winter apple, an oversize one!"

"They'd laugh even more if they could see yours, Luis! How long must we stand here spitting insults at each other?"

"Until I am ready." He stood in front of her, glaring up at her.

"I wish you ill-luck in the election, Luis." Yolanda stared straight ahead of her. "Not that you stand a chance, but you will never be more than the ruling mayor's pawn, a puppet to do the dangling."

"We shall see. You most certainly won't!"

"Tell me just one thing, Luis." She lowered her voice. The death squad warders were waiting outside, just victim and hangman left alone in this room, an old custom. "Why the sudden decision to hang me? Ruben doing a one-upmanship on Stu?"

"You were always shrewd in spite of your looks." Luis Diogene laughed, moved behind her. "Perhaps so. It is not my concern. But rest assured that I shall recall today for the rest of my life."

"I'm sure you will."

"I'm ready!" Diogene raised his voice, and the door opened to admit two warders. "At least the fog has cleared. It would have been such a shame had visibility been reduced!"

Max Frame sat on a wooden bench some ten yards from the heavy wooden structure that served as an instrument of barbaric execution. On either side of him were warders. He wondered if they had a part to play or whether they were merely interested spectators, for there was no mistaking their enthusiasm, partisan fans at a soccer match.

He looked around him, saw faces pressed against the bars of cell windows on all sides; row after row of eyes, he sensed their lust, their sadism. Jesus Christ, this was the very depths of depravity, the hell that his mother feared he might stray into as a child. Its existence had been known, guessed, for generations. Hidden. Death was but a step away from life.

The gasp of a thousand watchers was like a gust of arctic wind. It chilled his flesh before he saw the procession emerging from a doorway on the other side of the compound. The woman was in the lead, walking awkwardly because of her size, obscene in her nakedness, head held high in defiance. Max wondered how she would die if she was already dead. It was no more than a sick ritual, but what would be the outcome? Would she walk away with her neck broken, head lying to one side? It was a terrifying prospect, something that was only possible in the Ghetto.

He wouldn't watch; he would close his eyes and hope that nobody noticed.

The procession had reached the gallows steps. Yolanda stopped, then turned in a full circle as though making a final bow to her audience. Whistles shrilled across the open ground. Somebody shouted something that Max didn't catch; it was doubtless obscene. He saw that her wrists were bound behind her back. For the first time he saw her clearly. She was both revolting and strikingly attractive, a once-fine body sagging with fat while her features were finely cut, almost aristocratic. A foot on the bottom step, she swayed uncertainly, and one of the warders reached out a supporting hand.

Luis Diogene brought up the rear, now wearing an unnecessary mask, squat Death in its most horrible form. He grasped the hanging rope, caressed it with a bizarre tenderness. Yolanda was facing in the opposite direction, a haughtiness about her ungainly posture which had Max admiring her. He had never seen her before, he had no idea what her crime was, but she was facing the inevitable with courage.

Surely they would mask her. They didn't. Diogene extended the noose, draped it over her head, and let it lie as if it was some kind of ceremonial necklace, a decoration rather than an instrument of death. She seemed oblivious of it, almost unaware of what was happening. Perhaps they had drugged her, but Max knew that they hadn't. Mercy was an unknown commodity in the Ghetto.

He felt a touch on his arm, started. The warder next to him was whispering something, his mouth

so close that Max recoiled from the putrid breath
that everybody here was cursed with.

"This is the one we've been waiting for, mate.
Never thought it would come to it. Diogene will
take his time, you mark my words."

Max felt physically sick. They were all as bad as
the hangman, a form of sadism that transcended
cruelty. He just nodded. He switched his thoughts
to Nat, wondered where the boy had got to. The
other had not been in his apartment when Max had
checked before going to pick up Diogene. He might
have gone to work early, but it was doubtful. In
which case he had gone to look for his father. Well,
that was up to Nat; Max had decided to absolve
himself of all responsibility for his friend if he was
determined to go it alone. The Ghetto was a mine-
field of danger; if Nat wanted to take unnecessary
risks, then he'd have to take the consequences for
his own actions. All the same, guilt nagged Max
because he had persuaded him to come along. He
got to thinking about Shanifa; the situation was a
thousand times more difficult now than it had been
before. Surely she was not in love with a guy like
Stu Merrick. No, the prospective mayor had singled
her out for his lust. Max winced. She would doubtless welcome a means of rescue. She was obviously
still working at the cafe, so that was his best means
of contacting her. He must talk with her at the
earliest opportunity.

A movement on the far side of the exercise yard
attracted his attention. A door had opened, and a
couple of warders emerged, shepherding some be-
draggled figures who were obviously prisoners. Max
stiffened. Oh, no, this wasn't going to be a session
of mass execution, surely!

They were heading this way, toward the gallows;

two prisoners, two uniformed guards. The former were young. One of them lifted up his head, and the sight of his features sent shock waves through Max. Malformed, a pathetic creature who was instantly reminiscent of the trio who had feasted out on the Waste that night. *The rounding up of the Downers had already begun.*

But it was the second prisoner who almost had Max leaping from his seat and rushing across the open space, recognition that realized his worst fears, for the youth in the muddied leather jacket and ripped jeans was none other than Nat Bonner!

No, I can't let them hang Nat. If necessary, I'll die with him!

"Merrick'll do what's been needed since I was a boy," the man next to Max was whispering again. "He'll exterminate the Downers, the vermin who've preyed on this place for years. Looks like Quiles has made a start."

The latest deputation stopped in front of the huge wooden structure, the warders pushing their charges forward roughly. They stood there, watching with uplifted heads, eyes on the naked female on the platform, the executioner standing on the balls of his feet as he stretched to tighten the noose around her neck.

"Looks like we're in for a good session this morning!" Max's informant laughed.

Max did not answer. If they hanged Nat, then he would have to live with that on his conscience for the rest of his life. He wondered if there was some means by which he could rescue him. Don't be bloody stupid, you'd just end up on the gallows with him, Max Frame. These guys are hanging-crazy!

A hush fell over the yard, a silence that was poignant with expectancy, that moment before the kick-off at a big match. Yolanda Morrison stood erect on the trapdoor, a mountain of wrinkled, sagging flesh. Maybe she guessed, the thought crossed Max's mind, knew that it was impossible to die a second time, that it was all a sick game on both sides. *But did any of them know that this was hell? Or were they under the illusion that this was but a continuation of their earthly lifespan?*

Diogene's hand rested on the lever. He was in no hurry, playing to his audience, a man who had fulfilled his ambition, had become Satan in hell. Max did not want to watch, but suddenly it was impossible to drag his gaze away; this gross enactment had him in its frightening hypnotic power.

He found himself counting, tried in vain to stop. Four . . . five . . . six . . . He made it to eight, and then, without warning, the hinged floor slammed downward and the body poised on its boards disappeared from view. The rope snaked, jerked. In the silence one heard the threshing of legs, bare feet skimming the ground beneath them in a vain effort to take the body weight on their blistered soles. A crack like the report of a pistol, loud and sharp in the still atmosphere. Then a cheering from all directions that grew in volume until the yard seemed to vibrate with the noise.

Then silence. The spectators in their filthy cells were listening, perhaps unable to believe that after all these years Yolanda Morrison had been executed. Maybe they suspected a trick, some political ruse schemed by Quiles and Merrick, a sham hanging to be followed by a surreptitious release of the victim, a devious coalition between the rivals to spare them embarrassment.

But it was real enough. The warders were unbolting a door in the wooden gallows pit, wrestling with the tightened noose, dragging out the limp body by its legs. Luis Diogene knelt to examine the corpse, then rose and gave a salute to his audience which triggered off another deafening cheer.

Max wondered why he had not thrown up, possibly because he had not eaten so far today and it was unlikely that he would do so in the near future. Those who had accompanied him on the bench had gone forward to help, uniformed bearers carrying the dead woman toward a mound of rubble which so far Max had not connected with this ghostly business. Suddenly he understood only too well, saw the body thrown into this deep grave, heard it land with a sickening thud. Two of the men grabbed up shovels and threw earth and stones into the yawning hole. In all probability there was a layer of quicklime in the bottom which would dissolve the flesh and bones, a means by which the living dead were destroyed for good.

But this was no concern of his, Max told himself. The dead persecuted the dead, nobody could change that. He looked for Nat, saw him standing out there alongside the ragged Downer, staring across at the warders who were now leaning on their shovels, satisfied that they had covered the body. The youth's mouth opened; he shouted hoarsely. Whatever his cry, it was lost amidst the chatter of excitement from all around. One of his captor's grabbed him, pulled him back roughly, and struck him a blow across the side of the face.

Max tensed. Luis Diogene was back up on the platform, winding up the rope, reknotting the noose so that it ran smoothly. Smiling to himself throughout.

The warders were holding their prisoners, arms

wrenched behind their backs. The pain was evident in Nat Bonner's expression.

Max found himself screaming mutely. *No!*

Then he felt himself go weak with relief as the uniformed officials, pushing their charges in front of them, retraced their steps toward that forbidding gray stone building. Nat Bonner and his cell mate had merely been brought to watch, a preview of the end product of Ghetto internment. A deliberate mental torture.

Max sank weakly behind the wheel of the limousine and waited for Luis Diogene. The executioner would be in no hurry; probably he was already planning his next hanging. It might be the Downer. Or Nat. Whatever, Max was powerless to help; the might of hell was an invincible cycle of eternal torment.

Now he must contact Shanifa. There was no time to be lost, for events were sudden and dreadful here. She had walked out of here once; it was surely possible that she could do so again. Somehow he had to take her away, by force if necessary, before they subjected her to some awful, irrevocable atrocity that would condemn her to the Ghetto for eternity.

Fourteen

Much to his relief Max was not asked to work the night shift. Having taken Luis Diogene back to his apartment, he drove back to base and parked the stretch limo alongside the others in the underground bay. None appeared to have been used during his absence, and so far he had not seen any other drivers. He was beginning to suspect that the manager was the extent of the staff besides himself; what little business there was could be taken care of by one driver. The whole setup was a sham. But for what purpose?

"See you in the morning, chap." The moustached supervisor was engaged in some paperwork in his glass kiosk, did not even look up. "We've a pickup at seven-thirty so don't be late."

Max clung to the hope that by morning he and Shanifa might be gone from this place. He tried not to dwell on the night hours that lay in between. Dusk was creeping in through the drab, mostly deserted streets; it would be foggy again tonight. The conditions were both an advantage and a disadvantage; they provided a cloak for furtive movements while at the same time hiding obvious landmarks. In his pocket he carried his street plan, at least that was a bonus he had not had on his previous expedition here. But the map had no boundaries marked; he had no idea in which direction Northside lay.

But Shanifa must know! If only he could persuade her to accompany him back, then his only worry was prowling Downers.

Max stood by the headless statue in the Square looking across toward the cafe. Lights shone within, but the windows were opaque with filth, making it impossible to see inside. Shanifa *had* to be there. Unless Stu Merrick had taken her back to his apartment. But no taxi had been called, Max was sure of that.

The door scraped open, and a cap-and-muffled man shuffled out, pausing to spit on the pavement before slouching away in the opposite direction. Max attempted to peer inside as the door slowly narrowed his field of vision. The usual drab clientele hunched over tables whispering illicit gossip or stood at the counter. His view of the girl serving stewed tea from the huge urn was obstructed. But he knew it was Shanifa.

Max had two options with which to gamble. If he entered the cafe, then his powers of persuasiveness were restricted by the eavesdroppers. If Shanifa told him to get the hell outside, then he would have no choice but to obey. But if he waited for her to leave, followed her at a distance back to wherever she lived, then there was always the possibility that Merrick might arrive in the meantime. Max decided to wait. If he failed tonight, then he could always try again tomorrow. She had not recognized him in the taxi, he was certain of that, so it was safe to assume that she was not aware of his return to the Ghetto.

He was tense, wished that he had a cigarette. Tomorrow he would buy some. From the chain news-agents in Northside.

He heard a car approaching and pressed himself back against the cold moss-covered stone of the anonymous statue. No headlights even though dusk was merging into darkness, just missing a whippetlike cur that darted across the road. Max's heart stepped up a beat as he caught a glimpse of the garish lettering on the doors of the sedan. POLICE. It did not slow, was lost from his view within seconds. He was edgy.

People were filing out of the cafe. It was obviously closing time. Men and women hunched dejectedly along the pavement, the gloom swallowing them up. A girl was locking the door from the inside. He could only see her silhouette, but he knew without any doubt that it was Shanifa. Max's frustration was at a peak, and it was all he could do to stop himself from rushing across the road, pleading with her to open up. Pleading with her to leave with him. Now. But it wouldn't work, any more than it had the last time.

She was taking her time. He feared at one stage that there might be a rear exit and that she had left unseen. The dirty windows had steamed up. She was probably washing up the dirty crocks, wiping down the filthy tables. My darling, you don't *have* to do this.

It was fully dark before the lights went out and the door opened. A shadowy form emerged. For all he could see it might have been yet another of those head-scarved, prematurely-aged hags, but in his mind he saw Shanifa as she had always been: slim, blond and blue-eyed, a smile that even the Ghetto failed to destroy.

Max quickened his step in case he might lose her

in the darkness, his worn trainers padding noise-
lessly on the concrete. She was hurrying. Another
fear assailed him; she might be on her way to meet
Merrick, or heading for his apartment. No, he
would have sent a car for her, that was his way.
Possibly she had not yet risen to the status of a
live-in mistress; she was merely his whore when the
urge took him. The thought made Max angry. He
lessened the distance between them.

They had left the shuttered shops and boarded-
up warehouses behind them; the streets were now
lined with dingy terraced houses. An occasional
light shone from behind frayed curtains. This was
the area where the workers lived, one step up from
the slums inhabited by the Downers who had not
yet been driven out onto the Waste.

The girl in front did not slacken her pace; not
once did she glance behind her, apparently had no
fear of lurking danger, the foggy shadows holding
no terror for her. There was now less than ten yards
between them; if she saw him now, it did not matter. Max was tempted to catch her up, stop her in
case her destination was some place where it was
not possible to talk.

Suddenly she halted, and stretched out her hand
for an adjacent door handle. It clicked, and she was
pushing her way inside one of these unlit houses.
It was then that Max called out her name.

She turned in the doorway. His fear was that she
might dart inside, slam the door and lock it.

"Who is it?"

Oh, God, her voice was as soft as it had always
been, curiosity rather than alarm, peering behind
her as she spoke.

"It's me," his voice quavered; he thought for a
second that he might break down. "Max."

"Max!" Surprise but nothing more. Not even anger because he had disobeyed her and returned to the Ghetto. A slight intake of breath and then she said, "You'd better come inside; it's not wise to stand gossiping on the streets."

He followed her in through the door. The house smelled stale as though it had been shut up empty for years. It probably had. She flicked a switch, flooded the short, dingy hallway with dim light. The brown wallpaper was peeling down to the plaster; the matting on the floor was frayed. It was cold, too. Max shivered. He thought that perhaps they would go into one of the adjoining rooms, but she made no move to open either of the doors.

He saw her clearly now; she was just as she had been on that night when they had set off for the hospital, perhaps a shade paler. It was difficult to tell because her complexion was always pallid. He remembered how she used to pinch her cheeks in an attempt to put some color into them. There was an air of unease, almost furtiveness about her, the way her eyes met his, averted, stared down at her feet.

"I knew you'd come back, Max." There was resignation in her voice, a sigh. "But I couldn't talk in the cafe; it's dangerous to talk anywhere in the Ghetto."

"I want you to come back with me. Things can be as they used to be, Shanifa."

"No." He thought he detected a sob, and when she looked up, her blue eyes were shiny with tears. "Nothing can ever be as it was, we have to accept that."

"Can you tell me *why* you're here?"

"Because I died in the car that night. I thought you knew!"

The hallway seemed to lurch. He held on to the wall to steady himself. "I . . . I think it was all a mistake. They're trying to cover it up, the doctors, the police . . ."

"They're trying to cover it up just as they have been doing for years, centuries, but the fact remains that this place which we knew of as Pace Park or the Ghetto is really the hell we were scared of as kids. No eternal fires or anything so dramatic as that, just everlasting degradation and damnation. I came here because I died. Just as Wanda did. I've seen her, by the way."

This was crazy. Again Max tried to convince himself that it was a convenient way of disposing of the mentally sick by the authorities. A ghetto of lunacy. Shanifa had been brain damaged in the accident. He needed to take her back, get her some treatment. But he had seen too much already for him to believe the lie he was telling himself. He just nodded. He needed time to think. But time wasn't an available commodity in the Ghetto.

"What happened then?" he asked.

"I don't really remember." Shanifa touched his hand, held it lightly. "It was as if . . . as if I'd been asleep, maybe had a memory lapse. The next thing I knew I was here, standing in a queue at the Employment Office. They fixed me up with a job at the cafe in the Square, gave me this house, for what it is. If you accept your lot, then it's not too bad. I just wish that Stu Merrick hadn't fancied me."

"You don't like him, then?"

"He's vile!" she whispered. "He wants me to move into his apartment. I don't have any choice, not unless I want to end up in the prison. Or worse. He's fixing for me to go up to his place in a day or two. I suppose it has its advantages . . . for a short time, until he finds somebody else. I'm just hoping that when he does he'll let me go back to the cafe . . ." She was on the point of breaking down. "I don't want to become one of his army of whores!"

"You won't, I promise you."

"There's no way you can change things, Max." Her expression was pleading with him. "Don't try or else he'll fix you. Most likely his thugs will throw you onto the Waste . . . with *them*. Whatever happens to me, I don't want you to interfere. You can't win here; nobody does except the Ruling Council. Even mayors don't stay in office forever. A few years and it will be Quiles again. Then somebody else. Perhaps even Diogene!" She shuddered at the prospect. "But I want to know what *you're* doing here. You told me you didn't die in the crash. Maybe something happened to you afterward, something so sudden that you can't even remember it."

"No"— he tried to smile— "nothing happened to me. I survived. God, how I wish I hadn't, and then perhaps everything would be all right. I wouldn't be here if I hadn't glimpsed you that night on Northside. Which makes me think that you aren't dead, either, *because you walked out of here even if you did return!*"

Without warning Shanifa burst into a flood of tears, slumped against him, held on to him. *"Oh, Max, I broke all the rules that night. I wanted you. I was looking for you. I even went back to the house, but you weren't there. But I couldn't remain outside for long, so I had to return. It was all so pointless. If I had found you, then we couldn't have been together the way we used to be."*

His flesh was prickling, it was all so impossible.

"But the fact remains that it is possible to escape from here!"

"Yes, but it's futile. How could we live as we used to when I'm dead and you're alive?"

"Rather that than going on as we are." His lips found hers, and then she was kissing him passionately.

"Max." She fought to extricate herself from his embrace. "Don't, please! I don't know how you managed to find your way in here; it has to be a fluke, against all the laws of living and dying. I never thought you'd find your way out last time. Now you're back. Oh, God, I wish you hadn't returned for both our sakes!"

"Shanifa, I want you to leave with me tonight. If you're dead, then I'll accept that so long as I can have you. Please, come back with me?"

"I can't. Oh, Max, if only I could!"

"But you have already."

She was silent for a few moments, and he sensed how her body shook. "I don't know, honestly I don't. If only it *was* possible."

"We won't know until we try."

"I want to think about it first."

"There isn't time, Shanifa. Once Merrick gets you in his clutches it'll be a thousand times more difficult to get you out of here."

"You're right, Max. All right, I'll . . . listen!"

Even as he felt her begin to tense again, he heard the sound of a car drawing up outside, its engine dying, the slamming of a door. Footsteps, then a heavy pounding on the door.

"Max." She dragged him away and opened one of the doors that led through to a musty-smelling, darkened room. "He mustn't find you here. Wait in here, hide."

Max stood there in the total darkness, heard Shanifa opening the street door. Muffled voices, one was a man's, demanding and urgent. Whoever it was, he was inside, standing in the hall.

"I won't be a minute." Shanifa was hurrying upstairs, her feet tip-tapping across the floor of the room directly above. Drawers and cupboards opened and closed. In his mind Max saw Shanifa hastily stuffing belongings into a holdall, trembling as she did so.

He heard her coming back downstairs. Her visitor spoke gruffly, and then the outside door banged shut with grim finality, a sound that embodied hopelessness as it echoed through the deserted house. Shanifa would not be returning.

An engine started up in the street outside. Max heard the car pulling away from the curbside. That was when he sank down into a damp and moldy armchair, felt the broken springs sag beneath his weight and surrendered to tears of futility.

So close and now so far, perhaps the opportunity had been wrested from him forever. Another few minutes and together they would have been setting out on their attempt to escape from the Ghetto. It was as though it was ordained not to be, that some dark power had forestalled them and sent its disciple, in the form of Stu Merrick, to snatch Shanifa back into this domain of evil.

When morning dawned, gray and featureless as it always was, Max Frame was still slumped in that chair, staring unseeing at the undecorated wall. Perhaps, he decided, it was easier to be dead in the Ghetto than to be alive. At least, that way he would be here with Shanifa forever.

He went outside into the street and began to walk in the direction of the taxi station. For the moment it was back to the proverbial square one. Another endless day in this eternal hell was beginning. Without Shanifa he would not attempt to fight against it.

Fifteen

Shanifa had not returned to the cafe a fortnight later. Max had taken to calling in for a cup of their mahogany-colored tea after work each day in the vain hope that she might suddenly be there. By now he accepted that she would not be returning.

A slovenly woman of indeterminable age was serving behind the counter, uncommunicative except for a grunt when asked a question. She served stale sandwiches with her grimed hands and blackened fingernails; obviously there were no hygiene laws in the Ghetto.

"Where's the girl who used to work here?" Max enquired one evening when there were no other customers at the tables. With Stu Merrick, of course, but he was seeking an elaboration on Shanifa's absence. Would she be coming back?

"Gone." At least, that was what it sounded like. There was nothing further to be gained by patronizing this filthy eating house.

His reconnaissance took him up to the luxury apartment block where Merrick lived. It was much the same as when he had last seen it, a veritable fortress with a uniformed official in the foyer. Callers were required to produce proof of their identity, their reason for seeing whoever they wished to see, then sign a register on the desk. Any frivolous visi-

tors would doubtless be dispatched speedily. Or the
police called.

Tomorrow was Election Day.

There was now an additional peace-keeping force
on the streets, heavily outnumbering the police.
Gray uniforms and steel helmets, holstered pistols
or rifles, batons carried in readiness. The militia
had been brought in, for unrest was anticipated. Armored cars were parked on street corners; a dozen
or more soldiers guarded every polling booth.
Ruben Quiles was relying on the votes of the Downers, so the lowest strata of society would forsake
their nocturnal lairs and infiltrate the city; a kind
of uneasy ceasefire had been declared, a truce
which the rabble could not be trusted to observe.
The Ghetto streets teemed with the shame that usually lurked in its darkest places, the malformed and
diseased helping their less fortunate comrades to
the polls, for their very existence depended upon
Quiles' victory; tomorrow they would either halluci-
nate on free drugs or be rounded up for execution.

Max went to cast his vote around the middle of
the day. Not that he had any interest in the outcome
of the election, this evil society would prevail whatever the result, but the taxi manager had given him
time off for polling. He could have walked round
the streets, come back later, but he was interested
to see how the voting was conducted.

The Employment Office had been converted into
a polling booth for the day. A double queue
stretched from the main entrance right down the
steps and into the street: the rabble, mostly dropouts and recognizable Downers, formed one line;
the other comprised the expected gathering of trilbys, caps and head scarves. The silence was unnerv-

ing, the only sound the shuffle of feet as people moved on up the steps. Others arrived.

The militia made no attempt to conceal their presence; a line of soldiers, rifles, which Max thought from a distance looked like ex-World War I 303s, were held at the ready. Stoic expressions, robots primed to kill if the order was given.

He glanced upward, saw that the third floor windows were manned by marksmen. A tank was positioned threateningly across the street, an ancient Churchill but nonetheless menacing.

The atmosphere of escalating tension was all the more frightening in its uneasy silence. It was on such a tide of noiselessness that Stalin might have come to power in 1917. The fuse was lit, sputtering; ultimately there had to be one hell of a blowout. The only uncertainty was precisely when it would explode.

It took Max half an hour by the clock on the front of the building to gain entrance. That same clerk who had issued the work permits was distributing voting forms, rubber stamping the outstretched hands with an indelible ink as a means of ensuring that nobody voted twice. It would have been a practicable impossibility to keep a register of the lower echelon of this society.

The interior was heavy with a nauseating stench, the odor of uncleansed bodies, a hint of disease that emitted cancerous fumes. The Downers huddled in their queue, creatures of the wild overawed, seeking safety in numbers, a primordial hatred of those who had condemned them to be what they were. Many still had their mental faculties; only a lengthy incarceration on the Waste would deprive them of that, revert them to beasts of the wild. They aided those who had already succumbed, held their scrawny fingers, guided the pencil to make a shaky cross in the box marked "Ruben Quiles." Grunting, slobbering, bemused and angry, some having to be restrained as a basic instinct urged them to launch an attack on those who lorded over them.

An armed guard moved in on a huddle, cursed them as he pushed them aside, revealing a decrepit figure in the center, clawed hand clutching a voting paper. A pencil fell, rolled; the soldier trapped it with his boot.

"Ignorant bastards!" He motioned the rest away with his pistol, then retrieved the pencil. "Come here, you!"

The Downer stared uncomprehendingly. The paper was snatched from his grasp; the pencil made a mark on it. Low muttered snarls came from the watchers as they threatened to close in, but the pistol kept them at bay.

"Here, put this in the box!" A flourish that could not be misunderstood had the wretch taking the crumpled sheet, ambling across to the crate in the corner, and dropping it in through a slot in the lid. "There, that's better." A smirk, the gun moved in an arc. "It takes one of you to vote, not a crowd. Now, hold your papers out!"

Max watched as two more soldiers closed in. Ballot papers were taken, marked, handed back. A slow procession filed past the box, unwilling fingers fumbling the folded slips into the slot. The stench was suddenly much stronger as wasted flesh oozed perspiration out of its pores. The smell of fear was accompanied by throaty growls of resentment. Broken toenails scraped the floor as the dejected company made a slow exit.

"Come on, you fuckers, let's have your papers.

We close at seven." One of the guards laughed as
he marked the crosses. "With luck, you'll never have
to vote again. Come on, *move!*"

Max took his paper. Three choices: Merrick,
Quiles or Diogene. He voted for Quiles because he
had never met him, therefore he was the lesser of
the three evils. It didn't really matter a damn; rival
militia would determine the final outcome. In all
probability Quiles' men were monopolizing one of
the other booths. Only Luis Diogene didn't stand a
chance because he didn't have any soldiers.

Outside some fifty Downers had bunched on the
pavement, were spilling into the road. A long,
drawn-out howl split the uneasy silence. Max felt
himself recoiling from it, cringing. He was back on
the darkened streets, a flesh-hunting creature trailing him through the shadows.

A shot answered the cry, the report magnified by
the surrounding buildings, a vibrating echo trying
to find a means of escape. Max pressed himself
back into the doorway as people began to scatter in
panic. Downers mingled with the working classes.
If there was to be a massacre, it would be indis-
criminate.

Then the uneasy silence rolled back. Inside, the
voting continued. Outside, the crowds had dispersed, either returned to their places of work or
else were roaming the streets under the watchful
gaze of the posted marksmen.

Max walked in the direction of the taxi bay, frequently stepping off the pavement to avoid a huddle
of Downers. Deep-set, wild eyes followed his every
movement, fingers pointed, curled as though to pull
him back. He sensed the growls of lust rather than
heard them. Only the might of the militia was pre-

serving life; at any second they might exterminate it.

The manager was still in his small office, engulfed by that never-ending mountain of paperwork, when Max returned. Perhaps he had voted early on his way to work. Or not at all. He did not look up as Max slid into the driving seat of a limo and sat there with the door open. There were unlikely to be any call-outs; most of the streets were blocked off, anyway. Today the only traffic would be armored cars and tanks.

Occasionally a shot was heard, mostly in the distance, probably just warnings to quell any pocket of unrest that arose.

"I wouldn't go out tonight if I was you." Max started; the manager's approach had been silent. The other handed him a paper cup of tepid tea, probably from the vending machine in the cloakroom which never seemed to be in working order whenever Max attempted to use it. "There'll be trouble tonight, the worst we've seen for years. There's never been an extermination campaign against the Downers before."

"Suppose Quiles wins."

"He won't. You'll see."

Of course, he won't, not with the way Merrick's soldiers are rigging it. "I thought Quiles ran the militia."

"There's a lot thinks that, but he don't. If Merrick don't win legitimately, there'll be a coup. It'll be over by morning, and they'll be piling the dead up on the Waste to burn 'em. Soldiers and Downers alike, and any of us that's foolish enough to get caught out in the streets. That's what I'm saying, chap, stop in your apartment and don't open the door to nobody. 'Cause you're dead if you do!"

Max's guts churned. If only he and Shanifa hadn't lingered last night, they'd both be away from all this. She was safe, though, that was one consolation, even if she was a prisoner in Stu Merrick's apartment fortress.

"When will everything revert to normal?"

"Sometime tomorrow, maybe. But don't come in till the day after, let things settle down. I guess we'd do worse than to head for home right now before it all starts up."

"Why've the Downers come out of their holes, the voting's all a farce?"

"They don't know that, do they? A propaganda trap that Merrick's cashed in on. Free drugs that they'll never see, a bullet or a rope instead. They ain't got any intelligence; that was bred out of 'em generations ago. The newcomers fall for the ruse, drag the old 'uns along with 'em."

A sudden thought crossed Max's mind, had a little shiver touching the base of his spine. "Tell me something. Since I've been here, I've not seen any *babies or children.*"

"No"—the other shook his head—"you won't see kids here. I guess they're all . . . *somewhere else.*"

That shudder was up as far as Max's shoulder blades.

"Folks mostly come here after they've grown up a bit. *The women here don't get pregnant.*"

Max swallowed. Of course, this was the land of the dead; there would be no givers of life here. "Tell me, didn't they once used to call this place . . . *Pace Park?*"

"I think we'd better be moving while the going's good." The manager turned away. "We don't want to get caught up in what's boiling up out there, do we?"

* * *

Max sat in the window of his apartment just as
dusk was falling. He kept well back, left the light
off. He did not really want to watch; it was a kind
of morbid compulsion that had him gazing down
into the street below. Perhaps if he had had a book
or a magazine he would have read instead. Except
that necessitated artificial light which might have
been dangerous. He had already checked to ensure
that the door, frail as it was, was bolted.

He wondered if there was radio or television in
the Ghetto. He doubted it. The only purpose they
could have served was propaganda, and the authorities seemed to do very well on that count without
media broadcasting. Just one newspaper, because
there was only one version of events to be related.

The Downers were gathered in the street down
below. They had not travelled far from their designated polling booth. Max estimated that there must
have been close to three hundred of them, segre-
gated from the citizens now, a mindless, meander-
ing rabble of sub-humanity waiting for darkness to
fall so that they might regain their bearings. Lead-
erless and lost, a line of them squatted with their
deformed backs to the wall, staring upward. You
had the eerie feeling that they saw you, even at that
distance. *And that when night fell they would come for
you, satisfy their aching hunger.*

Max felt the floor and walls vibrate, a far-off
earth tremor, even thunder. He tensed, heard it
again. It was closer now. Stronger.

The Downers had crowded into the middle of the
road. Even in the encroaching dusk there was no
mistaking the expressions of sheer terror on their
grotesque features. A low moan that had begun like

a swarm of angry insects escalated into a whine, a
wail of sheer hopelessness. Heads were turned in
both directions; fleeing, turning back, trampling
those who had fallen in the rush, being herded to
and fro by some invisible force.

Max realized what was happening seconds before
the approaching tanks came into his view, one from
the north end by the Employment Office, the other
from the south, ancient Churchills that scraped and
ground the roadway beneath their caterpillars; steel
monsters of destruction bearing down upon their
prey which had been lured into this trap.

The apartment walls shook; a glass was dislodged
from the shelf and smashed on the floor. Now
more tanks, three abreast, filled the street from
both directions, grim-faced soldiers aligning this formation of death. There were no gunners; there was
no need.

Writhing half-naked bodies were being herded
into the confined, decreasing space, some attempting to scale the walls but there were no handholds.
The site of death had been earmarked with preci-
sion; there was not so much as a niche to squeeze
through between the oncoming death machines.

The screaming had reached its peak. Diseased
lungs collapsed beneath the strain. Bodies clambered
on bodies in a pyramid of malformation, avalanched
into a wriggling mass that was unrecognizable for
what it was.

The tanks slowed, then edged forward as though
savoring the final moments of this maneuver of
massacre. Crushing, grinding, serrated conveyor
belts pulping waste offal, rivulets of blood beginning to run sluggishly down the slight incline behind, the mighty vehicles elevated on the mound as
they allowed their weight to flatten it. Backing off,

coming forward again. Back and forth, rolling and rerolling until there was nothing left to see in the deep dusk. Only then did they reverse in their separate directions and return whence they had come.

Max was still vomiting in the darkness of the filthy toilet when he heard the fire engines arrive, heaved in time with their gushing hoses, spewed until his stomach was empty.

Even had he been able to sleep that night, the sporadic gunfire from near and far would have kept him awake. Once his door was rattled, but whoever it was went away and did not return. Sometime after dawn he drifted into a fitful, exhausted slumber.

Election victory or coup, there would be a new leadership before this awful day was out, and Max's greatest fear was for Shanifa, who would be compelled to succumb to the desires of the new Satan who ruled over this hell they called the Ghetto.

Sixteen

Roxy lay on the bed watching Ruben Quiles dress. Shit, he was a revolting bastard! His thinning gray hair reminded her of the parched weeds on the edge of the Waste that year when there had been a drought. His lean features depicted more than cunning and cruelty since the last time she had seen him, a fear that haunted him day and night. He had pulled every trick in the book, but he knew he was on a loser. Rigging and counterrigging, but in the end the votes wouldn't count for one wisp of that moustache that made a vain effort to hide his hair lip.

Let me have men about me that are sleek and fat, she thought to herself, and smiled. She had run the gauntlet, all right, from boring Ed to the dizzy heights of Stu Merrick, cast out to the street prowlers and now the crumbling mayoral suite. Whoring all the way, it didn't make any difference now. Ruben was the last stop-off; she'd go out in style.

They were still shooting out in the streets. They would leave Quiles until last. A kind of sick climax. Like the one she had just faked.

"You should have come to me before, Roxy."

"I didn't get the chance, Ruben." Which was partly true.

"I guess it's too late now." He went to the window, looked down into the forecourt below. A handful of his remaining loyal militia were crouched against the wall, rifles at the ready. Rifles didn't stop tanks. He closed the curtains, came back and sat on the edge of the bed. "He'll never annihilate the Downers, no matter. As long as you keep condemning people to the Waste, there'll always be Downers. I don't think anybody realizes that; they don't breed, you *create* 'em. Like playing God in reverse, take a human body, chuck it out to rot, see what it turns into. If they *died*, there'd be no problem."

Roxy was silent, thinking of Ed. He would be one of *them* before long. Which was why she had not run back to Stu. Sure, he would have protected his whores, but there was a limit to what your conscience would let you do. Sometimes even the price of survival was too high.

"How long before they come for us, Ruben?"

"They'll take their time." He laughed, a hollow sound. "Stu's enjoying this. He'll want to savor every minute of his day of triumph. You know, if the militia had stayed loyal, I'd've won. I'd've kept the Downers happy out on the Waste, given 'em what they wanted and they'd've bothered nobody. *I* massacred 'em, really, because I brought 'em into the city to vote when their votes weren't going to count anyway. Put 'em right where Stu wanted 'em. He's slaughtered a few hundred, but there's others he'll never kill. And all the while he'll be throwing folks out there to build up the numbers again. So the problem goes on."

Quiles got up again, went across to a wardrobe, and reached amongst the mothball-smelling clothes. He straightened up, and Roxy saw that he had a pistol in one hand, a battered gallon can in the other.

"Always kept these handy, just in case." There
was a sadness in his expression, a regret because he
had need of something that he had hoped never to
use. He laid the gun on the table, a Webley .45
revolver, another World War I relic. "It's loaded.
We'll use it if we have to. If you want to, that is."

"It won't make any difference." She laughed.
"You should know that, Ruben."

"No, I suppose it won't. But *this* will." He lifted
up the cannister, and she heard the contents swill-
ing about inside, smelled their pungent fumes
where the liquid had leaked around the cap.

She felt herself stiffen. From down below there
came a flurry of shots.

"Stu won't use the tanks or any heavy stuff,"
Quiles went on. "He wants the mayoral apartment
left intact for himself. He'll do it by weight of numbers. Those guys down below don't stand a chance.
Sounds like he's already made a start." He winced
as a fussilade of gunfire rang out. Somebody was
screaming; running footsteps sounded across the
forecourt.

Quiles unscrewed the cap and began splashing the
kerosene round the room, drenching the curtains,
then flung some at the door. Roxy wrinkled her
nose; the smell was overpowering.

"I'll see to it that he doesn't install himself in
here." A box of matches rattled. His head was
cocked to one side, anticipating footfalls on the
stairway outside. "Here they come now, Roxy."

"Open up!" The door was banged, rattled on its
hinges.

"Get fucked, and tell that to Stu Merrick, too."

There was a silence. Maybe they hoped that they
did not even have to damage the door, that the
former mayor would surrender meekly.

"There's only you left now, Quiles," the reply was gloating, an officer of the militia who would have been on the losing side if he had not opted to join the coup.

A rattling sound, Roxy saw the matchbox in Quiles' thin fingers, the tray open, spilling some of its contents onto the floor. A rasping as a brimstone head scraped the emery paper, sputtered into flame.

"The pistol's there if you want it, Roxy." For the first time she read compassion in his expression. "It's up to you."

"No." She smiled back. "You go ahead, do what you want to do, Ruben. I'll be all right."

He nodded, tossed the burning match at the door, and in an instant a sheet of flame was scorching the ceiling. Hungry, insatiable fire roared and spread, an inferno that vented its wrath, ran the length of the carpet, leaped at the curtains.

Roxy's eyes streamed as the smoke blinded her. She fought to breathe, thought about the pistol but changed her mind. She was aware of Ruben moving about, sensed his closeness. Then he was on the bed by her side, his arm around her. He, too, was apparently ignoring the gun.

There was shouting on the landing. Those footsteps were retreating back down the stairs; any thought of breaking down the door had been abandoned.

"I wish you'd come to me sooner, Roxy," Ruben said, "but at least we'll go out together."

"Me, too," she answered. In Ruben's case she had got it all wrong. Beneath his cruel exterior he wasn't the bastard she'd thought he was. Just another puppet ruler in the Ghetto's System; she found herself wondering about the Power that controlled it. It was a frightening thought, and she pushed it from her mind.

They were trapped in a ring of fire, the flames seeming intent on devouring the walls around them. Like Stu Merrick, they were leaving the best until last.

Somewhere sirens were wailing; the fire engines had not wasted any time. Roxy thought she heard the hissing of water as the invincible flames boiled it. This was one blaze they wouldn't extinguish. All they could hope to achieve was to control it, prevent it from spreading. In the end they would have to sacrifice the mayoral apartment block.

The bed dropped, wedged at an angle. She clutched at Ruben. The floor beneath was giving way; the supporting beams were being devoured by the fire. She felt its heat scorching her, drying out her flesh. It wouldn't be long now.

The bed was slipping, lurched another foot or so. They clutched at the headboard. Waited. Then, suddenly, the floor beneath them opened up, a fiery abyss that belched sparks, engulfed them in black smoke.

Roxy closed her eyes. Ruben was gone, snatched from her. A brief sense of vertigo, bracing herself for the final impact, rushing downward into a well of fire.

The Pit. She recognized it with her blinded eyes, just as she had always known it would be, the eternal fire of which the nuns at the convent had preached in her childhood. The real hell.

It was only then that she started to scream.

Shanifa was also lying on the bed listening to the sporadic shooting in the city. Stu Merrick's bed. Her

one consolation was that the self-proclaimed mayor
of the Ghetto was not by her side.

He was out there gloating over his spurious victory, had told her how he wanted to be present
when his troopers stormed the mayoral apartment.

"This is the end of the road for Quiles." Merrick
laughed. "I want to see him led out of there hand-
cuffed, thrown in the back of a truck and driven to
the prison. The trial will be first thing in the morning; it will be over before midday. Diogene can console himself with the fact that he'll have the honor
of hanging the previous mayor. It'll maybe soften
the blow of losing for poor old Luis. He polled less
than a thousand votes. Shitfire, who wants a bloody
executioner for mayor!"

She did not reply; Stu didn't expect her to. His
kind liked to do all the talking; they had no time
for listening. Now that he was gone, she would take
a bath, attempt to wash the smell of his sweaty body
off her own. She felt soiled, both physically and
mentally. He was a mass murderer, nothing less; he
had the blood of hundreds on his hands. She even
felt pity for the Downers. They had all been human
in some form once; it was the System that had
made them like they were. She had wanted to throw
up just listening to Stu's account of how the tanks
had trapped them in the streets and steamrollered
them into a mulch, pulped them so that the hoses
were able to wash them down into the sewers.

The luxuriousness of this apartment disgusted
her, the rewards of prostitution and drug peddling.
And murder. But now that Stu was in power the
Ghetto's streets would be turned into rivers of blood
on a scale never witnessed before.

It was some time before she mustered up strength
enough to stagger to the bathroom, where she

perched on the edge of the bath and tried not to
listen to the gushing taps because they reminded
her of the firemen's hoses. Stu had vented his lust
on her, but there was nothing remotely gentle in
his mating. No way could it be termed lovemaking;
he had thoughts only for his own pleasure. She was
nothing but a hind at the rutting stand succumbing
to the crazed thrustings of the stag, his bestial
gruntings making her want to throw up. She had
feigned an orgasm, but she doubted if he had even
noticed. And after he was satisfied he rolled over,
fell asleep on his back and snored loudly.

She attempted to relax in the warm water. Her
thoughts switched to Max. She had to find out if
he was all right. If only they had not dallied that
night, they might have made it out of the Ghetto.
Whether it was possible or not to return to the
world of the living, she had no idea. Maybe it would
have been different the last time if she had been
able to find Max.

Any attempt to escape at the moment was out of
the question; the militia would be patrolling the
streets, searching for any Downers or known Quiles
supporters who had escaped the coup. Stu had informed her that in a day or two they would be moving into the mayoral suite. Perhaps when everything
settled down an opportunity might present itself.

She was still in the bath when she heard Stu Merrick return. She could tell by his heavy tread and
the way he slammed the door that something had
gone wrong. She was in the act of drying herself
when he burst into the bathroom.

He towered there in the doorway, the bolt swinging like a pendulum where it had been ripped from
its screws. Tall and terrible, his lined face suffused
with blood, his eyes protruding, bubbles about to

burst. Saliva strung from his curled lips as his hands clenched and unclenched. Shanifa saw how the veins in his neck and forehead corded. She cowered from him, the bath towel wrapped around her, a coy virgin surprised by an intruder.

"You cow!" His words were slurred with rage. "You fucking cow! You'd laze in the bath day and night if you could; you couldn't give a shit what was going on outside!"

Her lips trembled, and she was temporarily robbed of her powers of speech. He was mad, demented, an enraged bull looking to vent his fury on the first available victim.

"I . . . I don't know . . . what you mean." She forced the trembling words out, a desperate plea for mercy.

"Sure you don't"— he advanced a step— "because you've been lazing in the bath. Let me tell you." A hand reached out, snatched the towel away, bared her trembling nakedness. "Ruben Quiles has gone and set fire to the mayoral apartment. The whole building is gutted, him with it. He's even deprived me of the pleasure of hanging the bastard!"

His face was close to hers now, a grotesque stone gargoyle that breathed fetid fumes, might split and crumble at any second. She gave a cry and tried to wrench her gaze away, but he grabbed her hair, pulling her back.

"Stu . . . I'm sorry . . . it's not my fault!"

"Isn't it?" He slapped her with the flat of his hand. "I made a mistake in picking you up out of the gutter, Shanifa. A bad mistake. I don't often make 'em but I made one this time. You're a slut, only fit for whoring, and that's what you'll do from now on!"

She tried to dodge his bunched fist, but he was

still holding her securely. Her head went back, bounced off the tiles; she tasted blood in her mouth. Screaming, sobbing, writhing as his fingers grabbed the soft flesh of her small breasts, twisted them, threatened to tear them from her body. Bent double, his teeth fastening on to the back of her neck, holding her down while he pummelled her with his fists. Scratching with his fingernails, stamping his booted feet on her slender toes. They would surely break at any second.

Stu Merrick felt her sag in his hold, backed off and let her crumple to the floor, then rested a foot on her stomach as he stood over her; he had failed to conquer Ruben Quiles, but on this occasion he was the victor. It afforded him a sense of euphoria.

He reached down, grabbed a limp outstretched arm and began to drag her out of the bathroom, pulled her across the landing toward the bedroom. Effortlessly, he lifted her up, flung her onto the creaking four-poster, and arranged her so that her legs were spread lewdly. He lifted an eyelid; the pupil stared sightlessly at him. He gave a guttural laugh.

"You strumpet!" He began to undress slowly, strewing his borrowed military uniform on the floor, stared down at himself and laughed again.

He leaned over her, slapped her bruised cheeks, lifted her head and shook it. She moaned but did not open her eyes. The ancient springs groaned their protest as he clambered onto the bed and knelt in between her.

"You bloody whore!" He shouted as he entered her.

Within minutes he was spent, his purpled features shiny with sweat, slapping her and shaking her until finally her eyes flickered open.

"You heard what I said?"

Her inarticulate reply was interpreted as an affirmative.

"You're only fit for whoring," he repeated, his eyes beginning to glaze again. "And that's exactly what you'll do. *Now!* Get your clothes on and get out into the streets. There's soldiers aplenty with time on their hands who'll know what to do with you. And they'll *pay* for you out of their wages. They'll queue up for you because you're Stu Merrick's ex-mistress. And you'll pay me back for what Ruben Quiles did to me. D'you hear?"

She nodded dumbly, mumbled through swollen lips. Her shaking fingers were scarcely capable of holding her clothes, but somehow she struggled into them. She carried her shoes because her feet were in too much pain to wear them, staggered from the room, and stumbled toward the wide stairway.

Yet amidst her pain and terror Shanifa experienced a feeling of relief . . . and hope. Not only had she escaped from the clutches of this madman who now ruled the Ghetto, but she was free to roam the streets, to search for Max. The price was high, but she would pay it willingly.

Seventeen

Nat had no idea what all the shooting was about. He stood at the barred window, watched palls of smoke in the sky, smelled death in the acrid stench. His thoughts turned to Max. His friend was out there somewhere. Sod Max, he means nothing to me now, the selfish bastard. I don't give a shit if he gets killed!

The Downer had crawled into a corner, cowered there in silence. Nat thought he slept, but in the gloom he saw how the other shivered. He felt sorry for the guy; he couldn't help his lot. A harmless, grotesque being who was a victim of hell's totalitarianism. The authorities would probably hang him before long.

There was a constant rumbling beyond the high walls. Nat knew it was tanks on the move. People screamed; gunfire came and went. Within the prison itself there was an air of unrest, warders hurrying to and fro. The prisoners had not been fed since last night; perhaps they were going to be abandoned, left to starve in their cells. Nat didn't care; he didn't worry about anything now. He had come here to find his father and had been rejected; all he wanted to do was to die and be like the rest of them.

Yolanda's execution had left its mark upon the

youth. The sheer barbaric brutality of the hanging
had numbed his mind, acted as a kind of anaes-
thetic that had possibly spared his sanity. Whatever
they did to him, even if he shared the same fate,
he was not afraid. He wanted to die, the means
were purely incidental. If there had been a way by
which he could have committed suicide, he would
have done so. But there was not, just bare walls and
a cell door, nothing with which to sever an artery
or strangle himself. He would die when they were
ready to kill him.

Nat ignored the Downer and sat in the opposite
corner with his back against the cold, slimy wall.
He was thirsty, but he resisted the temptation to
drink from the bucket by his side. The water was
stale, probably rainwater collected from the roof, la-
dled out of a butt along with algae and filth. For
the moment he would endure his thirst. Later, he
might be forced to slake it.

He looked up as he heard footsteps. One of the
warders paused by the door, looking through the
bars. Nat recognized the man. Heavy features that
usually wore an expression of cruelty were now
white and drawn, the stamp of fear upon them.

"Hey, you!"

Nat scrambled to his feet, sensing that something
was wrong. Normally this man had a jibe ready. If
he came in the cell, he gave you a kick. The door
was left ajar as the warder stood to one side. He
seemed uncertain of himself.

"If you want to go, go. The Downer, too."

Nat stared in disbelief, thought perhaps he had
misheard or else it was some kind of a trick. Run
and we'll catch you, hang you for trying to escape.

"Go on, if you're going. There isn't much time
left."

"Why?"

"Because they're taking over the prison."

"Who?"

"Merrick's militia. Any warders who are known Quiles supporters will be thrown in with the prisoners. Me, I'm going to make a run for it, too. Might as well, they'll hang me if I stay. You don't look a bad kid; that's why I'm giving you the chance."

"I . . . my father. Sid Bonner."

"Sid? You have to be kidding!"

"No, honest. I just want to find him."

"He's around somewhere, probably lit out already. But I can't hang about. Look, I'll leave the door open. You can make your own mind up whether you go or not. Best of luck, kid."

Nat glanced toward his cell mate. The Downer had not moved. If he had heard, apparently he did not understand. He did not seem aware that the door was open, that there was an opportunity to make a bid for freedom. Nat turned away, stepped out into the corridor, and caught a glimpse of the warder disappearing at the far end.

Freedom was a frightening prospect in the Ghetto. All the same, it was better than rotting in this stinking jail. He needed to make it out onto the streets, and as far as he knew, the only way was across the exercise yard.

One moment Nat was alone; the next the corridor was full of running, jostling people: men, women, warders and convicts, a silent throng, breathless, panic-stricken. An elderly man was pushed, fell; the rest trampled over him in their haste to find a way out.

"*Stop!*" A lone warder tried to bar their way, pistol at the ready. A shot, somebody screamed, but then

the crowd was upon him, dragging him to the floor.
They took his gun, surged onward. Nat brought up
the rear, cast a glance at the crumpled form of the
prison officer, then jerked his gaze away and would
have thrown up had his stomach been full. Jesus
God, they'd wrenched the poor bastard's head off,
set it up on its bloody stump as a grim warning of
the people's revolution that was just beginning.

The yard was full, mostly prisoners who had been
freed, not as a last merciful act by their former
warders, but to add fuel to the uprising. Quiles'
men had run the prison. If they had to surrender
it to Stu Merrick, then they were determined not
to leave him a legacy of untried inmates for the
gallows.

Nat glanced about him: young and old, men and
women, near-skeletal creatures who could barely
walk after years of incarceration, striving to regain
a freedom that they barely remembered. Somehow
a few had climbed up onto the wall, scaled a human
ladder, were walking along the top. Others had
dragged the huge gates open by sheer weight of
numbers.

Then the shooting began.

Those upon the wall crumpled, toppled by a hail
of bullets from outside. Concentrated fire blasted
the gateway, chipped the stone pillars, cut a swathe
through the scrawny mass who were on the verge
of escape. Nat threw himself to the ground as the
man in front of him staggered and fell, cut down
by a bullet which would have surely taken Nat had
the other not acted as a shield.

The militia lined the street outside, armored cars
drawn up in a semicircle to act as a barricade. A
deliberate ambush. They had anticipated a mass escape, allowed it to begin so that they might be

spared the time-consuming business of executing the inmates singly on the gallows.

Warders who had elected to join the breakout were returning the fire, revolvers against the might of heavy artillery. A blinding explosion threw bodies in all directions, grenade-blasted limbs airborne like dead branches in an autumnal gale. Nat felt the heat sear his face, pressed it into the sharp gravel and prayed again to die. Yet self-survival was instinctive. He could have staggered to his feet and been granted his death wish. He did not because he still clung to the vain hope that he might find his father, that this time he would not be rebuffed.

A group of soldiers made it on the run from the vehicles to the entrance, bent low, firing sub machine guns from their hips, a devastating arc of rapid fire that added to the numbers of the fallen. Some of the escapees were fleeing back toward the prison; a few made it back inside, but most were cut down in mid-flight.

In a matter of minutes the attempted escape was quelled. Uniformed militia were moving amidst the fallen, kicking inert bodies to ascertain if any still lived. Nat grunted as a boot took him in the thigh, and braced himself for the close-range shot that would blow half of his head away. It did not come. Instead, rough hands hauled him to his feet, his head was jerked back by his hair and the stumbling march back to prison began.

It was a different cell this time, roughly the same size as the previous one, but on an upper level so that the slatted window looked out into the permanently gray skies that dominated the Ghetto's drab landscape. Nat sat slumped in a corner, unaware for some time in the depths of his depression that he had a companion. Hours ago he had resigned himself to his fate. There had been a brief spell of hope, and now that had been dashed. The pick-me-up, put-me-down cycle that eventually reduced one to the state where the body functioned but the brain switched off.

He barely glanced at his companion, a dim outline that was definitely no Downer. Strangely, he would have preferred his previous companion to whoever the other was; the fellow had been no trouble, had left him alone. There was no way of knowing what kind of relationship might ensue with this stranger. If his cell mate spoke, then Nat would answer. In the meantime they would both be content with their own thoughts.

Nat was still thirsty. His craving for a drink had him searching for the water bucket. It was difficult to see in the half gloom of an unlit cell. Maybe the other fellow had it. Nat knew he would not be able to stick it out much longer; however foul and stagnant the rainwater was, he had to drink.

His bruised leg throbbed; his movements were stiff and painful, almost a crablike crawl across the floor. His companion moved, the shadowed features watching him intently.

"Nat!" A sharp intake of breath.

Nat's senses reeled; his hearing, his dimmed eyesight, had to be playing tricks on him. An hallucination, a very cruel one. The latest form of mental torture, induced by fear and pain, hopelessness, and thirst. No, it can't be, I won't fall for it this time.

"I need water," he tried to speak firmly, but his voice shook. "Let me drink. *Please!*"

A metal bucket scraped on the floor. He heard the slopping of water and reached out to drag it closer. I'm not going to look because it's all a lie. I'm exhausted, when I've drunk I'll sleep. And in the morning that guy will be somebody totally different. He won't be . . .

"Dad!"

It was Sid Bonner, all right. A shaft of gray light fell on those familiar features, enough to confirm that which Nat had denied. He forgot about the water, thought for a moment that he might faint.

"It's me, Nat." Sid Bonner smiled wanly. "I guess we're together now, locked up on *Death Row!*"

"Death . . . Row?" Nat repeated the words, experienced a sinking feeling, then shrugged it off. It didn't matter. If they hanged them both, then he and his father would be together. His search was over.

"Merrick's cleaned up the whole Ghetto," the man spoke in a hoarse whisper. "The way he intended to all along. The election was a farce, didn't mean a thing. Even the vote rigging was a sham because he had his militia poised for a coup all along. I guess he fixed the voting just so he could kid everybody, maybe even himself, that he'd won. There'll never be another election, he'll see to that. He's got total power, his own army, police, even his own prison warders. They'll massacre anybody who's against them. This is only the beginning. The hangings will go on and on; Diogene will get what he wants even though he didn't achieve it at the polls. They'll hang us, too. We'll be amongst the first. You're a damned fool for coming here. Tell me all about it."

Nat told him, about Max and Shanifa, and how they had walked into the Ghetto through the barriers on Northside. A sudden thought struck him. He asked, "Is Mother here, too?"

"She was." His father turned his face away. "I saw her once, just after I arrived. I was going on the night shift, and there were some women coming out of that cafe in the Square. A glimpse, that was all I got, across the road. It was her, all right. I shouted, hurried after her, but lost her in a side street. Never seen her since. There's a lot of folks you never see again in the Ghetto."

Nat fell silent. He cupped his hands, scooped some water out of the bucket and slurped it. It didn't taste foul as he had expected; it was sweet and fresh on his palate. He splashed some on his face. He felt clean, refreshed; the need for sleep was gone, too.

Sometime during the night a plate of food was pushed under the door, stale black bread and half-cooked grain. He shared it with his father, and they ate without talking.

Nat noticed the silence for the first time. There was no heavy tramping of warders' booted feet, no rattling of grills or clinking of keys. No shouts of abuse, no obscenities. Nothing except the sporadic whispered conversation between his father and himself.

That was when he realized that they were the only survivors of that prison yard massacre. Later that day they smelled the stench of incinerating corpses, the vile odor permeating their cell as a grim reminder that their fate was worse than the oblivion of a mountain of ashes.

The third day dawned and still Luis Diogene had not come to hang them.

Eighteen

Shanifa had found three customers that first day. Or rather, they had found her. All soldiers, all together.

Still bearing the marks of Stu Merrick's violent assault, dried blood streaked on her face, she had staggered along the only route she knew in the Ghetto, heading toward the Square. Her intention had been to go on from there back to the house where she had lived. Not that she expected to find Max there, but there was always the chance that that was where he would start looking for her. If he had successfully evaded capture by hiding in the living room, then he might still be safe.

Corpses littered the streets. Two men clad in somber charcoal gray smocks were gathering up the dead, tossing them into the back of a small truck. A Downer sat propped up against the wall, so she stepped into the road to avoid him. He might have been just resting his deformed body; there was no mark on him. She shuddered as his sightless eyes stared at her.

She heard an approaching truck, but did not look round. She had learned long ago, in life, that it was safer not to meet a passing gaze. The engine slowed and she tensed. Still she did not turn her head as it drew up alongside her.

"Hey, bitch!" Guffaws had Shanifa wanting to break into a run, but it would have been to no avail. In all probability they would have gunned her down, then done what they had in mind to her dead body. Merrick's death squads were shooting on sight; anything that moved was fodder for their bullets.

She turned slowly, saw their faces in the cab, blurred expressions of lust and cruelty. The doors were open. They were getting out, soiled green uniforms, holstered pistols.

"Well, well!" The largest of the trio approached her, reached out and uplifted her chin with a callused finger. "I guess you was pretty before somebody roughed you up, baby. Maybe you struggled, eh? Learned your lesson, maybe."

The other two crowded in on her, and she shrank from their pawing, hands groping her, squeezing her flesh through her flimsy garments, rubbing themselves against her.

"Guess you'll oblige us without any trouble. No charge, huh? Not for peace-keeping troops. Without us, you might be dead already!" More coarse laughter. She wanted to scream but dared not.

They took her hands and began leading her back toward the vehicle, feeling her all the way. The rear of the truck was covered by a torn canvas awning. They lifted her up over the tailboard, then dropped her inside so that she sprawled on the filthy floor. Then they were clambering in after her, the big fellow pushing the others to one side.

Shanifa closed her eyes and lay there while they ripped at her clothing. A button pinged against the metal surround. She would not struggle, no more than she had when Stu had lain on her, but this was far worse, bestial instincts that had to be satisfied in the only way they knew how, a primitive mating.

They hurt her but she did not cry out. Shanifa retched when their foul tongues threatened to choke her, the stench of their putrid breath and stale sweat almost suffocating her. Broken fingernails scratched her at the height of their combined lust, and then they were tipping her back over the tailboard, tossing her torn clothes after her, scorning her as she lay there in the gutter. A final insult, exhaust fumes pumped on her naked body as they drove off. They had satisfied themselves of all but the desire to kill. Farther along the street she heard the truck slowing again, a burst of rapid gunfire. Killing was all that was left to them. She did not look.

In the seclusion of a stinking alley she somehow managed to dress herself again. The buttons were gone from her blouse; there was no way of hiding her small, firm breasts with their bleeding scratches. Her body throbbed where they had abused it. Slumped there, her back against the wall, she waited for darkness to fall and hide her degradation.

The house was still unoccupied; she sensed its emptiness through the open front door and broken window. She did not want to go inside, had to force herself to step into the hallway, then stood there in the darkness, listening. Just the familiar scurrying sounds as the rodent inhabitants fled at her approach. She eased open the door of the living room, whispered, "Max?" in vain hope.

He wasn't there; she had not expected him to be. But there were no signs of a struggle, so at least he had left of his own accord. She prayed that he had escaped the massacre which had turned the streets red with blood, that he was safe somewhere, awaiting the opportunity to go out and search for her. If she had known where his apartment was, then she would have gone there. Now her only hope was that he would find her. Would he return here? She did not know. She might be safe for a day or two, but once the coup was completed, Stu would have his militia searching for her; he would not allow her to escape the net of prostitution which he was throwing around the Ghetto. In his crazed, illogical mind he blamed her for the destruction of the mayoral building. He would have his revenge on her, reduce her to an alley slut for eternity.

The stillness of that first night was interrupted periodically by the passing of a militia vehicle. Shanifa followed their progress with her ears, willed them not to slow or stop, feared lest the soldiers might be conducting a search of empty houses. Later she heard the chilling cry of a defiant Downer who had survived the purge and had succumbed to his basic instincts. The scream was cut short by a volley of shots.

She waited.

Max stayed in his apartment for the next couple of days. The troops did not appear to be concerning themselves with official workers' homes, instead concentrated on patrolling the streets. Vehicles rumbled to and fro, with only an occasional shot heard in the far distance. Any resistance to the coup, such as it was, was over.

On the third day he decided to check in at the taxi firm. Absence from work might evoke an investigation, and that was the last thing he wanted right now. The streets seemed much as they had been before, the usual trickle of huddled workers not even glancing in his direction. In the Ghetto you minded your own business, did not concern yourself with anything other than your own particular routine.

There was no sign of the moustached manager in his kiosk; instead there was a younger man with a long, sallow face wearing military trousers, his tunic hanging limply from a peg. He looked up, regarding Max with a disinterested expression.

"You're Frame," a statement, not a question.

"That's right." The stretch limos were nowhere in sight, the only parked vehicle a battered jeep with a torn canopy. Max was uneasy.

"You'd best go home, you'll be contacted in due course. There's no work for you right now."

"Oh, I see." Relief because he would not have to venture out into the streets where it seemed that anybody not wearing a uniform was a target for the soldiers' rifles. He would have time on his hands, time to search for Shanifa.

"Only military vehicles are permitted until further notice." The lips moved in what might have been a hint of a smile. "But, before long, everything will be back to normal. Just stay in your apartment."

Max returned home and spent the rest of the day lying on the bed, trying to sleep. He would need all his resources, mental and physical, for whatever lay ahead of him.

Dusk merged into darkness, but it was after midnight before he let himself out onto the landing. The streets were sparsely lit; perhaps a curfew had been imposed. If so, he had no way of knowing, for communication in the Ghetto was limited to one newspaper, and today even the news stalls were unmanned. You learned the laws by experience; misfortune could cost you dearly.

The road outside was deserted, the air heavy with the stench of charred flesh. The funeral pyres had been smoldering all day, the only means of exterminating the dead in this place where corpses lived for eternity. A means of preventing a population explosion. Max shuddered at his own logic; he was also frightened by his own foolhardiness. There was only one place where Shanifa was likely to be, ensconced in the mayoral apartment with that inhuman monster, a bastion of evil guarded by soldiers and tanks. There was no way he would even be able to communicate with her. But at least he had to make a reconnaissance, view from a distance and maybe come up with some kind of plan. So futile but he had to try it.

There were no armed guards outside the mayoral apartment. Because the building had ceased to exist, was nothing more than a mountain of blackened rubble that thickened the perpetual nocturnal fog with wisps of smoke from its smoldering rubble.

Max stared in disbelief, saw how fragmented stonework had spilled right across the road so that only caterpillared vehicles might pass. The mighty seat of totalitarian power had been razed to the ground and left to burn itself out, another hideous scar on this dreadful community that might well be left as a shrine to Stu Merrick, who had overthrown the lesser of the evil regimes.

A terrifying thought had Max swaying, holding on to a pile of masonry that was still warm. Suppose Shanifa had been consumed in the inferno! No, it was unlikely that Merrick had moved in yet. He would want to jettison everything that bore a reminder of his predecessor first. This was the re-

sult of a siege, Quiles holding on to what was rightfully his until the end, an act of defiance against
an unscrupulous rival who had turned defeat into
victory by the only means left to him. In which case
Shanifa would still be at Merrick's apartment. He
prayed to the God who had abandoned the Ghetto
to this fate that she was.

His destination now was Merrick's abode, less
than a quarter of a mile from here. Max clambered
over the debris, used the shadows to hide him from
the view of any mobile patrol. It was like that first
night when he had trespassed in these darkened,
deserted streets, when . . .

the Downers howled their hunting cry.

Max pressed himself back against a factory wall
and stared fearfully into the smoky darkness, the
scream still vibrating his eardrums, numbing his
brain with primordial terror. Surely not, for the militia had been scouring the streets all day in search
of their hated, primitive foe, shot them and burned
them so that the atmosphere was putrid with the
stench of mass cremations.

But you only needed one Downer to become the victim
of frenzied mutilation and cannibalism. And one had
slipped the net.

Max listened, thought he detected the wheezing
of diseased lungs up ahead of him. It might have
been the hissing of this smoldering demolition.
Whatever it was, it sent him creeping away in the
opposite direction, herded him out of Bontoft Avenue as though evil had been commanded to protect
evil, the lower echelon enslaved to guard the hier-
archy, wild animals trained to do their master's bid-
ding—to track down by scent and savage any who
dared to oppose the new regime of hellish terror.

It was coming this way! Max quickened his pace,

but it still kept up with him, an unseen lurker of
the shadows behind him, snuffling his scent through
its mucus-encrusted nostrils, slobbering its saliva in
anticipation of his flesh.

Unerringly it had driven him past the turn that
would have taken him back to the comparative safety
of Block 18. Unfamiliar streets, some unlighted so
that he hastened on in the hope of finding a streetlamp; falling once so that his injured leg reminded
him that it was not yet healed. Only the fear of
what the blackness ahead might hold prevented him
from breaking into a shambling, panic-stricken run.

At every street corner he stopped to listen. His
pursuer was relentlessly on his trail, wearing him
down, exhausting his body and brain until finally it
would be a relief to surrender and pray that the
end would be quick.

Still coming. And coming.

Until suddenly, unbelievably, it wasn't coming at
all. Max knelt there in disbelief, easy prey now that
his stamina was almost gone. Listening and hearing
nothing. Suspecting a trick, the game of the beast
of the wild.

But there was nothing. He sensed the emptiness
of the shadows, the desolation of a covert after the
hunt had passed through. Perhaps it had given up.
Or lost him. Whichever, all that mattered was that
it was gone.

He stretched out, attempted to ease his throbbing
limbs, rest his tortured lungs.

And it was then that he found the pistol, a Webley
.45, fully loaded.

It was sometime during the latter hours of darkness that the click of the front door catch brought

Shanifa out of her restless slumber with a start. She sat up in the armchair, listened in fear and hope. Her swollen lips moved, mouthed the name of her lover, prepared to scream if it was not Max.

Why should it be? Why should it not be?

Somebody was in the hallway, a stealthy step at a time, feeling his way along the walls until he came to the living-room door. Groping for the knob, finding it and turning it with difficulty so that the rusted hinges creaked.

Pushing it open.

Shanifa's fingers rested on the light switch. She did not even know if the power was still connected; all she knew was that her fear of the darkness had increased a thousandfold since her childhood. Whoever it was creeping into the room, however beautiful or terrible, she had to see him.

She flooded the room with light and screamed.

It was an apparition, for it could not be real. She had glimpsed Downers before, fled from one once, but none had been as awful to behold as the one who now confronted her, its barely human features disfigured by some blood-clotted wound. An eye was gone, the yawning socket open right into the skull, the nose flattened, splintered bone, the half mouth oozing blood and saliva. A close-range shot, perhaps a salvo of bullets, had taken a terrible toll, but here in the Ghetto death was not final. It was clothed in rags that failed to screen its wasted body. Shanifa stared in horror at a lust that was greater than its desire to sink its broken teeth into her tender flesh. An obscenity that was instinctive to a depleted race, the desire to procreate even though that was an impossibility.

She backed away, but there was nowhere to go. The intruder lurched after her. A hand that looked feeble moved with unbelievable speed and strength, threw her to the floor and lowered its cumbersome weight down onto her.

Nineteen

One morning the warders came for Nat and his father. Nat had no idea how long the two of them had been incarcerated; it might have been days, weeks. Months even. In the beginning they measured time by the grayness or blackness framed in the tiny barred window of their cell. It was impossible, pointless, to keep count of the alternating light and blackness, and they became numbed to an acceptance of their fate, eventually convincing themselves that they would never be hanged, that everlasting imprisonment would be their sentence.

Of course, eventually, Nat would die. Then he would carry on where he left off, nothing would change. Black bread and half-cooked grain twice daily, they ate it because it was a ritual, a mockery of a life that they were condemned to reenact.

It was a long time since they had last talked. To converse was but to repeat everything that had been said before; there would never be anything new to discuss. The coup was over. The air smelled stale, no longer stank of burning bodies. The ashes had been scattered, the dust dispersed. If there were any other prisoners here, then Nat had neither seen nor heard them.

The four uniformed officers opened the door and held it wide. An inclination of heads that said "come on, it's time" had Sid Bonner walking unsteadily out into the corridor. Nat followed, devoid of fear, for when there is nothing left to live for death is a welcome alternative.

Their footfalls echoed a desolation that confirmed Nat's suspicions that they were the sole occupants of this bastion of terror and hopelessness. He glanced into cells as they passed along the walkway, saw emptiness and filth, uncleansed stables whose inhabitants were long gone.

Luis Diogene was awaiting them in the interrogation room; his gloating smile seemed to have taken on a fresh eagerness: the gallows had stood idle for too long, and he was anticipating a renewed acquaintance with a friend who had been absent.

Almost lovingly, he unbuttoned Sid's prison tunic, even folded the soiled clothing over a chair, reduced his intended victim to a savored nakedness. Nat averted his gaze; embarrassment was a sensation that he had not experienced for a very long time. His pallid cheeks blushed as his memory recalled that night in boyhood when he had made an urgent trip across the landing to the toilet. His call had coincided with that of his father; they had met in the dim glow of an unshaded bulb. Sid Bonner had been stark naked; perhaps he always slept that way, either habitually or because he could not afford pajamas. Curiosity had prompted the boy to stare. Then he had rushed back to his room and wet the bedsheets in his guilt. He had never forgotten the incident. Which was why he kept his head turned to one side now, listening to the clink of weights on the antiquated scales.

Now it was his own turn. He flinched when the squat, black-cloaked executioner stroked his bared flesh, those fat fingers lingering obscenely on private places. He hoped that his father was not watching; embarrassment was a twofold curse.

A thick fog hung over the yard, had drifted in off the Waste and had not dispersed as it usually did. Cold and clammy, it enshrouded the unclothed bodies as if it sought to bestow some last measure of respect on them.

The warders held Nat's wrists, halting him before the bizarre structure. He remembered how he had stood in this exact spot the day they had hanged Yolanda Morrison. Now watch your own father hang, boy!

Sid Bonner stumbled on the steps, but Diogene caught him, pulled him roughly, guided him up onto the platform. Nat turned his head, but a slap across the cheek jerked it back.

Watch your father hang, boy.

Luis Diogene ran the rope through his fingers, draped it over the squat neck, and tightened the noose. He stepped back, turned and let his gaze rove along the lines of overlooking cell windows, bowed to them as he had always done. His shoulders were hunched. Nat detected a sadness about his posture, one who had gloried in death until there was no death remaining. The guns and tanks had done the job without ceremony, deprived him of what was rightfully his.

Nat met his father's gaze, and was shocked by the lack of expression in the gray eyes; not so much as a farewell smile. Just an acceptance, a blankness.

Nat's lips trembled, but no words came. His eyes misted over mercifully so that when the lever clanged it was but a silhouette that plunged down through the trapdoor. Only the sharp crack of breaking bone brought a cry of despair; he would have rushed forward had not his captors held him firmly.

Luis Diogene supervised the removal of the limp body, then ordered the two uniformed officials to lay it on the ground. Nat tried not to look, but it was impossible; he had to see what they had done to his father. This time a cry escaped the youth's trembling lips, for Sid Bonner's face was turned toward him, sightless eyes seeking him out, his neck stretched to a grotesque length, the head almost torn from the shoulders.

"*Hang me!*" Nat screamed. "*For God's sake, hang me!*"

Even in that bizarre moment of revulsion, Nat found himself ridiculing the executioner, the other's penguinlike posture and appearance resembling a comic book caricature, waddling toward the trio of spectators, stepping in a muddy puddle up to his ankles. He stood before Nat, looked up at him, and smiled with a pseudo benignity.

"So you're ready to hang, boy?" Silk-coated words that sent a shiver up into Nat's scalp, a terror that transcended the prospect of the brutal, instant death for which he craved.

Nat nodded, but he could not get any more words out. It was as though the rope was already throttling him. Mutely pleading to be executed, afraid that his executioner might fondle him one last time before condemning him to the living grave of the Ghetto, soiling him for eternity.

Diogene smiled again, but when he spoke to the warders his voice was terse, commanding. "*Take him back to rot in his cell!*"

Nat thought he might faint. The guards were supporting him, dragging him back in the direction of the prison entrance, scraping the soles of his bare

feet on the rough ground until they bled. They
pulled him, half carried him, up the long flight of
stone steps, only released their hold on him when
they reached the stinking cell, let him slump down
onto the floor and clanged the door loudly shut.

It was after the echo of their retreating footsteps
had died away that Nat began to sob uncontrollably.

Nat lay on the floor of his cell for most of the
day. At least, he thought it was the same day; he
might have slept and awoken on the morrow. A bowl
of gruel had been pushed under the door. It was
almost dark beyond the barred window; the only
light inside the cell was a glow from the bulb out
in the corridor.

God, he hated the bastards for what they had
done to him. They knew every trick in the book
where psychological torture was concerned. They'd
had him pleading to be hanged, desperate to join
his father in this hell of the living dead, but from
the outset Luis Diogene had had no intention of
executing him.

Nat wondered if they *knew*. If they did, then they
were making sure that he suffered the worst of both
worlds. We'll hang you, Nat. No, we won't. Tomorrow, maybe, we haven't decided yet. It could go on
until he died from natural causes, possibly years
hence, and then some more. They must know, he
decided, or they wouldn't be keeping him locked
up in a massive empty prison after they had massacred everyone else.

Once again his thoughts switched to Max. He was
probably lucky, killed in the purge, able to live on
in death with his girlfriend.

Nat gave up trying to work out ways by which he

could take his own life; there were none available
to him. *They* made sure of that. Escape was impossible; that mass attempt had proved that. And if by
some means he did manage to find a way out of
here, what then? The only refuge was the Waste,
with every chance of either ending up as one of
the new generation of Downers or else being boiled
in one of their cook pots. Without a doubt this was
the real hell; you didn't need eternal fire to be in
purgatory.

He wondered what they had done with his father's body. Doubtless it had been committed to the
Pit, dissolved in quicklime with due irreverence, just
as thousands of others before him had been anni-
hilated. And after that? The prospect was too terrible even to contemplate. *What happened to your soul
in the Ghetto once your body had been destroyed?*

Somebody was coming. Nat edged back into a corner so that the shadows might hide him from the
contemptuous, lusting stare of a patrolling warder.
Doubtless, before long, his body would be their play-
thing, the object of their depraved lust. The footsteps were slowing. He feigned sleep, not that it
would make any difference if they wanted him.

A jangle of keys, the door clanged open. He
squinted through half-closed eyelids, saw a uniformed figure supporting a form that slumped
against him. Another prisoner, possibly a Downer,
an unwelcome cell mate, a stinking sub-human creature to share his food and shit on the floor until
he learned to use the latrine bucket. Or perhaps a
twisted experiment to see how a Downer and a living being cohabited over the years. Another sick torture for their sadistic enjoyment.

The newcomer lurched, staggered against the
wall, and sank to the floor. He wheezed for breath,

edged back into the darkness as though he, too, was afraid.

"A friend for you, pretty boy." The warder laughed as he slammed the door shut and locked it again. "Have a good look at him when it gets daylight. You'll like him!"

The laughter receded with the footfalls, and Nat was left alone with that shape in the shadows, listening to its diseased attempts at breathing, aware that it was watching him the whole time, that it would not sleep because there was no rest for the dead. Oh, Christ Jesus!

A long night of intense blackness. Nat's only consolation was that he was unable to see the monstrosity incarcerated with him. It made no move to molest him. Judging by its breathing and snuffling, it was in no physical state to harm him, so better that it remained unseen. He dreaded the dawn when its deformed body would be revealed to him, the beginning of an unwholesome companionship that might last beyond his own death. He cowered, cringed, edged as far from it as the walls would allow.

He dozed uneasily, awoke once and thought that the other was using the bucket, a strangulation noise that could only be retching and vomiting. Poor sod, *they* were to blame for its very existence, an insidious apartheid that had brought about this sub-normal race on the Waste, a vile regression that was a blasphemy even in hell.

After a time the awful silence returned. Max succumbed to the exhaustion brought about by his trauma of the previous day, and when he awoke again dawn was throwing faint strips of half light on the opposite wall. He tensed, saw that the huddled indefinable shape was still there, and braced himself for full daylight.

The light was slow in coming; outside that dense fog had still not dispersed, its clammy, vapored breath creeping in through the bars. Nat thought about speaking, small talk, a false welcome to test the response of his companion. He dared not in case he provoked it. Better to see it first. They were going to be together for a very long time. Any form of comradeship had to be a slow progression of their acquaintanceship; they would have nothing in common except a sentence on Death Row.

The silhouette became more definable. Prison clothing, which was only to be expected. The body was squat, knees tucked up to the chest, hands clasped across them; not the ragged claws of a Wastelander, but nails that had been manicured on rough stone. The head was still in shadow, seeming to lie lengthways across the shoulders. It might have been a trick of the half light.

A movement startled Nat. He saw how the creeping daylight had spread, an infiltration of murky gloom, enough to see by if you stared hard enough.

Nat stared. *And screamed.*

For those ashen, twisted features were only too familiar, had been so for almost two decades. The lips tried to smile, trembled. That head, lying horizontally across the broad shoulders, attempted to lift itself up, but the dislocated neck caused it to fall back. The skull was devoid of support; it would have to be borne thus throughout eternal damnation.

Stubby fingers came up, somehow raised the head and held it in an upright position; that way it might have been almost normal had not the neck been

stretched to an abnormal length by the rope that
had taken the body weight.

The mouth tried to speak, but the vocal cords
were gone, severed by strangulation. The nostrils
flared as they strived to take in the cloying air, not
because the body needed to breathe, but because
such functions continued after death in a mimicry
of the life that had gone before.

Sid Bonner had been executed, and his living-
dead, mutilated body had returned to resume its
sentence on Death Row.

Twenty

It was some time before Max became aware that he was familiar with his surroundings. The fog had thinned slightly. A streetlamp cast its glow on a boarded-up shop front which he remembered having passed recently, had noticed the rusted advertisement for Wills' Woodbines which would have been a saleable antique on the other side of the Northside boundary. Of course, he had followed Shanifa along this road. Her house was in the adjacent street!

He hesitated, stepped back into a patch of shadow. There was little point in returning to the house; Shanifa most certainly would not be there. Stu Merrick had snatched her. She would be with him, wherever he was. Yet he had no alternative but to go there. Because somewhere between here and Block 18 a hunting Downer was on the prowl. Max needed somewhere to hide until daylight, and the empty house presented the obvious solution to his problem.

He studied the revolver in the glow of the street light. It felt good. Partly a psychological advantage, he accepted that, because bullets were a stoppable force in the Ghetto, not a killing force. The dead were dead; they could not be killed again, only mutilated. But a broken limb went a long way toward discouraging an enemy. Max tucked the weapon in his trouser belt; he would not hesitate to use it if the necessity arose. It was a confidence booster, at the very least, even if it was only a paltry weapon when compared with the heavy artillery of the undead militia.

He crept along the deserted street, wary even though his pursuer seemed to have abandoned his trail. It was inconceivable that he had encountered the only Downer left at large in the Ghetto. There had to be others, and faced with extermination they would be desperate; the vengeance of such a primitive, persecuted enemy was too terrible to contemplate.

He found the house where Shanifa had lived without any trouble, stood looking at it from the opposite pavement, trying to will one of the windows to light up, to see her silhouette behind the frayed curtains. But that would not happen; he had to face reality. He needed the place as a hideout until daylight, until the streets were safe to walk again. Or as safe as any street in the Ghetto was ever likely to be.

He crossed the road, paused again. An uncanny, inexplicable feeling came over him, one that had him tensing, his hand going to the butt of the .45 in his belt. Whereas he had sensed the emptiness of the deserted houses he had passed, this one exuded an atmosphere of total contrast. But it was not warmth, such as it might have been had Shanifa still been there, but of hostility. *His own inbuilt warning system screamed at him, yelled at him to flee while there was still time.*

He saw that the front door was open; he might have left it ajar after Shanifa had been taken away. His nerves were reacting to the train of recent events; no human being could possibly have withstood all that had happened these past weeks without suffering some kind of reaction. He tried to tell himself that it was just his nerves, that there was nothing threatening inside this shabby house. Nothing at all.

It didn't work. His mouth was dry; the revolver was in his hand. He took a tentative step forward, listened. *There was somebody inside*.

He pushed open the door, saw how a sliver of light shafted into the hallway from the room on his left, the one in which he had hidden to escape Stu Merrick's men. Beyond it something was moving, sounds that were unfamiliar, a kind of rhythmic shuffling that went on and on to the accompaniment of a rasping that could only be constricted, rattling breath.

Max hesitated, considered a stealthy withdrawal, for whatever was happening was no concern of his. He pictured a room filled with the dying dead, mutilated, writhing corpses left to await collection by the next corpse wagon. Bodies destined for incineration, their vile fumes polluting the fog-ridden atmosphere of the Waste.

He took another step forward. The gun wavered in his grasp, a comforting weight that would spit leaden destruction. His forefinger rested on the trigger. Beyond that intersecting door the wheezing was escalating to a whine. Whoever, whatever, made that awful noise was vibrating the floorboards. Max did not want to look. He had to.

Jesus God! He saw the wasted back through the partly open door, the emaciated frame shiny with grimed droplets of sweat where the rotted clothing had fallen away. Only vaguely did it resemble human form, twisted into bestial shape by an eternity of existence on the Waste, a creature that preyed on anything that fell into its taloned clutches.

It was kneeling on the linoleum. Max saw the blistered soles of its feet as it struggled to push itself to and fro, its efforts squeezing the tortured breath from its body. Max had no idea what it was doing, but its very posture bespoke the depths of depravity. It was almost spent now, supporting itself on its hands, sagging forward.

He shot it from close range, the Webley bucking viciously in his double grip, the report deafening in the enclosed space. It was as if he had triggered a slow-motion camera. He saw that malformed skull split raggedly in half, its contents exploding in a stringing mass. The body jerked upright, half turned by the force of the bullet, the cadaverous features transformed into a scarlet mulch. Faceless, seeming to cartwheel, it hit an armchair and overturned with it so that the creature was mercifully hidden beneath. Skeletal arms and legs protruded, twitching, bony heels hammering feebly on the floor. Still breathing but it was finished, only food for the Pit or fuel for the next cremation fire.

Max could not hold back his scream, almost fainted as the floor seemed to tilt toward him. The full horror of a beautiful female body, bruised and bleeding, lay strung with the mucus of this monster, lewdly displayed to taunt him, degraded beyond the realms of obscenity.

Shanifa!

He flung himself down beside her, wept as he saw those closed eyes, revulsion in her unconscious expression, her limbs in a posture of surrender, for to have resisted would have brought upon her a fate worse than the living death of which she was a victim.

He shook her gently, heard her moan of hopelessness. He whispered incoherent words of comfort
through shaking lips, used a strip of torn clothing
to wipe the slimy filth from her scratched bosom.
Thank Jesus she was dead, for no living female
could have survived such an ordeal.

"Max!"

The sound of his own name sent his lips in
search of hers, holding her to him and wishing that
he could die so that he could be with her. He
thought about the revolver lying beside them, but
it would not solve anything in the Ghetto. Death
was but a state of existence; it carried no guarantee
of eternal love.

"I'm all right, Max." He marvelled at her recovery, the way she sat up and groped for her torn
clothing. "It was bad, but it could have been a lot
worse."

Her gaze strayed to the form that lay beneath the
upturned chair. The limbs were still now, the curse
of everlasting life was temporarily stayed, but it was
not destroyed.

"We can't stop here." He helped her to dress.

"No," she replied, "but nowhere is safe. Especially for me when Stu Merrick finds out that I
haven't returned to his fold. I've got a change of
clothes upstairs, unless somebody's taken them."
She switched off the light.

"I'll come with you." He followed her up the narrow stairs. Her movements were sure, she did not
need a light; it would have been dangerous to show
one.

In the blackness of a stale-smelling bedroom he
heard the rustle of garments, marvelled again at
her composure.

"Can you find the way out of the Ghetto?" A question he had been afraid to ask until now.

"I don't know." Shanifa took his hand, and led him back to the stairs. "I found it that once, but then it was more by luck than anything." She squeezed his fingers, kissed him on the cheek. "I guess that's something we won't know until we try. Come on, we don't have much time. Once it gets light we'll be spotted on the streets."

Max held her hand as they left the house, the revolver pushed back into the top of his trousers. Now that he had found her, he would not relinquish her at any cost. If need be he would blow out his own brains at her side; at least that way they might be cremated together. But in the meantime he had to think positively. There was a route out of the Ghetto; they would find it and escape from hell back into the world of the living.

Max wondered if his companion knew where she was going or whether she was just following the streets and hoping to emerge on Northside. He did not ask because he preferred not to know. Just being with her was a bonus on the last few months.

Once they pressed back into a doorway and watched a militia patrol truck pass. It did not slow, disappeared from their view. Max wondered about the Waste, if they had to cross it. They must have been walking for at least an hour, and there were still houses all around them. Perhaps crossing the Waste had been his mistake; you stuck to the roadways and built-up areas, skirted it.

At length she stopped, and he sensed her uncertainty.

"What's the matter?" In the Ghetto hopes were raised, dashed; an eternal cycle.

"I'm . . . not sure." Shanifa was staring into the

murky gloom of reduced streetlight. "I thought . . .
I was sure that this street led onto . . ."

"Northside?"

"Apparently, I was wrong." He sensed her disappointment. "To our right, beyond the next turn, lies
the Waste. To our left . . . the road turns back on
itself!"

"But there has to be someplace off that road,"
he insisted.

She did not reply. The fingers that held his own
squeezed softly as if she was saying "I'm sorry, Max,
I really thought we might have made it."

"Let's . . ." His voice died away. His ears had
picked up a sound that was suddenly, refreshingly
familiar. Except that for the moment he was unable
to identify it. "Listen!"

"It's traffic," she said. "You can always hear traffic in the Ghetto at night when it's quiet."

"Yes, it's traffic, all right"— his grip tightened on
her— *"but that's not Ghetto traffic! It's high-speed, modern traffic, not antiquated trucks and old wrecks chugging
along. Unless I miss my guess, that's the Ring Road, the
Northside bypass."*

He felt her stiffen with him. "Is it? I've heard it
on occasions, never gave it much thought. But if
you're right, then it lies behind where the road
swings back on itself."

"In which case we have to find a way through
the houses and warehouses. An alley, perhaps, anything that will take us away from the streets without
leading us onto the Waste. At all costs, we have to
avoid the Waste."

"I can't remember how I found it last time." She
shook her head as if to jolt her memory. "I . . .
sort of got where I wanted. As if I was meant to!"

"And we're meant to right now." He began leading her along the curving street. "Because I'm not meant to be here at all, and I'm not going anywhere without you. Come on, then, we'll find a way."

Max's leg was no longer throbbing; he had forgotten all about it until now. He wanted to run, to pull Shanifa along with him, but he resisted the temptation. Only too well he remembered that previous nightmarish attempt to escape from here; that wandering on the Waste, the route that had led him back into the city of the dead. Northside, geographically, had to be nearer than the bypass; so near and yet so very far.

He slowed his pace, felt the wall on his right in the darkness, and followed it with his outstretched hand in the hope that he might find an alley that led through beyond the houses and deserted storage sheds.

There was none. Each building joined to the next, there was not so much as a passageway to separate them. *As if they had been built as a wall to prevent the dead from escaping from hell. And to keep out the living.*

Now the roadway was no longer straight. Beneath a streetlamp they saw where the gentle curve began, the unending darkness leading back into the bowels of the Ghetto.

Twenty-one

Nat had drifted into a state of total disorientation. After the initial horror of his father's return to the cell, it mattered not whether it was day or night. Conversation was out of the question; Sid Bonner's vocal cords had been reduced to uttering incoherent sounds, and any communication had to be effected by means of basic sign language which was no problem due to Nat's own impediment. These last few weeks his deafness had been no hindrance; the Ghetto was, in effect, a world of silence. Sounds such as gunfire he heard; vibrations he picked up easily enough. There was nobody to talk to; if there was, then he lip-read.

Sid Bonner sat in the far corner of the cell most of the time, found it more comfortable to let his head rest across his shoulders. After the first couple of days, Nat accepted his father's grotesqueness; it would always be like that, and in time he would forget that his father had ever been any different. Without the proximity of mirrors, he might even believe eventually that he was the same.

They rarely saw the warders. Food was brought twice a day; exercise periods seemed to have been abandoned. Nat feared lest his limbs might weaken to the equivalent of a bed-ridden hospital patient, so he took to doing basic exercises within the con-

fines of the cell. It was not easy, for there was barely
room to stretch his body out to do press-ups. Running on the spot was virtually his only means of
keeping his limbs mobile. Such movements for any
length of time irritated his father to the extent that
he hissed his annoyance.

Eventually Nat's listlessness turned to exhaustion;
there was little point in continuing to exercise if he
was to be confined in this small cell for the rest of
his life and, like his father, after death. He gave
way to the urge to sleep more, and his appetite
diminished so that often the food in the bowl was
left untouched.

Sleep was a pleasant relief from the constant
boredom, so he began to sleep heavily for long periods. Often waking was no more than a drowsy
interlude between deep slumbers. He did not even
trouble to check the window to see whether it was
light or dark outside. It did not matter. Nothing
mattered any longer.

It seemed as though he had slept for an eternity.
The hand that shook him awake was heavy and impatient, so he knew it was not his father's. He
stirred, and started to struggle up onto a callused
elbow when a slap across the face slammed his head
back against the rough stone wall.

"Wake up, boy!"

Nat stared in the grayness of an early morning,
saw the two warders bent over him. A third was
dragging Sid Bonner up onto his feet, the latter's
head lolling horizontally on his shoulders, vertical
lips protesting with mute curses and stringing spittle.

Nat shook his head, tried to clear it. Awareness
was a long time coming; he must have slept very
deeply. His arms were held behind his back. A

jerked thumb commanded him to follow behind his
father, who was being led out into the corridor. Nat
stumbled. If they had not been supporting him, he
would have fallen. Dizzying waves of vertigo came
and went. Doubtless, his condition was due to the
lack of exercise and reduced food intake. Or else
he was ill. Whatever was the matter with him, he
could expect no help. In the Ghetto there was no
medical treatment, for the dead needed none.

His confused brain tried to grasp the situation.
On Death Row they only took you down below for
two reasons: exercise or execution. Surely to God
they weren't going to put his father through all that
again. He tried to tell himself that it didn't matter
because Sid Bonner was already dead; and if it was
Nat they were preparing to hang, then he welcomed
the end with relish. Anything was preferable to his
present predicament.

Of course, Luis Diogene was waiting in the interrogation room. He was bound to be. The black attire, the smugness of his expression, told Nat that
an execution was about to take place. Him or his
father, that was the only issue in any doubt.

It was him.

Realization came as a shock even to Nat's confused mind. For a moment his own death wish wavered; he almost pleaded, might have done so
except that the words would not come.

"Boy, I've been waiting to hang you." Diogene
thrust his bloated face close, his breath was foul-
smelling. "I've longed for this day, and at last it
has been granted to me."

Nat stared past him, his eyes going in search of
his father's; found them. The warders had anticipated him and were propping Sid Bonner's head
upright on his shoulders, fairground sideshow men

attempting to steady a coconut on an uneven surface. The eyes had glazed as if covered by cataracts;
the lips were clamped tightly shut. Don't look to
me, son, I can't help you.

Diogene's fat hands were slowly divesting Nat of
his garments, the fingers smoothing over his flesh.
Nat shuddered and the hangman laughed.

"I've been hearing rumors about you, boy." His
tone was menacing, possibly to boost an underlying
fear. "I shall be interested to see how you react
when you drop." He turned and looked at the pathetic grotesqueness of Sid Bonner now that the
head had been laid back to rest. "Will you be like
your father, or . . . we shall see!"

There was an urgency about the execution prepa-
rations now, a haste that was accompanied by fumbling, shaking fingers. Even Nat sensed the awe that
the other tried to hide, the hollow bravado as he
was led down the gloomy, sloping passage and out
into the foggy yard. His guards seemed tense, held
him as though he was some species of repulsive rep-
tile, would have quickened their step still more had
it not been for the hangman's cumbersome walk.

Nat knew that his father was following, supported
by a third warder. This time Sid Bonner's role was
that of spectator. Watch your son hang; see whether
he walks with a dislocated neck or whether he is
lifted out of the gallows limp!

They guessed, but they did not know. Nat found
the courage to laugh silently to himself. He had
fooled them all along, just as Max had, wherever
he was. They would have to accept that the living
had infiltrated their secret hell, that the Ghetto was
no impenetrable fortress of degradation and purgatory.

Mounting the steps was not easy; Nat flinched

from Diogene's supporting hand. His weakness was
due to his confinement, the lack of exercise and
proper food. But in the end it would not matter;
the result would be the same. That last sleep, the
one they had woken him from, had been the best,
so refreshing. He felt as if he could have slept forever. It had certainly revitalized him.

He swayed on the platform, stared down and saw
that his father's head was being held upright again.
They were making sure that the father witnessed
his son's final agony. Nat started. He had not been
aware until now that there was another spectator
present, a tall, well-built man with rugged features,
standing some twenty yards away. For a moment
their eyes met, and Nat found himself swallowing.
Guilt, embarrassment, fear, he almost apologized
for his presence here, so powerful was the other's
personality, an invisible force that hit you like a
physical blow. There was no mistaking the evil that
emanated from this stranger, the malevolence in
those hooded eyes. Somehow he was vaguely familiar. Nat tried to remember where he had seen him,
but his concentration was broken by Luis Diogene
looping the noose over his head and tightening it.

"You are honored, my friend," a throaty, leering
whisper. "The mayor himself has come to watch
you die!"

Nat shuddered. Of course, Stu Merrick's picture
had been posted all over the Ghetto, an artist's impression, perhaps drawn in that same studio where
he had worked that first day. The likeness had been
crude but recognizable.

"Did you hear what I said, boy?"

Nat nodded with difficulty. He had not heard; he
had read those revolting thick lips.

"He's heard about you, too. That was the only

reason you did not hang with your father that day. We wanted to observe you, but in the end we couldn't be sure. And there's only one way to be certain . . . *to see whether you die on the end of the rope or if you are already dead!*"

Nat did not answer. They would find out for themselves in a moment or two when his neck snapped and he dangled limply. God, he only wished that he could observe their reactions.

Diogene had shuffled out of his view. Nat braced himself, looked for his father one last time. But if Sid Bonner saw and understood, then his features remained expressionless. A glance toward Merrick; the mayor was tense, head thrust forward with eager expectancy. *If you've tricked us, boy, then your eternal torment will be a thousand times worse, that I promise you!*

Any second now . . .

Nat would not hear the preliminary click of well-oiled mechanism; he might feel that split second vibration when the trapdoor was freed, just before he plunged down through it . . .

There was no advance warning. One second he was standing there attempting to pick up the slightest of tremors; the next he was plunging downward with a rush of vertigo. His fall was checked; there should have been instant oblivion, or at the most a few seconds of agonized strangulation.

There was neither. He felt something break. His body was being wrenched downward, his neck elongating as it took the strain, the flesh chafing down to the bone. He was swinging, gyrating; dizziness was the worst sensation. He swung one way, back the other.

Then daylight flooded in through the square, open doorway. Two warders stepped inside. For some reason, on this occasion, Luis Diogene was hanging back, unwilling to inspect his craftmanship at firsthand.

Hands reached up. The guards appeared to be standing on a small platform, taking his weight. The deftness of fingers experienced in releasing hanging corpses loosened the knot and pulled the noose over Nat's head. He slumped, but they caught him, lifted him down, and lowered him to the rough floor, then dragged him out into the misty daylight.

His vision was distorted, but he had survived the drop. That was the only explanation his bemused brain could come up with. He lay there on his back, but for some reason he could not see those clustered around him, only his father, who had been left unattended.

And as their eyes met on a horizontal level, Nat realized. He tried to scream his terror, felt his vocal cords struggling to move, but the sound became lost like a disconnected telephone cable.

They dragged him to his feet, and he recoiled from Stu Merrick's triumphant expression. Lipreading was not easy from that angle, with your head lying flat across your shoulders, but Nat understood the gist of the other's mute mouth movements.

"Our fears were unfounded all along!" There was no mistaking Merrick's relief, almost to the point of exuberance. "The boy was dead when he arrived; he could not have come here otherwise. Let's not waste any more time with either of them." He turned back to the warders. *"Throw them both in the Pit!"*

Twenty-two

"It's hopeless." Shanifa clung to Max and started to sob. "Absolutely hopeless. There's no way we're going to find a way out of the streets except onto the Waste, and nobody escapes from there!"

"I did," Max tried to sound convincing. It had been sheer luck, and their chances of repeating that good fortune were remote.

"I suppose we could give it a try." She shuddered. "At least it's marginally preferable to being picked up by the militia or the police. Exist out there and become one of them or else rot in prison forever. Some choice!"

The sky was starting to lighten in the east, a tinge of gray where a few minutes ago there had been blackness. The fog had rolled back, leaving a depressing dampness behind it. Another day was dawning.

Max knew that they had to make a decision soon, before they no longer had a cloak of darkness to hide their furtive movements. He considered returning to his apartment. If they could reach it unseen, then they could hide up there, wait for night to fall again. But would the next night be any different? Or the one after that?

They stood staring down the deserted street that doubtless wound its way back into the heart of the

Ghetto. All roads, it seemed, led back to hell. Dilapidated terraced houses, shuttered shops, warehouses that in all probability were empty. There was
just one vehicle in sight, a battered black Ford
Zephyr parked against the opposite curb. He experienced fleeting nostalgia, recalled the one his parents had owned when he was three or four, almost
a middle class status symbol in those days. Theirs
had been red. . . .

"Hey, just a minute!" He took Shanifa's hand,
began to drag her forward.

"What is it, Max?"

"I'm not sure . . ." He approached the car cau-
tiously, wiped the condensation from a side window
with his sleeve, and looked inside. Ripped upholstery, sweet papers on the floor, an overflowing ash
tray. Then he saw what he was searching for, a
bunch of keys hanging from the ignition.

He glanced up and down the street. The dawn
was coming fast now, but there was nobody in sight.
He tried the door, had to use his full weight to tug
it open.

"Get in." He pushed Shanifa in ahead of him,
then slid in behind the wheel.

"It's crazy," she protested. "If we can't get out
on foot, we certainly won't by car. And we'll be spotted that much more easily."

Max did not reply. He prayed for a second, the
first time he had prayed for a long time. The bat-
tery was probably flat or the starter motor had
seized up. There could be a dozen different reasons
why this abandoned car would not start. It was just
an idea; he had to try it.

The engine moaned its protest at this sudden in-
terruption. *It fired at the second attempt, ticked over
jerkily, threatened to cut out, then picked up again.*

"Eureka!" He turned, kissed Shanifa, revved the engine and belched out clouds of exhaust fumes from the rear.

"I don't see how it'll help us," she said. "We'll be even more restricted than travelling on foot. The soldiers or the police will stop us for sure."

"Maybe, maybe not." Max checked the petrol gauge, surprised to find that it registered nearly half full. "We've got nothing to lose, let's give it a go."

He laid the revolver on the seat between them. If they were destined to go out, then they would do it in style. He let out the clutch, the car shot forward.

Shanifa's hands had moved upward, groped along the side of the window. She laughed softly. "I was looking for the seat belt." Max laughed with her. It was the first sign of a return to normality.

"Any idea where you're going?" She noted that he turned right when they came to a junction.

"Not really. Just looking. I've got a street plan here." He fumbled it out of his pocket, then handed it to her.

"Keep going right." She flipped it open, held it so that she could read it in the faint light. "Any left turn will take you back to the center. There doesn't seem to be anything beyond the outer circular road. Maybe they just haven't bothered to mark it; this is merely a plan of the main part and the suburbs."

"Then we have to try to find what lies beyond." Which, on foot, they had failed to do.

Max drove on full beam, twin powerful beams that sliced through the remnants of the fog, illuminated the empty streets. There were a number of parked cars, all models of yesteryear, but no sign of people. Perhaps the occupants of the Ghetto were lying in, feared to walk the streets until the new regime had established its true role. All places of work were temporarily closed. Hell had ground to a standstill.

"There's a vehicle behind us!" Shanifa half turned, her voice tinged with anxiety.

"I've seen it." Max was watching in his mirror. "Driving on sidelights. It's turning off!" There was no mistaking his relief.

Another right turn, this street was narrower, cars parked on either side forcing him to drive in the middle of the road. He switched off the headlights; it was almost full daylight now. He was uneasy. His own experience of driving in cities had him thinking that this street might come to a dead end. Seconds later his misgivings were confirmed, had him braking.

"Shit! Just when I thought we might . . ."

"Those look like roadworks barriers blocking the way." Shanifa pointed. "Damn, the road does go on, but they've closed it. Probably got it dug up or something."

Max eased the Zephyr up to the barriers; wooden barricades on which the elements had partially erased the red lettering, unevenly spaced but sufficient to prevent a car passing through.

He nudged one with the bumper; it tottered, swayed precariously. He pushed at it again.

"Max." There was alarm in Shanifa's voice. She was half turned, looking through the rear window. "That car that was following us . . . *it's coming up behind us now!*"

He glanced in his mirror. A sedan with a wide grill was approaching them from the rear. He saw the beacon light on the roof, knew that across the

doors on either side would be the word POLICE.
They were trapped. There was no way back; the
road ahead was barred.

"Hold tight!" He accelerated, and the Zephyr
surged forward. There was a resounding crack as
it hit the wooden barrier with full force. A cross-
piece snapped, flew into the air. Rotting wood splintered and the car's tires crunched and powdered it
to sawdust as the wheels bumped over the debris.
Accelerating, hunched low over the wheel, he called
to Shanifa, "Get down. Just in case!"

Something hit the side of the Zephyr, a metallic
clang followed by a whine. Max swerved, the car
picked up speed.

White-faced, Shanifa was hunched in the seat.
"That was a shot."

"Too right it was! We just have to hope that they
don't hit a tire. Or worse!"

He tried to concentrate on the road ahead. The
surface was rutted, deep potholes full of rainwater,
piles of stones where digging had once commenced
and then been abandoned. An obstacle course, it
was difficult trying to avoid every obstruction and
keep an eye on their pursuers at the same time.
The wing mirror shattered. They were going for
the driver now.

His one consolation was that the Zephyr was powerful enough to keep ahead of the police car. His
concern was that they might meet with an insurmountable hurdle, perhaps a deep trench stretching
across the whole width of the road. Or a mountain
of rubble blocking their way.

The houses were petering out, mere shells now,
many of them razed to the ground, acres of demolition on either side. The chassis scraped on some

diggings which he saw too late; the exhaust system responded with a throaty roar.

"Well, we've put a hole in the exhaust." He cast a smile in Shanifa's direction. "It was probably rusted through, anyway. I'd say this road hasn't had a vehicle on it for twenty years, perhaps longer. Let's hope it keeps going."

The rear window shattered, the bullet glancing off it; another pinged on the trunk.

"Bloody hell!"

Shanifa half reared up, screamed as she saw the barriers across the road up ahead of them, another red and white wooden structure spanning between the crumbling pavements, an illegible warning notice in the center. So solid, the bases of the supporting posts buried in the ground. "Max, we'll never make it!"

"We don't have any choice," he yelled back at her, saw that the speedometer needle was flickering on sixty-five. "The only alternative is getting shot!"

Shanifa braced herself, closed her eyes. The impact threw her onto the floor, wedged her in the well between the passenger seat and the facia. Shards of broken glass showered over her; metal scraped, crunched on woodwork; the car slewed crazily, squealed its tires. But it did not stop.

"You okay?"

She looked up, saw Max's smile of triumph, and was just in time to catch the Webley as it started to slide off the seat. "I think so. What's the damage?"

"Nothing that will stop us, and apart from that I couldn't give a shit. Hey!"

"What is it?"

"That police car has stopped." Max was turning round to look back through the broken rear window.

"They've stopped at the barriers. But they don't need to because I've opened up the way for them to follow." His foot eased off the throttle; the Zephyr began to lose speed.

"Max, don't stop!"

"Just checking." He accelerated again. "Well, kick my arse, the buggers are reversing, turning back! What d'you make of that?"

Shanifa struggled back onto the seat, visibly shaken but smiling. She, too, looked behind them. "That's odd. Look, Max, the road here is smooth. The landscape is . . ."

"Northside!" He yelled his exuberance out of the window, then swung the wheel back as an overtaking truck blared its horn. A dual carriageway, the traffic was moving fast in both directions. Overhead the sky was blue; the bright early morning sunlight had him forcing down the windshield visor to shade his eyes. *"We're on the Ring Road, the Northside bypass!"*

It was true, but she still stared in disbelief. On either side of them a conurbation sprawled its ugliness, an unending architectural hideousness that was suddenly so very beautiful. And frightening.

"That's why the police turned back," she breathed. "We had breached the boundary of the Ghetto. They couldn't follow us any further."

"I guess I'll have to ditch this old wreck soon," he spoke with regret, a sadness. "Unlicensed, uninsured, no MOT, unroadworthy. And I don't have any certificate of ownership. Plus the fact we're carrying an unlicensed firearm." He laughed. "Once we get off the bypass I know a lay-by where the diddicoys often camp up. I'll dump it there. They'll have a field day with the scrap!"

Shanifa had fallen silent. Suddenly a distant

dream had become reality. She had no right to be
here; it was against all the rules of living and dying.
Last time she had run back to the domain of the
dead; that place beyond the grave had summoned
her to return. She had obeyed. It was sure to call
again, that pied piper of evil commanding her to
relinquish her hold on the living.

She had no right to be here. She was dead, a
corpse that defied the laws of the universe. Her
punishment would be too terrible to contemplate.
The Satan who had sent her out to whore for him
would exact his revenge, for her soul was his chattel.

Max's hand closed over hers, and he was shocked
to discover how icy cold her flesh was. He caught
his breath; she had not been like that in the Ghetto.
He stole a glance at her, almost recoiled from what
he saw, had more horns remonstrating with him for
his erratic driving. *For her soft, blond hair had become
gray and coarse; her cheeks had hollowed, resembling
wrinkled vellum. She had always been slender, but now
her figure bordered on emaciation. Instead of perfume,
his nostrils detected the faint odor of damp grave soil.*

My God in Heaven, what have I done!

It was going to be all right, though, he promised
himself. Whatever she looked like, she was his beloved Shanifa who had been snatched from him,
and he had reclaimed her. He would love her for
what she was. If necessary he would die to be with
her. His gaze rested momentarily on the revolver;
he would dump it along with the car.

"Are you all right, Max?"

"I'm fine." Somehow he managed a smile. "Just
tired, I guess. About another half mile and we'll
dump the car. Then, if you can make it, we'll walk
the rest of the way. I guess the first thing we both
need is a long sleep."

"Yes." She did not sound convincing.

"Damnation!" He changed down a gear. "There's a snarl-up up ahead. It's always the same at the height of the early morning rush hour. They designed the bypass badly where it filters onto the city road. Too narrow, a bottleneck. Still, I guess there's no hurry."

The engine idled, the exhaust rattling, vibrating. Max thought they had probably dislodged a bracket when they hit that pile of rubble. It didn't matter now, though.

The double queue was building up, edging forward a few yards at a time. Drivers were turning to stare at the battered Zephyr with its smashed rear window; one pointed, laughed. Fuck you!

A cloud formation had moved in fast, obscuring the sun. Heavy rain spots splattered on the windshield. Max tried the wipers. They didn't work. Only another quarter of a mile or so.

"I'm sure everything will be fine from now on," he spoke in an attempt to reassure himself. Because he felt it wouldn't be fine. He stared straight ahead, forced himself not to look at Shanifa.

"I hope so, Max." She did not sound convinced, either.

"It's all over now."

"Yes."

"I'll have to build the driving school up from scratch again."

They lapsed into silence. Suddenly conversation seemed forced, futile. The twin line of vehicles moved forward, stopped again. It was raining heavily now. The oncoming vehicles in the opposite carriageway had their headlights on.

Even before Shanifa screamed, Max had that unnerving feeling of déjà vu. An escalating sense of

terror which he had been trying to keep at bay with
small talk until finally the conversation dried up.
Through the rainswept windshield he saw the approaching headlights swerve, elevate, and seem to
become airborne. Even then he was still trying to
convince himself that it was an optical distortion
caused by the unwiped windshield. Or his mind had
played a cruel trick; the strain of everything had
been too much for him.

Refusing to believe until the last second when the
Zephyr became caught up in the line of mangled
cars, the articulated truck with the blown tire jackknifing and cutting a swathe right through to the
verge on the other side of the traffic jam. Even
then it was difficult to believe because Max had relived that nightmare so many times that reality became an impossibility.

But this time it was different because Shanifa was
all right. He could not see her in the darkness of
the piled vehicles, nor could he touch her because
his arms and legs were trapped, but she spoke to
him.

"Max, are you all right?"

"I think so." His concern was for her. "Where
are you?"

"Right here. I can't move, but I'm not in any
pain. If we're both okay, then all we have to do is
wait until they come and cut us free."

He wasn't going to tell her that he thought both
his legs were broken again. They were devoid of
feeling; the pain would come later. He was bleeding, too, probably from a cut on his head. Just a
trickle, nothing serious. They had been lucky. The
roof was caved in; another foot and it would have
crushed them.

Outside, there was screaming and shouting; a

blaring of approaching sirens. Steel cutters that had
you wincing however badly you were hurt. Waves of
dizziness had Max fighting to remain conscious, but
once they had freed Shanifa it wouldn't matter if
he passed out. She was still talking to him, but it
was difficult to catch her words, as if they were
whispered from behind a thin partition like the one
in apartment 417F.

Now the rescue team was starting on the roof of
the Zephyr, slivers of daylight lengthening and widening until, after what seemed an eternity, they
reached down for him through a jagged square.

"You're a lucky bugger, mate," a helmeted fire-
man joked. "Didn't expect to find anybody alive in
here."

"Is . . . is she okay?" Max found talking difficult.
A rapidly darkening haze threatened to engulf him.

"Just one guy killed back there," the reply
seemed to come from a long way off. "Mostly minor
injuries else, bloody miracle, I say. Now, just you
relax, don't you get worrying about nobody 'cause
everything's fine. We'll 'ave to get them to 'ave a
look at you at the hospital, though. Them legs don't
look too good, but they'll mend. Now, up you
come."

Thank God, Max thought, and fainted as they
pulled him clear.

Twenty-three

"I'm afraid you're confusing everything with your previous accident, Mister Frame." The tall, bespectacled surgeon standing at the foot of the bed was showing signs of increasing impatience. "I must be blunt with you; I have recommended that upon your discharge from hospital, you attend a psychiatric clinic."

"In other words"— Max's stitched lip curled in a sneer— "you think I'm a looney!"

"Come, come, Mister Frame"— a concerted effort at diplomacy— "there are many levels of psychiatric disorders. I'm not suggesting, indeed, I *know*, that there is no brain damage. Nothing like that at all. Your condition has been brought about by grief-related stress. It is quite common in the bereaved. You have to be rehabilitated."

"Shanifa was in the car with me."

"Yes, the first time. On this occasion you were alone."

Max closed his eyes. When he opened them again there was no sign of the silver-haired Doctor Mortimer.

Max hoped that the police would not return. The previous three interrogations at his bedside, within a week after his discharge from the intensive care unit, had been distressing. They kept on asking the same questions, but wouldn't bloody well listen when he answered them.

"Where did you find the car you were driving, sir?"

"I found it abandoned in Pace Park."

"Look, there are no cars in Pace Park. At least, no *driveable* ones. And if there were, there's no way you could get them out."

"Why not?"

"Because the area is barricaded off, has been for years. It's just wasteland."

"All right, tell me who the owner of the car is? Has he reported it stolen?"

"The car was scrapped in 1962. The DVLC have dug out the records. The gentleman to whom it belonged died in 1960, and his widow sold it to a scrap merchant because the cost of restoring it wasn't worth the value of the vehicle. Examining the wreckage, sir, that is quite evident. The car was unroadworthy. It was neither licensed nor insured, did not have a current MOT certificate. The tires were not within the legal requirements, either. There may be charges preferred; that depends upon the chief superintendent."

"Would you mind telling me the name of the previous owner, Sergeant?"

The policeman hesitated, glanced at his companion. "All right, but it doesn't have any real bearing on the matter. His name was Merrick."

"*Stuart Merrick?*" The color had drained from Max's face.

"Yes." The policemen exchanged glances again. "So you knew him?" A narrowing of the eyes, both heads thrust forward. "But you would only be about five or six then, sir!"

248 *Guy N. Smith*

"I've got a good memory for folks I knew when I was a kid." Max was trembling visibly.

"I see. Just a coincidence, then. As I said, it has no bearing on the case. But I must ask you again, sir, how you came to be in possession of a loaded .45 Webley revolver which had been recently fired!"

"I found it in Pace Park. Where I found the car."

The sergeant sighed, glanced up at the ceiling. "I'm afraid we shall have to pursue the question of the firearm at a later date, sir. Being in possession of a Part 1 firearm, without a firearms certificate, is, I must warn you, a serious criminal offense. However, what action will be taken, if any, depends upon the chief superintendent. We'll be seeing you again, sir."

They would be back, sooner or later. Max stared out of the window across the hospital grounds. The leaves on the big horse chestnut tree were already a rich golden color. Chestnuts were one of the first to turn. Spring was a long way away. He had been in the hospital for four months. Doctor Mortimer had hinted that he might be discharged next week. Max didn't give a shit. Next week or next year, it made little difference to him. But no way was he going to a brain clinic.

He went home because he had nowhere else to go.

There was mail, maybe a dozen letters, lying on the hall floor; he recognized Janice's handwriting, another from the insurance company. Doubtless more documentation, it was too early for the settlement check yet. Some junk mail. He swept it into a pile with his foot and hobbled on through to the kitchen.

He switched on the kettle for something to do. The house smelled stale; there was a thin film of dust on everything, reminding him of the Ghetto. Dust and decay.

He drank his coffee black because there was no milk. The fridge motor was still humming, that faithful old clock on the Belling told him it was two-forty-five. Whatever your predicament, life went on around you. At three PM he decided to go out; there was nothing to hang around here for. Today was as good as tomorrow.

Walking was more difficult than it had been the last time; human bones could only take so much punishment. He relied on his crutches to take the weight off his legs. The hospital might have kept him in another three weeks except that they needed his bed. He had agreed to both physiotherapy and psychiatric treatment, lied his way out.

It took him half an hour to reach the city center. The librarian was typecast, almost a caricature, sharp featured with glasses, a middle-aged spinster with an abrupt manner who mutely reprimanded him for letting the swing door slam behind him.

"Yes?"

"I'd like to look at the *Herald* copies going back thirty years or so, please."

Her expression asked "what for?" but she pointed to a glass door on the right, muttered "in there" and returned to whatever she was reading beneath the counter.

Max allowed the door to bang, on purpose this time. The room was small, shelved on three sides from floor to ceiling; scuffed binders with letroset dates on their spines. He pulled down the one purporting to contain fifty-two issues of the 1958 local weekly newspaper, then settled himself on a stool.

It was a laborious task, scanning every page, a jumble of townswomen guild meetings, social functions. A blurred photograph of a civic reception had his pulses racing. His mouth went dry when he recognized Stu Merrick in his mayoral regalia, holding a mace almost threateningly. The bastard had not changed any since dying.

It was on the front page of the June 11, 1959, issue that Max found what he was searching for, bold headlines that had him trembling: MAYOR RESIGNS.

> *Councillor Stuart Merrick this week resigned from his office following the recent allegations of vote rigging in the local election. This coincides with police charges of living off immoral earnings, following raids on two establishments in Southside. He was bailed to appear before a special magistrates court.*

June 18, 1959: EX-MAYOR COMMITTED TO CROWN COURT.

Max's trembling fingers flicked page after page, but it was in the following year's binder that he discovered that Merrick had not appeared before the Crown Court. January 14, 1960: EX-MAYOR FOUND DEAD.

> *On Tuesday morning, ex-Councillor Stuart Merrick was discovered dead in his Ford Zephyr in the garage of his Southside home. A length of hose pipe was attached to the exhaust. Mr. Merrick was due to appear before the Crown Court on Friday, charged with living off immoral earnings.*

Max let both doors bang behind him on his way out. It seemed that death was but a continuation of life. Nothing changed, which was why he found his thoughts of Shanifa comforting.

His progress was agonizingly slow. The sky was turning saffron before he reached Northside, trying to hurry now in case everything was not as it had once been. The tire factory was gone, the site levelled, boardings announcing the opening of a giant D-I-Y Superstore next spring; the old corner shop had finally succumbed to the supermarket opposite. His pulses raced. There was an aching void in his stomach. He let the crutches fall to the pavement, left them there; whatever the outcome, he would not be needing them.

He turned into Cemetery Road, ignored the churchyard on his right, for there would be nothing there for him, just a shrine that was meaningless because he *knew*.

Empty houses, everybody was gone, driven back by the tide of so-called progress. It was almost dark now.

He stopped to listen. Perhaps it was a trick of his imagination, an echo that had lingered until now in his mind, but he thought he heard the fast tip-tapping of light footsteps way ahead of him. He tried to hurry, but they receded into the night until he could hear them no more.

Please, God, let it still be there!

It was. A ragged outline of weathered timbers stood starkly across the end of the road, a barricade that had once screamed in scarlet lettering to turn back, lied in its reasons for denying access. Road Works. The road beyond was gone; it would never be resurfaced, just a rutted cart track that led away to eternity.

Max found the narrow gap, squeezed through. There was a mist beginning to roll across the desolation that stretched in front of him, gray vapor that swirled to greet him, cloyed his nostrils and smelled of rotting vegetation. In the far distance he heard a cry that might have been a wild animal emerging from its daytime lair now that night had fallen.

He hurried forward, did not glance back, for this time he would not be returning.

Here, nothing had changed.

HAUTALA'S HORROR AND
SUPERNATURAL SUSPENSE

GHOST LIGHT (4320, $4.99)
Alex Harris is searching for his kidnapped children, but only the ghost of their dead mother can save them from his murderous rage.

DARK SILENCE (3923, $5.99)
Dianne Fraser is trying desperately to keep her family—and her own sanity—from being pulled apart by the malevolent forces that haunt the abandoned mill on their property.

COLD WHISPER (3464, $5.95)
Tully can make Sarah's every wish come true, but Sarah lives in terror because Tully doesn't understand that some wishes aren't meant to come true.

LITTLE BROTHERS (4020, $4.50)
The "little brothers" have returned, and this time there will be no escape for the boy who saw them kill his mother.

NIGHT STONE (3681, $4.99)
Their new house was a place of darkness, shadows, long-buried secrets, and a force of unspeakable evil.

MOONBOG (3356, $4.95)
Someone—or something—is killing the children in the little town of Holland, Maine.

MOONDEATH (1844, $3.95)
When the full moon rises in Cooper Falls, a beast driven by bloodlust and savage evil stalks the night.